THICKER THAN WATER

DEDICATED TO
CAROLYN JEAN PHILLIPS
AND ALL THOSE WHO FOUGHT

AN ANTHOLOGY TO BENEFIT BREAST CANCER RESEARCH

THICKER THAN WATER

DEDICATED TO

CAROLYN JEAN PHILLIPS

AND ALL THOSE WHO FOUGHT

EDITED BY

RON EARL PHILLIPS

TABLE OF CONTENTS

THICKER THAN WATER

INTRODUCTION

Ron Earl Phillips

I ALMOST DIDN'T WRITE an introduction.

This anthology and its dedication are an extension of my grief for the loss of my mother Carolyn Jean Phillips who after a very long battle with breast cancer lost her fight. Sadly, she was not alone as 1-in-8 women in their lifetime will develop breast cancer. The survival rate for women who have non-metastatic breast cancer is 85% over a 10-year span. For many, remission follows successful treatment, but recurrence remains high for the next 5-10 years. That is when women, like my mother, fall into that 15% mortality.

I did not want to set the tone of this collection because of my grief. By my nature, something I shared with my mother, I am not outwardly emotional. I do not intentionally share my burdens, whether by pride or by modesty I keep them buried away. There are times I wish I would, and times I wish my mother had. It causes unnecessary ostracization and complicated relationships. My relationship with my mother was complicated.

As a child I called my mother by her given name, Carolyn, well into my teens. I was Ronnie, for the rest of her days. Later in life, she would call that name with a grin, knowing I thought it was childish. It was her way of separating me from my father. Ron was an abusive, womanizing son-of-a-bitch. Ronnie was her son. I miss hearing her call me Ronnie.

In 1972, my mother left my father in a beat-up Vega crammed with all the possessions she was allowed to keep. That included a three-year-old me, of course. That is when my mother became Carolyn, again. She had lost much of herself during her 10-year relationship with my father. Who my mother would have been had she stayed, I can't even imagine. I just know had she stayed with my father, I wouldn't be the person I am today.

Carolyn was my mother, my friend, my adventure buddy. She made me appreciate the outdoors as we traveled from Florida to Maine, all along the Eastern coast staying in tents and motor lodges. It wasn't all travel and fun, Carolyn was also a dating single mother working days as a social worker, helping others like herself, and attending night school for a graduate degree. We lived with her parents, who were built in babysitters. One summer, when I was 7, my grandmother who was eccentric (code for bi-polar) went away. I wasn't old enough yet to be interesting to my grandfather, so I attended night school too. That is when my mother gave me a gift her mother had given her: *The Wonderful Wizard of Oz* by L. Frank Baum. It was more than a sentimental gift passed from one generation to the next, but it was the gift of reading. I wasn't a particularly good reader, but I was interested, and my mother always encouraged my interests ever how fleeting. By the end of summer, I finished the novel and had become a reader for life.

Life with Carolyn wasn't perfect. Those complicated moments that may have lingered are not important enough to mention and are so insignificant compared to all the gifts she gave me in life. I am thankful for those gifts which include a father-figure in Larry, my sister Alicia, the years of being a doting "Grammie," and showing me that a woman isn't defined by a single role.

It wasn't my intention to make this introduction a eulogy. And there is no simple segue to introduce the stories that follow. Like my mother, the women at the center of each story are strong, determined, and sometimes ruthless to retain or reclaim their agency. The outcomes aren't always pretty, but I hope they will make you think, feel, and even empathize.

I want to conclude by thanking all the authors who took this journey with me to complete this special anthology. To you the reader, I hope you find at least one story that you truly enjoy, and that you will recommend *Shotgun Honey Presents: Thicker Than Water* to your friends, family, and strangers on the street. All profits will be donated to benefit breast cancer research.

Ron Earl Phillips
August 11, 2023

ON THE FIFTH DAY

Francelia Belton

GLORIA HARTMANN DIDN'T GET five golden rings from her true love on the fifth day of Christmas, as the song would say, but she did find her husband's wedding band and a note with these five words: *I don't love you anymore.*

She stood in front of the walnut double dresser in their bedroom, Albert's sock drawer open. She looked towards their bathroom door. The shower water was running and great plumes of thick steam poured out of the cracked open door. The scent of cedarwood and juniper body wash filled the air. Albert hummed to who knew what tune playing in his head.

Gloria regarded the piece of paper in her hand again, not quite sure what she was reading. It was definitely Albert's messy scrawl, but she couldn't understand why he would write this, and worst of all, lie about his wedding ring. The ring he claimed he lost in the men's restroom at his doctor's office. He had said he would call to see if anyone turned it in.

That was two weeks ago.

I don't love you anymore.

Gloria did not know where this was coming from, or what happened. As far as she had known, their marriage was happy. Not blissful, mind you, but happy enough. Married for 37 years, straight out of high school. Raised two daughters, both of whom were now married and with children of their own.

She dropped the note and ring in her front apron pocket and closed the bottom sock drawer with her foot and contemplated the open bathroom door. She would need to decide what she was going to do. Should she confront him about this? Now? But it was Christmas. The season of good tides and cheer, and most important of all, it was a time of spiritual reflection.

Since Albert hadn't finished his shower, she walked across the room and sat at her vanity table and opened her jewelry box. She picked up the hidden compartment and found their high school class rings. She and Albert were high school sweethearts, and had exchanged the rings on their senior prom night. In the center of hers was a sapphire, her birthstone. Albert's birthstone, a diamond, was in his. They got married when they were eighteen because she was pregnant, and it was the proper thing to do. They put their college dreams on hold, and Albert got a job. Then the next year, she discovered she was pregnant with their second daughter. Albert seemed disappointed at first, yet, despite it all, and with God's blessing, they had done very well for themselves.

Albert was devoted to his family. He loved his girls.

The plumbing pipe squealed and clunked when Albert turned off the shower. Gloria startled out of the past and the rings clinked in her hand. The shower door opened, and she stood from her chair, replacing the hidden compartment shelf and slammed shut the jewelry box lid. She performed a quick survey of their bedroom to make sure there was no sign of her snooping and exited the room.

Hurrying down the hallway, she reached the living room and stopped in front of their Christmas tree. The glittery pear ornaments intertwined with gold garland and the lights twinkled and danced. Maybe she should have guessed something was wrong when she got the Cuisinart food processor on Christmas morning, rather than the sapphire and diamond tennis bracelet she found in her husband's sock drawer two weeks ago. It was the reason she was rummaging through there again. She wanted to see if the bracelet was still there. Because maybe he had forgotten he hid it there. He'd been doing that a lot these days, misplacing things. His car keys, his reading glasses, his worn leather wallet. Supposedly his wedding band. But no, the ring was in the drawer, along with the upsetting note. Her hand slid into her apron pocket. The paper crinkled in her fingers.

The closet door rolled along its track and floorboards creaked as Albert shuffled around in the bedroom. He would be going through his morning ritual now. Shave, brush teeth, morning prescriptions, watch on last.

Gloria ran her hand across the fireplace mantle and the stockings that still hung there. She left the living room and headed for the kitchen. She opened the dishwasher and began putting the dishes away. There were extra dishes in this load because the girls and their families had dinner with them last night. They had stayed with her and Albert for the week for Christmas. What a wonderful time that had been, visiting with their daughters, playing with their grandchildren. How things had seemed so normal.

She had always known about Albert's various affairs throughout the years. She told herself they were flings. It was what men did. He never left her for any of them, and he wasn't about to now. It was something he must have been going through, writing the note, claiming he lost his ring. He didn't mean it.

She picked up the kitchen towel and wiped down the counters.

When she finished, she opened a bag of organic coffee beans, put them in the coffee grinder, then set them to brew. Soon the aroma of dark roasted hazelnut coffee hung in the air.

They were a very traditional family, and they had very traditional ways. And first and foremost, they honored their vows. They followed through on their word, especially to God. It was a virtue they passed on to their daughters. Family is the most sacred of all covenants.

God gave the world his only son who died for our sins.

If God could forgive mankind for what they have done, she could forgive Albert.

She always has.

And this time was no different. She knew what she would do to help save her marriage. Today she would bake something special for Albert!

Every year on the first day of Christmas, she baked a pear dessert using the fruit from the pear tree they planted in their backyard during their first Christmas together after they got married. These desserts were a Hartmann family tradition.

Five days ago, she made the pear custard pie because it was the girls' favorite. In fact, she had made four of them on Christmas morning; one for each girl to take home, one for the dessert that night after dinner, and one for her and Albert for the week.

But maybe that was a mistake. Maybe she should have made Albert's favorite Christmas pear dessert that morning. It had been quite a few years since she last made it. Maybe he wouldn't want to leave her if he remembered her cooking was the one thing he loved most about her. He had always said that no one could do magic like her in the kitchen. Maybe her cake could be the first step in curing what ails their marriage. Her mother always told her that food was the way to a man's heart. It was true for her and Albert. She had made him a lemon plum cake

on their first date back in high school. They had been inseparable ever since.

She pulled her Christmas recipe binder from the shelf under
the kitchen island and flipped through the pages. Apple-pear
crisp. Caramel pear cookies. Brown butter upside down pear
cake. She turned one more page and smiled. Ahh, this was it...
Spiced Pear Cake with Buttercream Frosting.

She opened the lower cabinet doors and pulled out the cook-
ware she would need, including the new food processor from
Albert. It was a state-of-the-art piece of machinery. All shiny
stainless steel. Cuisinart's top of line, top chef's model. Not as
expensive as a sapphire and diamond tennis bracelet, but it
wasn't cheap.

She ran her hands along it, admiring its gleam. All she could
think about was all the wonderful things she could make with it.

She had always told Albert she wasn't interested in material
possessions. She wondered if that was another mistake on her
part. Husbands liked to buy their wives beautiful things to show
how much they loved them. Perhaps by poo-pooing such things,
she didn't allow Albert to fully express his love for her. Men liked
to show they were giving and caring and loving husbands. The
other woman must have required such flashy gifts.

She opened the cupboard and started pulling out the ingredients. Flour, sugar, baking powder, salt.

She was sorting the ingredients when Albert walked into the
kitchen. He didn't say anything but pour himself a cup of coffee
from the coffee maker. He got the half-half from the fridge and
put in six large spoonfuls of sugar in his cup. She used to tease
him often early in their marriage by saying, "You sure you don't
want coffee with your sugar?"

She thought about what Albert told her his doctor said, about
him being prediabetic, so instead she said, "One of these days

that sweet tooth of yours is going to be the death of you." But she said it with a teasing smile.

Albert held the extra spoon of sugar mid-air, then dropped it back in the sugar bowl. The utensil clinked against the crystal. He said, "It hasn't killed me yet. Besides, coffee tastes like crap unless you add a little something to it." He noticed Gloria's concerned expression and changed tack. "But I, uh, appreciate you looking out for me. The doctor wanted me to cut down my sugar consumption."

She smiled an acknowledgment and opened the refrigerator to grab some plain yogurt and unsalted butter. She turned and set them on the island counter.

Albert added a touch more coffee to his mug, then looked at Gloria again, as if seeing her for the first time. "You look nice today. Did you do something with your hair?"

She brought a nervous hand to her hair. "No, nothing different. But this is a new blouse." She smoothed the red silk sleeve with her other hand.

"That must be it." He took a sip of his coffee.

Inside she beamed, triumphant. She knew it! Everything was fine. Albert did care about her. He had no intention of giving her the note. That's why he hid it in his drawer. Albert believed in the institution of marriage and family, the same as her. Albert wouldn't break that sacred trust. He wouldn't tear apart that bond. No matter how much he thought he loved this other woman. Albert wouldn't do that to them, hence the reason the note was still hidden. He had no intention of going through with anything.

Gloria almost pranced about the kitchen.

"Um," Albert cleared his throat. "It's poker night with the guys tonight. So, I'll be going out after dinner."

Gloria's heart paused mid-skip and her stomach flipped, flopped, and splattered on her forgiving soul. She took out two cinnamon sticks from its box and set them on a plate. She mustered a cheery smile. "Of course. It's your weekly game night with the boys. I forgot."

He nodded his head. "Yep. We never miss a week. Not even during the holidays." He chuckled.

That was true. Albert and his friends met every week, unless game night fell on Christmas. Then they would push it forward one day. But she wasn't sure about tonight. She distinctly remembered Albert mentioning that Ed and his wife were taking a cruise this year, and would miss the last two game nights of the year. They would be down a man. They needed four to play.

Albert must be going to see his mistress this evening. It had been five days. He couldn't go anywhere over the last week. The girls and their family were in town. How would that look, leaving every evening with houseguests? No, this was the first and best opportunity to see *her*.

But that's okay. That's what men do. And it was a women's place to be by her husband.

God. Marriage. Family. The holy trinity of a good Christian woman's existence.

"Excuse me," Gloria picked up her wicker hand basket and opened one of the patio's French doors. She stepped outside and let the chill December air calm her. She needed a moment to pull herself together and not overact in front of Albert. She gazed up to the overcast sky as if in communion with God. Looked like a cold front was coming in. The weatherman said it was going to be in the sixties, but how often is the weatherman right about anything these days?

The first hard pellets of sleet began to fall and one landed on her eyelash. She doubted Albert would be going anywhere this evening. A storm was coming in, no matter what the local weather channel was saying.

She shivered, then hurried to the pear tree and picked six pears, dropping them in her basket, then ran back inside.

Albert was still in the kitchen, rinsing his cup, and putting it in the dishwasher. He raised his head when she came in and closed the door behind her. He looked as though he wanted to tell her something…his mouth opened, then closed. Instead, he left the kitchen without another word.

She commenced with her baking, but soon realized she forgot about the apple cider vinegar. She went out to the garage to get it from the second refrigerator where she stored her extra staples. After finding what she needed, she came back into the kitchen and finished baking the cake. Soon the nutty brown butter aroma of juicy pears and fall spices overtook their home. The lovely rendition of "Silent Night" and other Christmas music from the radio its accompaniment.

Sometime later, as she was putting the finishing touches on the cake, Albert's curses floated into the kitchen. She had always disapproved of his language, but to give Albert credit, he made efforts to not do it around her. She sighed and put down the cake spatula and ventured out to the living room.

Albert stood in front of the television, which was on the weather channel. The weatherman confirmed what she already knew—God's divine intervention at work. Upholding their venerable vows to each other, and to their Lord Almighty, being paramount.

Nevertheless, and because it would be expected, she asked, "What's wrong?"

"There's a God damn blizzard happening. I won't be able to go out tonight!"

She cringed inwardly at his blasphemy, but said, "That's too bad. Maybe you guys can try again after everything thaws."

He grumbled, "Maybe."

She drew in a deep breath and said, "I made you something

special. It's your favorite. I know I only make the pear desserts on the first day of Christmas. But I figured we would be stuck indoors because of the weather. Also, I feel a little guilty about making the pear custard pie for the girls. It's their favorite, but not particularly yours."

He flipped through the channels, trying the local news. "It's fine. The girls are most important."

"No, it's not fine. I should have thought about your wants, your needs."

Albert clicked off the television and turned to gape at her.

She continued, "I know we didn't get the life we wanted. You wanted to go to college, see the world, but then I got pregnant with Dorothy, and that changed everything. And though it was a sin, God forgave us when we did the right thing and joined in holy matrimony. Then Irene came along, and well, our fate was sealed, forever blessed under God. I know that things haven't always been easy, but I have always appreciated you and what you have sacrificed for me and the girls."

Albert looked truly gobsmacked, and he only stared at Gloria in silence. She would have laughed if things weren't so serious between them right now. His cell phone beeped. He looked at the screen and put it away. "Gloria, I don't know what to say."

"You don't have to say anything. I wanted to do something special for you. Yes," She held up a hand to forestall any objections. "I am breaking my tradition of only making a pear Christmas dessert on the first day of Christmas, but I figured I would give you a small token of my gratitude."

Albert looked a little uncomfortable. "Well, you didn't have to go through all that trouble."

"It was no trouble. Plus, it was the perfect opportunity to try out the new food processor you got me. It worked wonderfully, I might add. It blended all the ingredients to creamy perfection."

Albert puffed out his chest and his face broke into a broad

grin. "Glad to hear it. I got it for you because I know how much you love to bake."

"I do. Baking in my meditation. The answers to all of life's difficulties reside in the beauty of baking and prayer." She felt her smile turn pensive, then willed it to brighten. "So anyway, I made you the spiced pear cake. I even whipped up some honey caramel syrup. I bet that will cheer you up about not seeing your friends tonight. Now, I know we're supposed to watch your sugar intake, but it's only one slice. I won't tell Dr. Graham if you won't." She gave him a conspiratorial wink.

His eyes lit up at the mention of the dessert, and a genuine grin spread across his face. "I thought I smelled something good baking in there. Mmmm." He closed his eyes in anticipation. "It is my favorite." He opened his eyes, and he reached out and took her hand. "Gloria, you know me too well."

A sincere warmth entered her body and radiated from her like a heavenly aura. "How could I not? I have known you for more than half my life."

"Yes," The light in his eyes dimmed a bit. "We have been together a long time."

"Through thick and thin." She smiled a smile that didn't show teeth. "Let me get our dessert."

She retreated to the kitchen and started a fresh brew of coffee because that's what he drank with his desserts. As the coffee percolated, she sliced two pieces of cake and placed them on small plates and set them on a tray.

Then she poured them both a cup of coffee, and she sweetened Albert's just like he liked it. Might as well go all the way. She carried the tray out to the living room, setting it on the coffee table. Albert sat down on the sofa and she handed him his cake and coffee.

He ate a bite. "Marvelous! I don't remember it tasting so good. It is so sweet, but perfect."

She sat on the loveseat across from him, setting her cake and coffee on the table. "I hoped you would like it."

He finished the cake in between sips of his coffee.

"Can I get another slice? It is Christmas, after all. We're allowed to cheat a little. I mean, it's not like doctors don't know that people eat more during the holidays."

She laughed, picking up her plate and handing it to Albert. "That is true. How would the gyms sell all those memberships if folks didn't have lose weight as their number one resolution?"

"You're not going to eat your slice?"

"Hm, you know I have always been partial to my pear and berry cobbler."

He dug into her slice, gobbling it down faster than she had ever seen him do. "Man, this is so good."

"Yeah, but maybe I'll make the cobbler for me tomorrow."

He nodded his head. "That sounds good, then I can finish off the cake by myself." He belched and blew out a puff of air. "I never did like the cobbler. Too tart."

"Yes, I know. That's why I seldom made it. Not sweet enough for you."

Albert's stomach gurgled, loud, and he put his hand over it. He groaned a little. "Oh boy, I ate too much."

Gloria cocked her head. "Did I mention we were out of apple cider vinegar? I wasn't planning to make the spiced pear cake for Christmas this year, so it wasn't on my shopping list last week. But it's one of the ingredients for the cake. I bet you would have never guessed that considering how sweet the cake is. It's never been enough to make a difference in the taste. All the other ingredients help mask it."

Albert moaned even louder.

"So anyways, I panicked. What can I use as a substitute? I can use white wine vinegar, or rice vinegar. And I even read that if you're in a pinch, you can use lemon or lime juice, which by a stroke of luck, I had a bottle in the garage refrigerator. But while I was standing in front of the open door, I wondered, what if I used something sweet instead? I know how much you like your sweets, and I thought, I know! I can make Albert's favorite Christmas dessert even better."

In a fit of violent discomfort, Albert moaned again and doubled over in pain.

Gloria ignored his interruption.

"And you know what? I was right. You loved the new version. It was sweeter than ever. Just like you like it. Adding the antifreeze was the best idea bar none."

"What?!" Albert twisted in his seat and his mouth dropped opened.

"I didn't believe the articles on the internet that said antifreeze had a sweet taste. I mean, how would anyone know that? Did you know there are people out there that have ingested it? On purpose?"

"Jesus fuckin' Christ, Gloria! What the hell are you telling me?"

"So, I thought, well, if people have actually tried it, how harmful can it be? After all, I only needed a quarter of a cup. Though I added a couple of tablespoons to your coffee too."

Albert vomited on the carpet.

Gloria wrinkled her nose. She was going to have to clean that up later.

Albert fumbled in his pocket and pulled out his cell phone. He tried to punch in his password on the screen look.

Gloria stood and walked over to Albert and snatched his phone out of his hand. A picture of a woman who Gloria could only presume was Albert's girlfriend was on the screen. The woman was wearing nothing but black lace panties and a see-through bra. The sapphire and diamond bracelet hung on her left wrist. A frown creased Gloria's brow.

Albert tried to pull himself up to the coffee table, scattering the

Christmas décor, magazines and dishes in his wake. Writhing in pain, her husband clung onto the table for dear life. "For God's sake, Gloria, call 911. I need help."

"Yes, you do, but I'm not carrying this marriage anymore." She reached into her apron pocket and set his ring along with the now wrinkled note down in front of him. "I found your wedding ring. Turns out you hadn't lost it at the doctor's office, after all."

Albert gaped at the ring. Then his body contorted in agony.

"I have always known about your other women, but that's okay. That's part of being married; your husband sleeps with other women. What is the poor wife to do?" She shrugged. "God doesn't approve, but men have been doing it for millennia. It's a weakness God put in men. But God must have had some purpose for making it this way, and I will not question God's ways."

She removed her wedding ring and placed it next to Albert's on the note. "It's the leaving me that I cannot abide by. And worse of all, during the Christmas season. What kind of heathen are you?"

Albert moaned a death croak and tried to get up. Instead, he crashed into the Christmas tree, knocking it over.

She stood and rushed to the crystal manger scene on the end table and moved it before Albert stumbled and toppled it over. With reverent handling, she placed the heirloom nativity scene on the fireplace mantel out of harm's way.

She turned her attention back to the squirming, twisting Albert on the floor. "Divorce is out of the question. Our wedding vows are an oath to God. You remember, for better, for worse, in sickness and in health, till death do us part."

Albert ceased his futile prostrations and laid still.

Gloria returned to the coffee table to where their wedding rings rested and looked down on them. The musical melody of "O Come All Ye Faithful" drifted in from the kitchen. After a few moments of quiet contemplation, she spoke. "Today is the fifth day of Christmas, we're supposed to give five golden rings." She reached into her other pocket and removed their high school rings. She placed them on the scrap of paper with the others. "We're a ring short, my love, but I suppose that's the best we can do."

THE KNIGHT'S TALE

Jay Butkowski

IT'S LIKE IF JOHN Waters filmed an adaptation of a Philip K. Dick novel by way of Clive Barker, Executive Producer. Weirdos in thick black-and-green eye makeup, cyber punks, techno goths, freaks in neon-frosted mohawks, outcasts with gaged ear lobes stretched to the near-breaking point. Fishnet shirts and vinyl pants are worn like school uniforms. Men dress like women; women dress like hood ornaments. The black-clothed shadow people of the club are punctuated by pale, translucent skin glowing purple beneath the black light.

Pervy old men leer across the bar at the daughters of the women they used to leer at "back in the day" while the music pulses, tribal and enduring. Sweet-smelling fog billows across the bar, catching and bouncing the glow of ever-present smartphones around the small space.

Why do you keep coming back to this fucking place?

The drinks are cheap, you tell yourself. The bartender's a

heavy pour, the weirdos keep to themselves, or at least leave you the hell alone.

And then there's "the girl."

She knows everyone and has a story about everything. When she leans in to whisper, she puts a hand on your shoulder for emphasis. You can feel the heat of her lips on your neck as she reveals the secret history of the world. You whisper back and smell her shampoo, hibiscus and honey and teenage wet dreams.

You'd follow her straight into the depths of hell to challenge the Devil to a game of Yahtzee.

"You wanna dance?"

She takes your hand and leads you effortlessly through the crowd to her place of honor on the dance floor. People move out of her fucking way.

She's royalty in this building. And you could be her knight in shining armor.

The thump of the electronic drums whips the dancers into a hedonistic frenzy. Her hands explore your body—ass, hips, tits. The heat of her body sends the flush through her and into your skin. Her lips, soft and wet, press into your own, her tongue tracing the outlines of your mouth ever so gently.

"Babe, why are you playing with that dyke, when we all know that what you really want is some dick?"

She laughs and pulls away—it's all a big fucking joke—but you don't understand the punchline. Why is SHE with HIM? Why is he even here?

He doesn't belong to this place. Not the way you do.

He looks like a reject from an Abercrombie catalog, cosplaying as a goth. He's wearing a long black duster over a tanned, exposed torso. Tan, as if any self-respecting goth would ever spend time enough in the sun to accumulate melanin. His teased long hair is carefully stylized—each strand meticulously placed; each lock positioned just so—to give the fake impression of some wild, untamed beast. The guy-liner helps to lend some intensity, and the long, braided beard with runic beads hanging from it is something that would be more at home in Game of Thrones than in Wrath's Night Club.

He's wearing a pair of skin-tight leather bondage pants, and he obviously skipped leg day at the gym to focus on his abs and pecs. The whole thing, working together—the chicken legs under a tanned six pack, the hairspray mane and Khal Drogo goatee—made him look like a satyr from Greek mythology.

Or the Devil himself.

Roll the dice, motherfucker.

"We're dancing here. Do you mind?"

You can't believe the words came out of your mouth, defiant and strong. You're actually going to challenge this alpha douche?

For her, you would. In a heartbeat. She deserves so much better than him.

"Listen, Ellen, why don't you go to one of those queer clubs in the Village, and find you a nice hefty bull dyke who's interested in—I don't know, what do you people do? Scissoring?—or whatever. This girl's taken. You coming, babe?"

"You don't have to listen to him," you tell her. You feel righteous and strong, and you want her to feel that too, to know that she can stand up for herself, and that you'll always be there for her: a partner, a friend, and more if she'll have you. "You don't have to go with him."

"Yes, she does," he says, and then a moment of realization. "Wait, is this some kind of crush? Are you crushing on my woman?"

You feel the righteous strength drain from you with that word: *crush.*

She looks at you with pitying eyes, knowing what comes next.

"Has she been leading you on? Making you think like you had a fucking shot in hell?" There's a twisted, perverse joy in his voice, as if tearing down another human being is the best fucking high in the world. "What, are you in *love*?"

He says *love* like it's a curse word. His laugh is more mock than mirth. He gets up in your face and drops any hint of humor from his tone.

"She could never love a freak like you," he tells you. "Not in a million years."

You glare, but he's cracked the armor, and you worry that he's probably right. He's won.

"Stay the fuck away from her, do you hear me? Because I will not hes-i-tate" he emphasizes every syllable to drive the dagger deeper and deeper "to knock your fucking teeth down your throat. Do you hear me?"

He reels back a fist, and you flinch. He laughs and shoves you hard as he charges past you. His other arm snakes around her waist to lead her away, further into the club. She looks over her shoulders as he escorts her away to make sure you're okay.

You're not okay. You're definitely not fucking okay.

As soon as he passes with his prize, you make a beeline for the ladies' room. You enter one of the stalls, lock the door behind you, and collapse in a heap on the dirty bathroom floor.

Outside of the club, you're quiet, closeted, mousy. Your family doesn't understand you; your friends, what few you have, are all tied to this space. Here, you could be who you were always meant to be. You can be open, and honest, and real, and raw. You can vanquish the dragons of self-doubt, of loneliness, and of fear. You don't have to hide away your true self, and you can get the girl and live happily ever after.

He took all that away with a couple ignorant remarks and too much Axe body spray.

He doesn't even belong here.

• • •

In the next few weeks—Months? Years?—you retreat back into yourself. In a sanctuary for outsiders, you've become an outsider. Your already short hair gets shaved off, and the stubble is usually covered by a ballcap pulled down low enough to nearly eclipse your eyes. You lose 20 lbs. because food isn't interesting anymore. Nothing tastes right.

You stick to the bar and avoid the dance floor like a vampire avoids garlic bread. No one notices you amid the hustle and bustle of the bar. You wonder if they ever really noticed you at all.

Looking in from the outside gives you a vantage point you didn't have before. You see things that weren't initially obvious, but in hindsight, are clear as day.

The old pervs at the bar? The one in the middle has an indentation on his ring finger from where a wedding band used to sit and the other pervs seem to be coaching him to re-enter the wild. The bartender is reading from a textbook on forensic psychology in between pouring another drink special—some sugary sweet abomination that all but guarantees a hangover the next day. The club owner is watching the thinning clientele base and wondering how he's going to keep up with ballooning rent payments at the end of the month.

The end may be nigh for this place, this haven for the strange and unusual, the budding Lydia Deetzes of the world, or at least your corner of it.

Then, there's her. She still comes regularly to hold court in her kingdom, but a little luster is missing; the bloom is a little off the rose. She's drinking more and talking less. She no longer has that same joie de vivre that initially attracted you to her, but instead, seems like she's faking it to keep up appearances. She looks tired and upset, and the act of putting on airs appears to cause her pain.

He's still there too, and he's starting to become even more controlling, even more dominant. He laughs a loud, obnoxious laugh with his friends and demands that she cater to his—and their—every whim. She's shrinking and he's thriving. He's openly rough with her, and to him and his buddies, it's all a big fucking joke but you still don't get the punchline. When you notice the bruising on her arm, that's when you decide that something must be done.

The Devil is owed his due. And you're happy to pay up.

• • •

The plan still takes months to engineer to get it just right. You're still going to the club, but only for surveillance purposes now, to keep an eye on his transgressions, and to screw your nerve on even tighter. You don't give a shit about the music anymore, or the atmosphere, or really, anyone else in the bar except her, and him. The bartender occasionally grumbles because you sit at the bar and nurse a ginger ale, but you can't afford to get drunk. Not now, when you've got to keep your wits about you.

When you're not at Wrath's, you practice in the mirror, to make sure the moves are fluid, quiet, and fast. You know that if this is going to work, you're going to need speed and stealth on your side. You're going to need the element of surprise, and you're going to need him to be nicely buzzed. You're also going to need to be plenty strong.

You start lifting weights. You gain back the 20 lbs. you lost to depression, and add another 20 more in muscle for good measure. Your shoulders are broad and defined, your back a rippling mass of sinew and bulges. You feel decidedly more powerful and decidedly less feminine, and you're fine with it—happy about it—because it's what you had to become to execute on your plan. Your grandmother stops asking when you're going to meet a "nice boy." Guess she's given up.

You watch for an opening. They're coming to the club less

frequently, and some weeks, you don't see them at all. You won't give up that easy. You've put in so much work, and this fucker is owed his Yahtzee.

Two months go by. Three. And then finally, he shows his face back at the club.

She's nowhere to be found. You tell yourself it's better that she's not here.

He drinks like a semi-pro drunkard, laughs loud, and enjoys his homecoming, except this isn't his home. He doesn't belong to this place, and neither do you. Not anymore. But this is where your paths first crossed, and this is where they should part. It's poetic.

He gets up from the bar to take a leak. You follow.

Wrath's has enough gender-fluid patrons that no one bats an eye when you walk into the men's room. You're bigger than you used to be, so maybe they didn't notice that you don't belong there.

He's standing at a urinal, head lolled back, enjoying the best piss of his life. You grab the back of his head and slam his forehead as hard as you can into the tiles behind the urinal, leaving a dent in the sheetrock underneath and cracks that spider-web out from the epicenter in the porcelain tiles covering the wall.

You move like you've practiced—lightning quick and confident in muscle memory. You've got one arm looped under his armpit and wrapped around the back of his neck in a modified half nelson. He struggles to wriggle free, but you're too strong for that now, and he's dazed, and has missed more than just leg day at the gym these last couple months. He's doughier than he used to be, and you're made of cold steel.

The scissors in your other hand snaps open with a sound like unsheathing a sword, the honed edges razor-sharp and held against the shaft of his dick.

"You asked her once why she was playing with a dyke when

all she wanted was this dick," you hiss. "What's so special about *this dick*?"

"Who the fuck are you?" he asks, fuzzy and semi-conscious.

"Not so special," you say, and with a quick snip his manhood flops and drops onto the pink urinal cake at the bottom of the stand-up toilet.

He tries to scream, but the sound gets caught in his throat, as you jam the closed scissor blades into their new home in the Devil's neck. Rinse and repeat. You stab him several times in the areas where you think they'll do the most damage and allow for the quietest kill – windpipe, Adam's apple, general vicinity of the carotid artery. You've done your homework and reviewed the anatomy books at the local library to learn how to inflict maximum damage with minimal opportunity for mistake. Each time you pull the scissors free and prepare for another plunge, you paint the wall with a splash of red.

After you're satisfied that the job is done, you drop him to the floor and let him bleed out and into the urinal. You rinse your hands and your scissors in the sink, and walk away, out the bathroom, out the club—this place where you could be yourself and where you found yourself. You take in a deep breath of cool night air and smile for the first time in months.

● ● ●

A few days later, they hold a memorial at Wrath's for him. You can't help but attend, drawn like a moth to revel in his absence from this plane of existence.

They found him a half hour after you left the club. No one saw anything. The cameras in the club caught nothing. The police have no leads. There were obvious signs of struggle, but nothing tying it back to you, and since it all went down in a men's room, the main suspects were all men.

Being invisible has its perks.

She walks into the club, a queen in mourning, returning from absentia. She's dressed in black, a bulge in the middle curving the lines of her dark dress around her expanding belly.

So that's where she's been.

She's shaking hands and giving and accepting hugs, thanking everyone for coming. You're at the bar, watching the receiving line processional—first dozens of people, decked out in their gothic vestments, then a few stragglers who gaze awkwardly at their feet and mumble condolences.

And then her eyes drift over the crowd and lock onto yours.

Shit.

You're starting to panic as she makes her way through the club to your position at the bar. You're supposed to be invisible, you tell yourself. It was a mistake to come here, you lament. You shouldn't have been so cocky.

You start to move towards the door, and she stops you with a warm hand placed on your shoulder.

"Thank you. From both of us," she says as she rubs her baby bump. "For coming out to the memorial, I mean."

"Yeah, uhh . . . sure," you stammer.

"I know he wasn't . . ." she trails off in thought, trying to find the proper eulogy for an abusive, domineering prick, but the words seem to be too far away at the moment. "Just, thank you."

"No biggie," you say, immediately kicking yourself for sounding so stupid.

"Hey, I know we stopped talking under . . . well, under bad circumstances," she says. "I just . . . with everything happening, and the baby coming . . . well, I could use a friend. Could we grab a coffee sometime? I know I'm not supposed to drink caffeine, but . . . I guess I'm just a little lonely. Not here, though . . . the coffee in this place sucks."

Bad memories, you think to yourself. Maybe the queen is ready to give up the kingdom?

"Of course," you tell her, a glimmer of hope sparking in your heart, even as your lizard brain—the one trying to help you avoid getting caught for murder—tells you to run. Far. Now.

She knows, right? She has to know. She knows everything in this place; everything everywhere. Maybe she knows and she's okay with it? Maybe she's happy about what you did for her, and maybe she was just waiting for someone to rescue her, so you two could be together, and live happily ever after raising the baby of the man you murdered at the toilet.

"What're friends for?" you offer with a shrug, not knowing whether to laugh, cry, or run.

ASHES IN YOUR MOUTH

James D.F. Hannah

AND HERE I AM, sitting in my pickup outside the Shop 'N' Go, underneath a cluster of oak trees edging along the parking lot. It's strategy—far enough away the security cameras won't see me, close enough to make a run for the entrance without wearing myself out.

Willem usually works nights. The store doesn't do much business, not since the state widened Route 89 to four lanes and moved coal truck traffic off the two-lane here. Made it where no one goes this way without a reason. You don't notice this lonely little convenience store with its pair of gas pumps underneath buzzing canopy lights and a faded vinyl sign advertising beer and lottery tickets.

Which is the idea, I suppose.

I tug my mask down over my face. A horse's head staring back at me in the rearview mirror. I lift the old Army backpack from the floorboard over my shoulder. Pause for a heartbeat.

You know those moments when you're about to do something

so monumentally stupid that your body doesn't wanna listen to your brain as it barks out those electrical commands from your synapses? Your hands sit idle in your lap. Your feet ain't fallen asleep, but they won't move, neither.

Right now is one of those moment.

We doin' this? Really?

Shane's voice. Trying to give me the out.

We.

Guess we are.

Everything is about moving fast. Feet hit the concrete. To the entrance and then inside. Know that when the door closes, there's no turning back.

The Oak Ridge Boys are singing about Elvira—

(*Giddy up, um-poppa-um-poppa, mow, mow*)

—as I get inside. Willem's at the counter, licking a finger and flipping a page in a porno mag. He sees me and has the split second of blank-faced bewilderment you expect when someone in a horse mask appears and they've got a gun aimed at you.

He's reaching underneath the counter for an alarm I know doesn't go to 911 or to the sheriff's department when I cock the hammer on my pistol and step toward him.

"You push that button, Willem, and I'll put what brains you got all over those cartons of Marlboro behind you."

He freezes, raises the hand back into view.

"You want what's in the register, I—"

"Not here for the register. I want what's in back."

Tiny pinpricks bubble across Willem's greasy forehead. "Time lock. Office safe won't open up 'til morning."

"I didn't say the office; I said in back." I use a low, easy, "do not fuck with me" tone.

"You don't wanna do this," he says. "You—"

I shoot him in the shoulder. The sound echoes between the cooler section of cheap beer and expired milk and carafes of ancient coffee caked thick on the heating elements. He screams, reaches for the fresh wound and fingertips touch the ragged hole in his flesh and he screams louder and falls backward off the stool.

I square my gun into Willem's face. He seems to consider this, then knits his eyebrows together into one seamless line marching across his forehead.

"Jesus Christ, is that you, J?" he says, choking words out between tears and gasps. "You know what they're gonna do? They'll—"

I tap at his shoulder with the toe of my shoe. He lets out this giant sloppy sob. A stain spreads across the crotch of his pants.

"I done asked twice," I say. "I ain't asking a third."

Willem pulls himself to his feet, using the stool as leverage, leads me past short aisles of chips and powdered donuts to a door marked "Cleaning Supplies." Taps numbers into the keypad and the door buzzes open into a storage room that smells of disinfectants and damp mops. The harsh glow of a single bulb hanging loose from the ceiling shows the wheeled bucket and shelf full of cleaners, as well as a wall decorated with some of Willem's favorite centerfolds.

I push the barrel of the gun into Willem's neck. "Keep going."

Willem peels back the poster of an anatomically impossible redhead to reveal a safe cut into the wall. This isn't the safe for the store. The one that keeps whatever meager cash and credit card receipts the mini-mart earns during a business cycle.

No, this is where the real money lays.

Inside are rubber-band-bound stacks of cash. A mish-mash of singles, fives, tens, the occasional twenty. At least a few grand, probably more. There's also a plastic grocery store sack that I rip open.

I pull out handfuls of cellophane baggies. Some filled with a white powder, the baggie stamped with "AoS" and a playing card spade on it. Others full of small white crystals—none of that blue shit like on the TV show—and these get stamped with pictures of a robot.

Everything gets a brand in America—even the dope.

I jerk Willem out of the supply closet, march him to the front of the store. Prop him next to the coffee pots and position myself near the entrance.

A clock somewhere in the mini-mart ticks off seconds. Nearly two in the morning.

Now's the waiting.

I can handle it. I've been waiting this long.

• • •

Shane did two tours of duty in Afghanistan, when we thought it was a war we could win. He came home knowing how to handle explosives but no goddamn clue how to handle the nightmares. He'd haunt the house on those sleepless nights like a spirit looking for vengeance. Eventually he'd land out on the front porch, the world bathed in a sheen of moonlight. I got to the habit of bringing his first cup of coffee straight there, him in a chair watching the sun chisel away at the darkness every morning.

Someone at his old man's construction company recommended he buy himself a Harley, which he did, and on weekends we'd cruise the highways together, no one in the world but me and him and open road through West Virginia mountains like a snake wrestling with bad decisions. My arms around his chest, wind whipping through my hair, he felt like the man I've loved since I first laid eyes on him.

But it didn't solve the sleeplessness or the nightmares. They remained ever present, sucking up air and space and time we didn't know we didn't have.

I don't know how the Steel Skulls happened. I think his dad's company did work on the clubhouse. Whatever it was, they drew him in. They liked ex-military, and they welcomed him with wide open tattooed arms.

Everyone knows the deal with the Steel Skulls. They weren't bikers doing poker runs for charity, collecting toys at Christmas. They had bad teeth and jailhouse ink and wives and girlfriends who looked like a bad idea at closing time on a Saturday night.

Looking back, I should have asked Shane what he thought he'd find. I got focused on him sleeping again at night. I never found him on the porch again.

It took me about a year before I caught him tying off a vein. I came home from pulling a double at the hospital and saw his ride in the driveway, thought it'd been a while since we'd sliced ourselves off a piece of afternoon delight, and we could rectify that.

There he was, edge of the bed, a whole kit set up on the mattress, and that piece of rubber piping tight around his arm.

After the lying, the crying, and the denying, for the first time ever, he told me about his nightmares. A patrol in Kabul. Seeing this kid, no more than nine or ten. Eyes that should have been nothing but innocence, but Shane recognized something else. Something that didn't belong. It's why he wasn't surprised when the kid dropped a cloak and showed them the suicide vest and the C-4. The detonator in his hand.

Shane turned that boy's head into red mist with one pull of a trigger before he had the chance to think about it.

"People told me I was a hero, Jessie," he said. "I kept remembering hunting with my dad, how proud he was when I got my first buck. But he never knew I puking afterwards, 'cause I thought about the way that buck had looked at me. That little boy looked at me the same way. That kid knew he was dying that day. It didn't matter how it happened, 'cause it was happening no matter what. I realized there's something in the universe that decided that boy and that buck, they both been born with no other purpose than dying. And that's all any of us are, is born with the clocking running, waiting for it to run out. How fucked is that, Jessie? You tell me."

Shane decided to sweat out the dope. I begged him to call the VA, get some help, but he said he had to do it like this. It was just me and him. And it was worse than whatever you'd imagine it to be.

Locked him in the bedroom and waited. It took a day and a half for him to beg me to get him some junk, that he knew he was dying. After that came the screaming and the cursing and calling me every name to shame our Lord in Heaven.

Jonny B showed up four days in. Like the rest of the Steel Skulls, that you hear him before you see him, and the roar of that chopper is like a prophet foretelling doom. I wouldn't let him into the house. I ain't never let none of that trash into my home. I told Shane that'd be a rule early on. He tried to argue it with me, tell me these were his friends, his brothers in arms, and I told him in no uncertain terms how few of fucks I gave about such shit.

Jonny B had on the club cut and a black T-shirt and oil-splattered jeans. I met him at the door, just before he could ring the bell. He smiled like I should be charmed. I wasn't.

"You're looking good, J," he said.

"What do you want, Jonny?"

"Ain't seen Shane of late. Checking on him."

"He's under the weather."

"He catch a cold or something?"

"Probably."

He let his eyes go past me and into the house. Shane was at the top of the stairs. Shivering with that ratty old blanket wrapped around him.

He'd busted the bedroom lock when he heard Jonny B coming. The asshole.

"How you feelin' there, brother?" Jonny said to Shane. "Get yourself a bit of the flu?"

Shane just stood there trembling beneath the blanket, looking like he wished he could vanish himself out of existence. A magic trick—Poof!—and the blanket would collapse onto the floor.

"There's club business me and your man need to discuss," Jonny said. Eyes back to the stairwell. To Shane. "Ain't that right, brother?"

Shane's face bleached white.

Jonny said to me, "You get your man right, J, 'cause me and him got conversations to have."

I found Shane in the bedroom, struggling to put on jeans. He didn't have the strength to pull them up, and they just pooled there around his ankles.

"I gotta leave, Jessie," he said. "They're gonna come for it."

"What are they gonna come for?"

The Skulls were moving dope, he said. No big secret; everyone knew the Skulls push whatever could smoked, snorted, jammed into a vein or shoved up your ass.

The rule was, no one in the club used. If "Scarface" taught us nothing, it's to never got high off your own supply.

Shane got high off his own supply. The club's supply, more to the point. Him and one of the others, a guy everyone called Montana. Another ex-military they'd been responsible for running smack and meth through the club's territory. There was a convenience store, he said, with a safe where they'd drop off the drugs and pick up cash left by dealers they used. The logic being you didn't want to get busted with both money *and* dope.

Montana started using when he was in Afghanistan. There were miles of poppy fields, and you could get the purest, cleanest dope imaginable. It was like buying fresh bread at the bakery, except, you know, smack.

What the Skulls sold wasn't near as good, Montana told

Shane. He'd tested it—just to find out. But shitty dope is still dope, and soon enough Montana was back on the needle. Skimming a little off the top in every delivery. Enough for himself, and never any more.

Not enough to notice. Right?

Sure.

Shane, who was still having nightmares, said he looked at Montana, a guy who seemed to have his shit together, and thought if Montana could handle it, so could he.

That's doper logic at its fucking finest.

Dealers the Skulls supplied noticed orders were coming in light. Jonny chalked it up to wiseasses trying to lift a few bucks, so they went and busted the appropriate heads and that still didn't fix the problem. You don't gotta read business management books or Agatha Christie novels to know how the rest of this pieced together.

They were coming for Shane and Montana. The Skulls would let 'em live long enough to admit they did it, then leave the bodies somewhere animals would get fat off the remains.

We needed to get out of town, Shane said.

Let's run for it, I said.

It seemed so fucking simple. Like we could get away clean. Walk away and move on. That's what the world is supposed to be, is a second chance.

The Steel Skulls don't give a fuck about your second chance, however. Or your first chances, for that matter.

I left long enough to put gas in the pickup and get food for the road. I came home and found Shane in the bathtub, shotgun barrel in what was left of his mouth, the rest of him scattered on the wall behind him like a jigsaw puzzle thrown by a temperamental child.

There was a note. Apologizing. Telling me how much he loved me. Saying what our time together had meant.

"Get out of here, J. This place doesn't do anything but suck the marrow from your bones and leave you empty. You deserve better than this, J. Know I loved you."

Had him buried at the cemetery off the four-lane. He didn't want any military stuff, but a few Army buddies still came to pay their respects. His family showed, methed up and making a show of their sorrow and asking if he'd left 'em any money.

The Skulls came also. Jonny leading the charge.

"Goddamn shame about this," he told me after the preacher was done talking about damnation and forgiveness. "But you don't ever know what's in a man's heart, huh?"

You don't know what's in a woman's heart, either, motherfucker.

Lemme give you a hint: Same shit as in a man's.

Anger.

Rage.

Wrath.

· · ·

Montana didn't get any better. He was found dangling from a rope in his basement. Wasn't even a note. His girl, this sweet thing named Beth, she left town right after the funeral. As in, she drove straight from the cemetery into a new town.

Because sometimes all you can do is run from the pain. You can't get away from it, but you can make it work to find you.

Always does, though. Every goddamn night.

I gave them six months. Time to relax. Two whole seasons to imagine life would go back to normal.

No one touched the convenience store, Shane told me. Sacrosanct, he called it. 'Cause two things you don't fuck with are money and dope, and especially not the Steel Skulls' money or dope.

I crouch behind the rack of gum and candy bars as the roar of the motorcycles get closer. They go silent in the parking lot and the doors open. Jonny B and some young guy, blond and fresh-faced and looking dumb as the dog, swagger through the entrance.

I come up fast over the rack and shoot the kid in the chest before either of them see me. His body slams against the door and slips to the floor, his eyes already as empty as old soda bottles. Jonny, reaching for a gun under his cut when I step into view. He locks eyes on me and the pistol and he stops moving.

He's staring at the clown mask, a faint smile threatening the corners of his mouth, at odds with the situation at hand. Sometimes all you got is bemused uncertainty.

I tug the mask off and drop it to the floor. Jonny's eyes widen in realization of the face in front of him. The smile gets real.

"Well ain't you a fuckin' plot twist, J?" he says. "You lookin' to wreak some havoc or what?"

I tell him to take his gun out slowly and kick it toward me. He does so without argument. I'd counted on him offering more fight. Jonny B, legendary tough guy. If my heart had room for disappointment, it might have found a little lodging there,

"What's the play, J?" he says. "What do you want here?"

That's the question, isn't it? What do I want?

I want Shane back. But that's can't happen. I wanna pull the trigger and kill Jonny and have it be the end, but that's not what I want either.

I say, "I wanna know why you did it."

It's such a simple request, Jonny's struggling with it. He could try to deny it, but why bother? No better time for honesty that having a 9 mm pointed at you.

"He was stealing from us," he says. "He was junked up. Him and Montana both. You start using, you ain't worth nothing then. Not to the club, not to the world."

"He was getting clean. We were gonna leave. We were gonna be gone for forever."

"That's what he told us. Thing is, people knew he was stealing. That makes us look like punks. When that happens, it's over for us."

"I'd have hated for y'all to lose face."

"It's business, J. Nothing more."

I shrug and let the backpack fall. Set my foot behind the it. Like a kicker readying up for a punt.

"Everyone in this goddamn town calls me 'J.' Everyone except Shane. Said it wasn't right to take a person and make 'em nothing but a letter. That's how I knew it wasn't him that wrote the note. He'd have never called me that."

I kick the backpack. It skips across the tile into Jonny's feet.

"Go on, now," I say. "Your money and your dope. Get out of here with it."

Jonny's confused as a toddler told to solve a calculus equation.

"The hell's going on here?" he says.

I gesture with the gun for him to pick up the backpack. He finally does.

"I needed the truth, Jonny. I knew it already; I just wanted someone to tell it to me. That's what you gave me. Now get your ass out of here."

"That's it?"

"Indeed."

He's almost to the door when he stops, looks back at me.

"You know this ain't all there is, right? The club'll know. And Willem, he's gonna tell the cops."

I shoot Willem. Don't even bother to look at him. Just swing the gun around and pop two shots. He grunts and thumps onto the floor.

"Guess it's just you," I say.

Jonny kicks his motorcycle to life. It's practically a sonic boom as he takes down the road.

I get the gas can from my truck and douse everything inside the store. Strike a match and light up the night.

As the fire burns, I dial a number of my cell phone. The number of a cheap burner phone I bought at the dollar store. A phone sewn into the lining of the backpack that Jonny has.

Shane's backpack.

In the fear and frenzy of everything, I'll bet Jonny never notices the extra weight. More than money and the drugs inside.

It's the few ounces of C-4, from Shane's father's company. Acquired because the old man, in his grief, forgot to ask for his son's keys back. Sitting in a false bottom in the backpack along with two pounds of ball bearings. The cell phone wired into the C-4.

Jonny won't hear the phone ringing. He'll never feel the heat of the explosion or the force of those ball bearings tearing through him. The bastard'll be dead before he knows it.

But Christ do I want him to suffer. He's owed it. Suffering the way Shane suffered.

Everyone's deserving of hurt here, and I've got no shortage to share.

WHATEVER HAPPENED TO JILL DAWN MEADE?

Karen Harrington

TEXAS: 1989

I TOLD THE POLICE that I don't know where Mama is now and I've never heard of the dead man, but they don't believe me. She was escaping from the Stop N Go last I saw of her so maybe they should check around there. It's not like I had any control over anything. Nobody listens to my advice. For example, I told Sally that her black eyeliner and blue eye shadow made her look hideous, but she insisted it looked great. Her school picture is the awfullest thing I've ever seen. She looked like a racoon went to the drugstore.

Now I sit in a jail room and try to overhear what's going on while this lady cop makes phone calls. The officers out in the hall drink coffee and talk about me. They think I can't hear them. People don't think much of eleven-year-olds so it makes eavesdropping a snap.

"The kid must be upset," I hear one of them say. "We're

waiting for her father to come and get her. A Brian Meade of San Antonio. He didn't sound too happy about the women."

I hear another officer say that blue vinyl had stuck to the dead man's face and peeled off when they pulled him out of the car.

"He was done for, plain and simple, probably headed to Mexico after the business with the women," he said. "An eye for an eye and all that jazz. Justice on earth or on a piece of toast."

I wish I had a piece of paper to write down what he said. I want to remember "justice on a piece of toast." As it is, I only have a Styrofoam cup of water the lady cop gave me an hour ago.

Now, she swishes back into the room and sits down. "Jill, I want to know how the day all started."

"The women are named Cheri and Beth," I tell her. "And you can tell your friends out there in the hall that they already spilled the beans. I know about the car headed to Mexico. It crashed. Someone died. The end."

The lady cop is surprised. You can tell by the way her mouth opens into a perfect O.

"Your mother is a pretty lady. And she has a pretty daughter too," the lady cop says.

"What about my mother?"

"We'll get to that."

I don't like that she is trying to be nice. I already know my mother is pretty. Pretty enough to attract drunk men. That's what I overheard Beth say one night. They never thought they were pretty enough, but I still thought they were, in the magazine sense.

"Is my mama okay?" I don't want her to know I'm afraid, but I am. This day feels like a dead end road where you have to turn around.

"That's unclear."

"What about Beth?"

"You want some more water?"

Well. Now I know something is up.

They could have been sisters, Mama and Beth. Dark brown hair they home-permed and Benson & Hedges menthol in their pockets. Both of them, just alike. Mama read somewhere that, "curls around the face get you a date." They plucked their eyebrows so high that I thought they looked like they were waiting for an answer to a question. They looked especially this way when they wore blue eye shadow, which looked better on them than poor Sally, you can take it from me.

Beth and Mama have long legs and pretty pink-painted toes. I always told Mama she was pretty, but she didn't listen. She said she attracted plenty of fists to the face. She got those fists from the "game."

"The game?" The lady cop asks as a question so now I realize I've been a motormouth, which is what Mama calls me. Well, if the cop wants to know more, I want to at least get something more than water. That's what Mama would do. Trade for trade.

"Can I have a Coke? And something to write with?" I add this in case there is another interesting phrase I need to write down.

It works because in no time, there is an ice-cold bottle in front of me, a pencil and a piece of white paper.

"The game is a way to stretch things out like the way you can add tuna fish to anything to make it stretch into a meal. Do you ever do that?"

The lady cop grimaces. I like that I made her do that. "I don't think so."

"Well, we eat a lot of tuna. That's because paychecks from working at the A&W and the Lucky Lady gas station didn't add up to much, even if you did stuff stolen cheeseburgers or lottery tickets into your purse," I say. "Which they did all the time." A smashed cheeseburger from Mama's purse is an awful thing. But I still ate it. I'm not stupid.

"What is it like at home?" the lady cop asks.

I take a long sip of Coke. Too much so that when I start to talk, I want to burp.

"Do you have curtains?" I ask.

"Well, yes, in some rooms."

"Mama thinks curtains make a place look homey. Is that true?"

"Depends on the window."

Our curtains didn't match anything else. But it really gave the place a sad look like the inside of one of my friends' trailer. I share a room with Mama most days. That is until these men spend the night. Then my room is the closet. I got a set of those glow in the dark stars and stuck them on the wall. Then I'd spray them with the flashlight and lay there, watching their glow fade out, hiding from sounds beyond the door.

Some of the furniture in the apartment was stuff from slow drives down neighborhood alleys, the kind of neighborhoods where people get tired of perfectly good flowered couches and faded green plastic patio chairs. We even found a TV that didn't have any sound, but showed the picture well enough. And it was fun to sit and wonder what the people were saying, or make up stories to go along with the action. That's how I started my talent for imagining things.

I would sit on one of those old flowered couches, and they would watch TV with a drunk man until he got drunker. When he passed out, it was time for the daughters' part of the game. We searched the men's pockets. Most of the time all we found was those little minty toothpicks or an off-brand condom. Then Mama would say "Yeah, right. In your dreams, bucko," or something like that.

"And how often did you play the game," the lady asks. I take another sip of Coke.

"I mean, not that often. Maybe only twice a week, but less if we struck gold."

"Gold?"

"If gold was a wad of twenties, I mean."

She frowns. It seems to be something she does a lot. "I see."

With a twenty, we could get an ice-cream sandwich or a package of colored ponytail holders after they bought smokes. It was those times I guess I didn't mind so much what we were doing. But being one of the pocket-searching eleven-year-olds made me know more about the world than most people under twenty, which Mama said was a good thing. She said I was lucky and smart to already be aware of the cruel world, of men and what they will try and do and take.

I don't say all of this. If you want to know, I don't understand all of this.

"And what did you think about this?"

"I'm eleven and even I know it was weird, lady. Geesh." I should ask for another Coke, not because I'm thirsty, but just because. And I'm tired of her face. And she better not call me honey again.

"Sorry, honey."

I crack my knuckles because I know that annoys most adults. It's my only super power. "You probably think she was terrible, but I know things that some girls don't. Mama says this is education money can't buy."

Maybe I'm making Mama and Beth sound completely rotten. I mean, they were at times. They could think of really creative ways for us to "get it" as they warned us all the time. *Jill Dawn Meade, you're going to get it! Don't look at me like that, girl, or you'll get it.* Sometimes "getting it" would include things like cigarette burns. Other things I'll never tell anyone.

"They don't sound like they were always good to you, Jill," the Lady cop says.

My Coke is empty now and all there is to do is swipe the cool water from the sides of the bottle. "Do you have kids?"

"Well, no," she says, fidgeting with her pencil now.

"Mama says people who don't have kids think they have all the answers. You think you have the answers?"

She slides her chair back and it squawks against the floor. "No one has all the answers, Jill."

I'm wondering what else I can ask for now. I'm not hungry, though, but it might speed things along.

"I think they didn't get that they were moms who were supposed to know better than us girls," I say.

They flipped through the TV or magazines and told us what boys they thought were cute and which famous people we should date, like Rob Lowe. They told us they wanted to buy more pink things for our room and spent too much money on fancy-label clothes. They wanted us to fit in at school. I guess you could say we didn't really look like girls living in an apartment with sad curtains and drunk men on weekends. We were always neat and clean. We had the latest Ghostbusters lunchboxes, metal squares with our white bread sandwiches inside. We had this even though there wasn't much to eat on the weekends. This was as confusing as it sounds and proves how mean she could be. All show on the outside, *look, my daughter has plenty* and then if you look closer you might see…nevermind.

We weren't allowed to smoke or have our ears pierced even though we begged to have them done. And we wanted perms, but no. They dropped us off at the library, not the mall like other kids, which would have been bitchin'. No, we had to hang at the library and giggle about getting into all the adult books, like the romance novels Mama hid under her bed. We read the lines out loud and imagined what it would be swept up with desire. But that is really, really a whole 'nother story because the truth is, we didn't really have to act out the romance novels or imagine them at all. We could hear them being acted out inside our apartment. And then we'd really giggle because we'd say, "Hey, that sounds like Marisa and Rip" from one of the forbidden books.

"Does this sound like a good mother?" I really want to know.

"She sounds…complex."

"Right. Complex." I want to write that down, too.

"Anything that made yesterday unusual?"

She cares so much about yesterday and all I want to know is what happens today. "She's going to make me wait, right? Teach me a lesson."

"Does she often leave you places? To teach you a lesson?"

"I mean, not often. Where is she now?"

"We are trying to sort everything out," the lady says.

"Well, can you sort faster?"

"How did the day start yesterday? You said your mother went to work, right?"

It was a day when the beds are still unmade at noon and the sink is full of dirty dishes. So, like every day really. But there was a stack of dirty clothes by the bedroom door that smelled like something wet and sour had been there a while. But the smell could have been the trash with all the cat litter stuff. My cat, Dave, seemed to make as much smell as us. According to Mama, the only thing he is good for is fending off bad people who searched the trash. She's got this thing about putting old bank statements and the men's stolen stuff in the same trash bag with Dave's dirty litter. This will be the penalty for anyone trying to get into something they shouldn't. And I guess this is an okay thing to do, although I think there are more uses for Dave than just that.

"I did the laundry before she went to work," I say.

"The laundry."

"There would be at least three baskets of it, that is if we had baskets, but we don't so we usually hauled it in old white pillowcases that you can easily drag across the pavement along with your box of soap. I wanted one of those little red wagons to make this work easier and kept hoping we'd find one on one of our grab-n-go drives down the alleyways, but I suppose they're too useful to throw out. Not like our flowery couch, which we grabbed on a full moon night last October. Do you have laundry baskets?"

"I have two," she says. "So, laundry. That's what you were doing this morning."

Since it was Saturday, we watched morning cartoons. Mama got ready for her shift by putting on her A&W uniform with a large plastic name tag that says CHERI in big black letters. She's worked there a while but is saving to finish her education at beauty college because she had to stop getting educated when she married my father.

Before she left, she barked out some chores toward my back. I pretended to acknowledge what she said but was really fast-forwarding my mind to a half-hour later when she would be gone and I could be lazy until a half-hour before she got home like always. Mama says I have a rebellious streak a mile long and that I'm just more of everything, good and bad. *You are just more, Jill. It exhausts me.* Well. I've been called worse on account of the way my teeth are coming in. All wonky.

Sally sat next to me, doing the exact same thing. Nothing. Beth was still sleeping with last night's "Rip." Sally had a sad face over that because Beth had promised to take her to get a haircut. Her bangs are beyond bangs now, as they say. She might as well grow them out or let them cover her horrible make-up.

During a commercial, I went into Mama's room to gather up my clothes. I stopped at her dresser and pulled out her silver charm bracelet. Sometimes she would let me wear it around the house, so I slipped it on and let all the charms dangle around my wrist. I was in no mood, as Mama says, to do the laundry. But then I saw a new romance book under her bed, and I suddenly wanted to get to the laundry room and read. According to the back cover, the story featured Cassandra Langdon and

Bolt Kensington, "two star-crossed lovers who rendezvous on the great stony moors of an English country estate, only to find a dead body. If they report it, their passions will be discovered. What should they do?!"

I couldn't wait to get into it because I wondered what I'd do if I ever came across a dead body. Of course, there was sure to be a lot of hot sex and all that stuff, most of which I skimmed since every book had a lot of it. Plus, I figured I knew how it felt. Once, I asked Mama what the big deal was and why people want to do it all the time. She told me to think about how, when you get out of the shower and you grab a Q-Tip and run it around in your ear, it feels so good. I am fortunate to know this information.

So I went ahead and got the laundry bundled in our laundry pillowcases. I didn't really want to be there when that new Rip guy stumbled out of Beth's room. I'd had that experience before and I prefer these men when they're drunk, and it is okay to search their pockets.

I begged Sally to come with me, at least to get it started, but she wasn't having any of it. I stuffed the box of soap into the pillowcase. I knew it would get dented and smushed as I dragged it down the stairs and I would "get it" later, but I thought, what the hell, I'm doing the work, aren't I? That's the kind of logic that didn't go over real well with Mama, but sometimes it felt good to picture myself saying it out in the open.

I suddenly realize that the lady cop has a perm and I ask her if she gets many dates because I want to see if Mama is right.

"Honey, let's talk about that later. I just want to hear about your day. Do you want something else to eat?"

I say that I do and she leaves and comes back with a cheeseburger and fries. It is like I'm on vacation almost.

"Whenever you are ready, finish telling me the story, honey," she tells me when I start to eat. And I notice now she is calling me honey again.

"You're about to tell me some bad news, right?"

She takes a deep breath. She would be no good as a mother because she doesn't hide how she is annoyed with questions. "Just keep going. You were doing laundry."

I dip a French fry in ketchup and explain how I got to the laundry room and how it smelled like soap and underarms. I put quarters in the washing machine and looked at the new book. One of the first words is "rendezvous." I make a mental note to look it up in the dictionary. It sounds like a word I would like to use when Sally and I playact.

I read while leaning against one of the warm dryers, so warm I wanted to crawl inside and lie down like I'd done before. But instead, I settled in and read the first page, which started on page ten, so I'd already made progress. Because I decided I might want to write these kinds of novels someday, I turned down the corners of pages that said things in a new way. By the time the first laundry buzzer went off, I had turned down three pages. I unloaded the clothes, put another load in and settled in for more reading. About this time Sally came racing in and told me to get home right away. She said Mama was home early because she'd finally gotten herself fired.

"She's throwing things," Sally told me, all upset. "I think she hurt Dave. She threw him against the wall."

"Dave is your cat?" the lady cop asks.

"Do you know if he's okay?"

"I'll check in a little while, honey," she tells me. "What happened when you and Sally got back to the apartment?" Now I know the bad news might be about Sally or Dave or both because that's three 'Honeys.'

We ran back home. Sure enough, Mama was still tossing things around, smoking and trying on new outfits. Dave was under Sally's bed and we couldn't get him to come out. Mama screamed at me because one of her tank tops was still in the laundry room. It didn't seem to count that I'd been washing it.

She settled down in front of her make-up table and applied blush galore. She said she'd been fired for taking money from the cash register, even though she'd sworn she wouldn't do it again. Then she was putting on her "get 'em in the net" outfit, which is a purple sweater with a scoop neckline and this great gold and pink necklace with specks of gold that sat just right around her neck. It was supposed to be a necklace that had been in the family for decades, maybe centuries. I wanted it.

So I took it as a good sign when she put it on and we both smiled at each other in the mirror. She always told me that, even if you're feeling low or look like crap, a necklace will make you look pulled together. She said she felt much better. I told her she looked pretty. And I wasn't lying.

I'd seen Mama like this before. It's all lightning before the thunder, calm before the storm, I have read that in books and it's true. If you pay attention, you can see a person has a forecast. Getting out that necklace meant the storm was coming.

If it's a big love, Jill Dawn, you'll get a big mess. Remember that. Men make babies and wars and then leave the scene of the crime for someone else to clean up.

This lady is impressed that I could say this because she nods her head and puts her hand up to her mouth, probably to stop the word honey from coming out.

"Do you know what shoplifting is, Jill?" the lady cop asks. Well, she used my name, so this is serious.

"Do you?" I ask.

"Of course."

"You ever gone hungry?"

"Can't say that I have."

"We only get things we really need. Usually. But I got the can of cat food, and that's not Mama's fault. Is she dead?"

"You wanted to help Dave. I understand that."

"Yes." I stab the empty Styrofoam cup clear through with the pencil.

We'd done this trick before. I'd go in, get a few things. After I'd made sure they'd seen the box of female products in my basket, I'd pretend I forgot to get something from another aisle. Then, the cashier waits on the next customer and forgets all about me. Mama sits in the car right by the curb outside the store like she always does, and as soon as the electronic doors swing open, I run like a bat out of hell with snacks and maybe a lipstick hidden under my coat. She drives away fast. We get to a stop and laugh. Then she would kiss my head and brush my hair back and tell me how proud she was of me. We've only done it a few times, ten maybe, when she was between paychecks.

"Just so you know, it was me who suggested the grocery store thing," I say.

"You're a helpful girl, Jill."

"I guess."

We were in her hatchback, driving up to the front of the store. I went inside and put the stuff in a shopping basket. Then I saw the red and blue cans of cat food, which were only forty-nine cents, so who would care. Besides, Dave needed a treat that might make him come out from under the bed. But when I got to the door, someone grabbed my arm with such a jerk that the stuff in my basket went flying and I saw Mama's eyes cut across me like a cold wind.

"Mama, wait!" I called as she sped away. I pulled free for a moment from the arm holding me back and I tried to run toward the red taillights of her car. But she was gone.

"And next thing I know, I'm sitting in this room with a woman who has no kids and never goes hungry. That's you in case you didn't figure it out."

She looks down and holds her head.

I'm so tired and I really am starting to worry about Dave. Plus, all our laundry is still in the laundry room and sometimes people steal it and I don't want to get in trouble for that too.

The lady cop tells me I'll be staying here for a while longer and that I'm doing a good job and do I want something else to eat. All she knows to do is offer food. Then she takes me to a different room, a place that seems like a jail cell, although she tells me it isn't. There's a cot, a sink and a small table in the center. They bring me some fried chicken and I eat it pretty fast because it's free.

The lady cop comes back in with a Scrabble game and lays it all out on the table. The letter tiles. The timer.

We play a long time and in between the spaces, the lady cop tells me little bits of information. Crumb by crumb, like she's seeing if I can take it.

"They took her to the hospital, Jill."

She lays out the word BIRD on the Scrabble board. "They weren't able to save her."

It is my turn to move the letters on the board and I use the D at the end of BIRD and spell DARK.

"Had she been to a bar?" I ask.

"Yes."

"With a good for nothing man, I bet."

The lady cop says nothing and then spells out the word FIESTA.

"Some bad things happened at your apartment," she says finally. "Gunshot. Witnesses say your mother put up a fight. Sally was fatally shot. The police came and the man was gone."

"The one who wrecked in the Buick?"

"I forgot you heard that."

I close my eyes and see the red taillights of the hatchback smear into a blur and I know in my bones that my life is worse off than before.

"Oh, honey." This time I don't mind hearing her call me honey.

"What is your name?" I ask her and she looks like I said part of a joke.

"Why, it's Rose, honey."

"That's a nice name."

"This is my card. You can call me anytime. And I'm going to give you a call when you get to your new home, okay? Your father is coming to collect you."

To collect me. I'd never heard that before. It didn't seem like the thing you do when you pick up your daughter who you haven't seen in five years.

Rose gives me a plastic bag with my Mama's necklace in it and tells me my father can help me get my stuff from the apartment. Then she gives me another hug and takes me to another room that has a bathroom and shower. After she leaves, I take a long shower and think I should cry over Mama, but nothing happens. Then I wrap myself in a scratchy towel that smells like bleach. I keep wondering why Mama was alive until they got her to the hospital. That seems like just the opposite of what it should be to me.

And I wish I knew what happened to Dave, if he's still hiding under the bed. I know he thinks all of this is his fault and can't understand why no one has come for so many hours. No one has come to collect him either. Thinking about Dave is what finally makes me cry. I hurry up and get it over with. No man wants to see a girl with the waterworks going. That's what Mama always says.

Police: Woman arrested for murder in South Dallas
DALLAS (CBSDFW.COM) A 43-year-old woman has been arrested and charged with murder after a fight led to a shooting at an apartment complex in Dallas Saturday evening, police said.

Police responded to the shooting around 9:45 p.m. at the Bonita Gardens apartments on Fordham Road.

Arriving officers found the victim, 42-year-old Darryl Lee Weber, with gunshot wounds. He was pronounced dead at the scene.

Police said the suspect, Jill Dawn Meade, was immediately detained. During an interview with detectives, police said Meade admitted to shooting Weber following a fight over her cat.

Saturday's incident is not the first time Meade has been charged in connection with a crime. According to court documents, Meade was sentenced to five years' probation as a first offender on charges of carrying a weapon on school grounds and subsequently convicted of probation violation in 2000 after being charged with shoplifting. In 2016, Meade was accused of stabbing her former roommate. Police said Meade threatened to kill the roommate if he didn't leave the home. Police say charges were later dismissed because the victim was not cooperative.

Meade was booked into Lew Sterrett Jail on a murder charge. Her bond has not yet been set.

SHIFTING THE BLAME

Curtis Ippolito

WHEN THE DRIZZLE TURNED into a driving rain, Beverly Stewart was left standing alone outside Sheriff Dale Hap's home. The righteous chants from the small group of women had ceased; the unseasonable weather this summer morning ending their protest without notice.

Rain smacked against the pavement.

Pretty soon, car engines started up around Beverly. She paid them no mind as they drove away.

Her eyes remained fixed on the stone house. Her fists clenched at her sides. One light shone inside, on the far left of the second floor. Sheriff Hap's home office, she'd bet. Beverly wondered if he was aware of those protesting him for the last thirty minutes. If so, he plainly hadn't given a damn. No one had come out of the house to object. No deputies called to chase them off this time. Their grief-stricken voices had to have penetrated his walls.

HAPLESS HAP!

STOP KILLING OUR CHILDREN!

She considered the latter too long and clumsy, and the former a weak indictment of the rottenness persisting in Hap's department. What happened to her son, Roger, wasn't hapless. His death was devastating. Unconscionable and unforgivable. And his wasn't an isolated case: seven other men had died in the sheriff's jails over the previous eight months. In total, one hundred and fifty inmates had died in Hap's custody in the ten years he'd served as county sheriff. Sounded like fiction. She wished it was. The total death count was an all-time state record and would surely continue to grow with each successful reelection campaign he undertook.

The next only two months away.

A burning mass throbbed in Beverley's stomach, an ulcer she'd given herself in the months following the call she received from the downtown men's jail.

She walked to her Acura two blocks over, and flopped behind the driver's seat. Pressed a hand to her belly until the pain backed off. She tugged at her soggy cashmere sweater and picked out a few hairs belonging to a litter of strays she'd recently scooped up. Siamese mixes. She'd received a few scratches for her trouble, but the kittens were easier to move than some of the other rescues she'd transported. Beverly started the car. Between the pouring rain and her heavy breathing, the windshield and the front windows had fogged over. She pressed the defroster button and turned on the wipers. Then she dug for her phone while waiting for the windshield to clear.

• • •

Sipping his morning coffee, Sheriff Dale Hap watched the group of women protesting him from behind one side of the thick curtains adorning his home office window. He let them. Whiners got no audience with this cowboy. If he called in his deputies to break-up their pathetic display, the media would come running. And the less those windbags meddled in his day-to-day, the better.

The eight women below shouted, and shook homemade signs in his direction.

Hap snorted at their chants. These hags actually thought he snuck into jail cells and personally squeezed the life out of their sons? Drama queens. Sure, prisoners died in his custody. For a lot of different reasons, too. Junkies OD. The crazies and guilty kill themselves, and others plain drop dead for no diagnosable reason other than criminals ain't the healthiest sort. So what if he encouraged his deputies to get creative with "difficult to handle cases," and sometimes that meant a few prisoners got roughed up and died as a result? Who cares? They were lowlifes. Gutter trash whose only purpose was gumming up the intakes of his five county jails every damn day of the week. The general public was better off. Listen, you live a rough life, you're gonna die a rough death. Pretty simple. Where you end up dying might happen to be in a jail cell.

Hap took a big sip of his coffee.

Other groups of mothers similar to this one had banded together over the years and protested him about the same thing. Initially, the media got a spider up their skirts about the jail deaths and covered the first few protests with fervor. But they eventually dropped that old bone, convinced it had no meat on it after Hap turned on the charm and helped reporters see the situation logically. All they needed to hear was the truth: Hap's jurisdiction sprawled across the largest geographical area of the state with hundreds of thousands of residents living therein. Simple math accounted for more prisoners dying on his watch than in a county half the size. Wasn't hard to square.

Why should the media care anyway? Not like voters did, and at the end of the day they were his only supervisor. If the public kept electing him, where was the problem? He also focused the media's attention on his department's accomplishments. Reminding them of how the crime rate decreased year after year during his tenure. Fed them feel-good stories too, including "The Sheriff's Department Holiday Gift Drive" benefitting terminally ill children, and the program where deputies delivered lunch to shut-ins once a month. Yep, the media ate out of the palm of Hap's hand, all right.

Outside, the sky cracked open and rain drenched the protestors. Hap smiled, watching the women scatter in defeat. There would be no media coverage of this pitiful show; nothing to tarnish his good name so soon before the election.

A sense of relief washed over Hap.

He looked again and one woman still stood in the street, doing what, he couldn't tell. Probably that Stewart woman. Bitch wouldn't leave him alone. She got her answer about her son's death, having sued him. What else did she want? He strained his eyes to examine her, but the rain was coming down in sheets. Didn't matter. Eventually, she skulked off too.

Hap shrugged into his suit jacket, snatched up his Stetson, and downed the last of his coffee. Time to get to work and keep his county safe.

· · ·

Beverly called Channel 10. The receptionist who answered told Beverly that Andrea Vazala had just returned from the field and needed some time to get settled at her desk. It would be a minute. But where did Beverly need to be with her husband of forty years passed away of a grief-stricken heart attack three months earlier, and her son in the ground as well?

"I'm happy to wait on hold, dear," Beverly said.

Scratchy audio simulcasting the station's morning news served in place of hold music. The lead story: the rain. Traffic hazards caused by the rain. Its potential impact on wildfire season. On the drought. Also, an update on the county election races. And there was a jumper off a highway overpass.

Beverly's thoughts drifted to six months earlier when she'd waited on hold in the middle of the night for someone from the downtown men's jail to come back on the line.

"Ma'am?" a male voice had asked, finally.

"Yes, yes, I'm here," Beverly said.

"I'm sorry to inform you that your son, Roger Stewart, was found collapsed in his cell earlier this evening and could not be revived."

"The last person already told me that," Beverly said. "I asked to speak to the sheriff. Are you the sheriff?"

"No, ma'am. I'm the spokesperson for the Sheriff's Department."

"How did he… die, or collapse, or however you put it?" She tried her best to keep her composure.

"A cause of death hasn't been determined—"

"He was only in jail because of an argument at home, and you're telling me he's dead now for no damn good reason?"

"No, ma'am. I'm not saying that."

"What then?"

A pause.

"Did your son have a history with drugs?"

Beverly tried to stay calm, tried not to get annoyed with his insinuation. "He'd been clean for years, but he recently relapsed. Why?"

"I really can't say any more," the spokesperson said. "Not during an active investigation. But know that with someone like your son—"

"Someone *like* my son?"

The spokesman went quiet. Beverly held her breath, hoping she hadn't ruined her chances of finding out more information.

"It's… it's not a surprise with someone with a history of drug abuse," he said. "The deputies found residue. I'm sorry. That's all I can say."

What did he mean? They'd found drugs in Roger's cell? He'd overdosed in jail? That was the last place she would have expected. How'd he get drugs in jail, first off, and so quickly?

"Did my son overdose?"

"I'm sorry, but I can't disclose any more information until the investigation is concluded," said the spokesman.

"When will that be?"

"Could be up to six months."

"Six months? Are you insane?" With that, Beverly hung up the phone and called her lawyer, who informed her that they could find out the cause of Roger's death if she sued Sheriff Hap.

So, she did.

Beverly received Roger's cause of death two months after filing suit, and ever since had wrestled with the fact that he had indeed died from an overdose. But suing the sheriff didn't produce any further answers into the circumstances of her thirty-one-year-old son's death. Like how had Roger procured the Fentanyl-laced Oxy? Why had no one been monitoring his cell? And why didn't anyone administer Narcan when they found him unconscious? They hadn't or he might still be alive. He could have survived the overdose if he'd been at home. Beverly kept a can of the antagonist in her purse for emergencies, just like with the EpiPen when Roger was a boy, due to his bee allergy.

No one would give her any answers, despite the numerous messages she left for the sheriff. And the media said it couldn't find out anything even if they tried. Her son's death being an active investigation.

Beverly blamed herself. If she hadn't called the police when she and Roger had gotten into that fight, he'd still be alive. Stupid her for thinking a couple of nights in jail would give him the time to clear his mind and want to get clean again. All she accomplished was sending him to his grave.

Her lawyer advised her to file a wrongful-death lawsuit against the county, but Beverly didn't need money. She had plenty, and the irony was all the money in the world couldn't keep her son clean.

No, what she wanted was to stop Sheriff Hap.

It would take some ingenuity to accomplish, but she'd discovered a way after hearing a story on public radio about a non-profit that was buying properties and transferring the land deeds to homeless individuals.

The news loop over the phone ceased and a voice spoke.

"Channel 10. This is Andrea Vazala."

"Hi, Andrea. It's Beverly Stewart."

"Mrs. Stewart. Sorry I didn't make it to the protest. My producer wanted me on rain coverage."

"It's fine, dear."

"Are you planning another protest? Is that why you're calling? Because my producer told me we're beating an old horse at this point." This didn't come as a shock to Beverly, as she'd heard basically the same thing from every reporter and producer in town before.

"Forget the protests," Beverly said. "I've got a much bigger scoop for you."

●　●　●

Hap wasn't at his office more than an hour when he overheard an incoming call about a large-scale animal seizure out in the east part of the county. Animal Services needed hands, as well as law enforcement support. Sheriff licked his chops. This one rang all the bells associated with the potential hero praise he craved—and frankly deserved—for all his hard work. The perfect story to help him clinch a third-consecutive five-year term. He could see the front page of tomorrow's newspaper now. The headline, "Sheriff Hap Rescues Abused Adorable Animals," with a photo of him directing his deputies on the scene.

Nothing the public loved more than an animal lover. Media too. They all gobbled it up.

"Jones, Sherman, Hemlock," he shouted out into his bullpen. "Tell Dispatch that I'm responding personally. You boys follow my lead. When media arrives on the scene, they come to me and only me for any and all comments and interviews."

It took them half an hour to drive from downtown to the three-acre parcel of land out east. Driving up a dirt road about five miles off the highway, Hap knew they were at the right place when he saw an army of vehicles parked in front of a dilapidated double-wide. It looked like when a circus rounds up its animals to get on to the next town, except with white Animal Services trucks being loaded instead of tractor trailers.

"What's the situation," he barked into the clear midday air. No sign of rain out in this part of the county.

A short woman with a severe haircut lumbered up to him.

"Sheriff. Thank you for coming." She offered a hand, which he shook firmly. "Donna Glazer, Animal Welfare Officer.

Hap tugged the brim of his Stetson.

"Fill me in, Officer," he said.

"Extreme hoarder situation, sir. Cats, dogs, small farm animals—all of them living inside this trailer in horrible conditions and exhibiting poor health. Mange, dehydration, emaciation."

"Jesus, that's awful." Hap feigned concern. "You found farm animals inside? Like in the living room?"

"Actually, there were cages of Siamese kittens in the living room. We found dozens of old rabbits in the bathroom, a pygmy goat in one of the bedrooms. Roosters in another. Adult cats and dogs running around everywhere. Pretty much every kind of old, unwanted, or stray animal—this person took them all in. It was a madhouse."

"Where's the owner?" Hap climbed the trailer's rickety porch stairs. The stench of barnyard overcame him. He whipped out a handkerchief and covered his nose and mouth.

"We don't know," Donna said. "We couldn't find any signs that the structure was occupied by… a human. We're hoping your department can assist us with locating the owner."

The scene inside disgusted him. Animal feces were smashed into the floor and what remained of carpet. Paw prints and claw marks decorated the wood-paneled walls. Cages were stacked everywhere. The air thick and foul.

He scowled. "You better believe it. I'll find the sick piece of crap responsible for this and string 'em up." Donna recoiled, so he added, "In a manner of speaking."

"Thank you, Sheriff. I'll be outside helping process things."

Hap followed her out, not wanting to spend a second more breathing in the vile animal by-product. When he stepped off the porch, he saw a Channel 10 van parking in the ditch off the road. A female reporter and a cameraman jumped out. Hap turned to his deputies leaning on their cruisers. Clapped his hands and yelled.

"Make sure these poor animals are comfortable and have access to water—"

"Sheriff?" said a female voice at his side, quicker than he expected.

He turned to her. "As duly-elected, sweetheart."

"My name is Andrea. Ready for comment?"

She raised her microphone below his chin. Hap straightened,

gave the camera held by a sloppily-dressed punk kid over Andrea's shoulder a big smile and winked.

"Please look at me, not the camera, Sheriff," she instructed.

He nodded, cleared his throat. "Andrea, what we found here today, frankly, it was very disturbing."

"Tell us what you found, Sheriff Hap."

"The trailer behind me was overrun with abused, neglected pets. Dogs, cats—kittens. Chickens, rabbits, even a goat. All left to fend for themselves. Feces everywhere. Poor things. Many will require specialized medical care. Sadly, I'm betting some will have to be put down."

As Hap waited for a follow-up, he caught movement on the road. Shielding his eyes, he watched a maroon Acura pull in behind the news van.

"Do you know the identity of the person responsible for this, Sheriff?"

Hap refocused his attention on Andrea, gave her the appropriate amount of sincere contemplation before answering.

"No, not at this time. But rest assured, I'm personally going to find the owner of this place and make sure they're prosecuted to the fullest extent of the law."

"Well, Sheriff. I already know who the property belongs to," Andrea said.

Hap glared back at his dumb deputies standing there. "You don't say. Aren't you resourceful?" Why hadn't one of his men looked up the deed to the address? Now he felt foolish, having a reporter best him at his job.

"Sheriff Hap." Andrea's voice was firm. "Can you explain to your constituents why you imprisoned these animals in the reprehensible conditions you just described?"

Hap bristled. "Now, hold on, sweetheart. What are you saying to me right now?"

"The deed to this structure is in your name. Dale Hap."

"I know my own name." He whipped off his Stetson.

Andrea pulled out a folded piece of paper from her back pocket, and handed it to him. She kept the mic raised as he opened it.

Sure enough, a printed copy of the official deed to the trailer and three acres of property where they stood with his name listed as the rightful owner.

"This dump ain't mine," he shouted. "I've never stepped foot here a day in my life!"

"It's there in black and white, Sheriff," said another female reporter now bodying him, raising her microphone to his mouth.

Hap heard tires locking up on dirt, and scanned the road to see two more news crews parking. Reporters streamed out of the vehicles.

Andrea got his attention, said, "If you say you haven't been here before now, Sheriff, does that mean you instructed someone else to gather and house these poor animals here?"

"What? No, of course not." Hap waved his arms. "No more questions! No comment. No comment."

But the reporters didn't budge; they weren't going to let him off that easy. Hap quickly found himself in a full-on scrum. Six more media members—three reporters and three camera people—ran up and joined the four already in front of him, walling him off. He felt smothered, trapped.

Back at the road, Hap spied a woman with gray hair now standing next to the maroon Acura, arms folded. *Beverly Stewart.* What was she doing here?

Then clarity struck him.

She'd done this to him, hadn't she? She'd somehow orchestrated this whole thing. A new headline popped in his head: "Sheriff Hap Accused of Hoarding, Abusing Defenseless Animals."

Goddammit.

No one gave two shits about her dead junkie son, so she went and pulled this stunt? He should march out to that road and arrest her for fraud right this instant!

No, no. That would only stir up more trouble than it was worth. Make the media wonder why she went to such lengths to pin this on him, place her in the spotlight, and open him up to intense scrutiny.

He'd have to try to ride this storm out. Start by getting his name removed from the deed. Still wouldn't matter though. There wouldn't be enough time for him to rehab his image after the news broke. Come election day, the public would only see him as an animal abuser. The one thing people won't stomach. He'd be lucky to get ten votes.

Hap slumped.

Reporters were shouting their questions at him now.

He plopped his Stetson back on his head, stole another look at Beverly.

She was standing tall. Waving at him with one hand raised above her head. She kept waving.

WE HAVE A WOLF

Meagan Lucas

MAGGIE WAS PISSED. She did not think that the partner who cooked, and cleaned, and chauffeured the child all over the state, should also be the partner who had to wrestle the garbage bins to the end of the driveway at this ungodly hour. John definitely could have taken care of these before he left for the airport last night. And fuck feminism, trash was not the wife's job. So, she was willing to admit that she was a little distracted when she saw it. It wasn't totally black outside, the security lights were on, and the sun was coming up, but it was still dark enough that she wasn't worried about the neighbors seeing her bare face, or bed head. And she had just manhandled the full-to-bursting cans up the driveway to the road; and there was something sticky on her right hand, so she was trying to tighten her robe around her with just her left, because it was much colder than it was supposed to be for November; and she was making a list in her head of all the things that she needed to do to get Henry to school, when something moved in the tree line to the right of the house and she stopped to look. She expected deer, or maybe the neighbor's poodle, or maybe a fox, but this was not what she was expecting at all.

• • •

"We have a wolf," she said to John when he called that afternoon. By then she had forgotten all about the garbage and how he needed to bring her something pretty home from Vegas to make up for it, because she couldn't stop thinking about the eyes in the trees and how it was way bigger than she'd imagined a wolf would be.

"They don't live here," he said.

"Sure, they do. We saw them at the nature center." Their son had gotten a kick out of howling at the wolves and having them howl back. They called him wolf boy, and wolfie, and the wolf whisperer for a month until he decided that he liked dinosaurs better.

"A long time ago," he said. "I bet it was a coyote, or a dog."

"It wasn't a fucking dog." She could hear the murmur of people talking, the clink of dishes. He was in a restaurant. He hadn't even found somewhere quiet to call her from. "You never believe me."

"That's not fair," he said with his mouth full.

"You never pick my side. You don't trust my judgment. You won't believe something just because it's me who told you. With me you always have to test it for yourself. When I said I fixed the pool skimmer, after you couldn't? You pulled the damn thing apart trying to figure out how I made it happen. When I asked you to go to the store because we were out of toilet paper and you searched the whole fucking house claiming it wasn't possible. When I told you what your mother said to me at our wedding—"

"You'd both been drinking."

"Does that make what she said MORE or LESS likely?"

"I don't see what this has to do with whether there's a wolf in our neighborhood or not?"

"I've never given you any reason not to believe me. I've always told you the truth."

"I don't think you're lying. I just think that the State department of wildlife would be exceptionally surprised to know that there was a wolf in our gated neighborhood."

"That borders the state forest!"

"Still."

"Still," she said. "I have to go do car line."

• • •

Henry was happy not having to pooper-scoop. Their tiny dog Ernie was not happy that he now had to do all of his business at the end of a leash. She didn't let either out of her sight outside. She found herself standing at the window watching the tree line more times than she wanted to admit. She heard howls and the sharp cry of injured animals and whimpering in her dreams, but she could never find the bodies in the dark. Could never save the unseen victim from the invisible horror.

• • •

John came home. He didn't have any glitter in his laundry, and he handed her a paperback copy of a hardcover she already owned. Airport presents. But she could tell that he was waiting for her to bring up the wolf. He'd probably spent the trip home looking up wolf population and migratory stats in preparation. But she had done the same when she couldn't sleep. And doubt had snuck in. It was probably a German shepherd, or a big coyote. She still wasn't letting Ernie in the yard alone though. So it was that they were strolling by the creek at the far edge of their property and Ernie was sniffing at every rock and leaf and withholding his poo even though she could tell he had to go, while Maggie tried to stomp the feeling back into her frozen toes when she saw it. A mass of brown fur, a small rack, and a lot of blood. She scooped Ernie and ran.

John chewed his lip, looked down at the deer. "How do we get rid of this?" It was drizzling, and he wiped drips off his glasses with the arm of his coat.

"If you drag it to the road the department of transportation would take it."

"I think I just threw up in my mouth."

"You know that this means though right?" This was the moment she'd been waiting for, when he would have to say it. She needed to see his face when he conceded. She needed to see the horror that she'd been feeling spark in his eyes. The danger that was lurking in their yard.

"We have a rotting deer on our property?"

She looked into his eyes and crossed her arms. She could not believe he was this stubborn.

"It's not a wolf," he said.

"Did you look at the back end? It absolutely was a wolf."

"Maybe you should email the neighbors and see if anyone else has seen anything suspicious? Ask if anyone knows what to do with a carcass, too," he said.

She wanted to punch him in the face.

* * *

Neighbor number one replied all with a long story about seeing a wolf one time when they were on vacation in Colorado.

Neighbor number two replied all saying that her dad said that an injured deer would usually run toward water, and that scavengers like coyotes like to start with the rump. Neighbor number three replied all saying that her cat Snowball had been refusing to go outside and that she thought it was the weather, but maybe the cat knew.

No one had seen anything unusual.

No one knew what to do with the rotting meat.

• • •

"Henry is turning into his father," Maggie told Charlotte after the server dropped off their lattes. "Same laugh, same goofy sense of humor, and Henry has even started giving me the same look that John does when he doesn't believe what I'm saying."

"Oh, that's pre-nagers for you. Parents are stupid. We know nothing. It's not like we've lived three times as long as them or anything. Because I don't know who Yung Gravy or SZA is I'm ignorant. I asked Chloe the other day who Eddie Vedder was and she shrugged!" Charlotte's index finger stabbed the table top and she sighed. "I'm just saying it's not just you, Mags. The kids think we're old and the men think we're naïve and over-reacting. Just let them. It's easier."

"But I'm afraid," said Maggie, "what if—"

"What if what? They go through life without the pleasure of Pearl Jam? I think they'll be okay."

Maggie watched Charlotte's face as she went on to talk about her new love of refinishing furniture and the virtues of chalk paint, and she realized that even her closest friend didn't believe her, and she took a big gulp of hot coffee and let it scald her mouth to keep from screaming.

• • •

Maggie bought a trail cam and set it up. The man behind the counter at the store spent a lot of time looking at her manicure and chewing on his lip. On the second night she got a blurry shot and ran to John and shoved the screen in his face. "Coyote," he said.

"Too big," she said.

"German shepherd," he said.

She rolled her eyes to his face, but when she left the room she did a little dance. She was going to catch the goddamn thing, and then he would have no choice.

• • •

Nothing happened for a week. And then two. And then Maggie decided the wolf must have moved on, and it was for the best because she really didn't want to embarrass herself anymore. But then she was coming home late from book club and when she pulled into the driveway her headlights swept across the yard and eyes glowed from between the trees. She stomped on the brake. The car threw her forward and her chest hit the steering wheel, but she didn't take her eyes from the trees. Bright white eyeshine. Too far from the ground to be a small dog or a cat. But too deep in the shadows for her to see anything else.

She didn't dare breathe. Her toes cramped on the brake, but she wasn't moving. Her hand searched wildly for her phone in the passenger seat, but she knew if she turned to find it, the eyes would be gone.

A groan, and then a grinding, as the garage door began to open, and the eyes and the trees disappeared. "Fuck," she said, and looked to see John standing in the garage bay scratching his head. She pulled in.

"What were you doing?" he said. "I thought maybe you gotten stuck. You're awful late."

"I saw it!" She nearly screamed, scrambling from the car. "I saw the wolf. Right there in the tree line. I'm not nuts, it was there. I was about to get a picture when you opened the door and scared it away."

"It wasn't the neighbor's cat? Or raccoon?"

She ran out into the driveway, the security light behind her turning her shadow into gumby on the concrete. "Fiery white eyeshine. Just like a wolf."

"How do you know that?" He followed her out, but while her eyes were on the trees, his were on her.

"Bobcats are yellowish. Bears orange."

"But how…"

"Research." She turned to him and clapped her hands together. "We have a wolf on our property." Clap. "I did research." Clap. "We need to know these things." Clap. "We. Have. A. Wolf."

"How much wine did you have at book club?"

She went inside. There was nothing he could say to ruin this. She saw it with her own damn eyes.

• • •

She knew better than to drink sweet wine, especially that much sweet wine, after dinner. But Allison had been so convincing, kept saying "skip to the part where you do," which was so obnoxious that she did, and now Maggie's stomach turned, and her esophagus was on fire, and she was not getting to sleep anytime soon. John was snoring. She could wake him up, but he would want to fuck. She didn't want that. She wanted to talk about the wolf, and how to convince the neighbors, and he would sigh and roll over, and then be awful tomorrow. She needed to get it on camera. That was the only way they would believe her. And help her get rid of it. And protect themselves. And the only way she could be certain that she'd get it where she needed it was to bait it. So, she bought an extra chicken at the grocery store and while John was at work, she slipped out to her trail cam and tied the chicken to a tree. And then she waited for dark.

Waiting was the absolute worst. At first, she couldn't stop herself from checking the feed over and over. Nothing. Then maybe a big moth? Nothing the first night.

It's too fresh, she thought, it needs to start stinking. On the third night the raccoons and at least one possum came. They destroyed everything. Maggie nearly threw up at the smell when she cleaned it up. Her stomach kept trying to jump out of her mouth. How the fuck was she going to get it to come back? And then it hit her. A wolf was a predator, it didn't want a dead chicken.

She needed live bait.

• • •

John came in the kitchen, Ernie's leash still wrapped around his wrist. His eyes were wide and his face pale. "You were right," he said. "There is a wolf." Maggie looked up to make sure that Henry was out of earshot.

"What are you talking about?"

"I was walking Ernie back by the creek and..." He swallowed hard. He was green. "Let's just say we found a, scene, that could only have been made by a major predator and, and I think the Jones' cat might have met an unfortunate end."

"Oh no," she said. Oh shit, she thought.

She hadn't been sure where to go for the live bait, but she ended up at a pet store. She'd thought maybe a guinea pig? They seemed big enough to be an interesting meal, but not fast enough or smart enough to be a challenge. But when she was in the store, they all had these heating lamps on them, and she realized that the cold was going to be a problem. But then there was a whole crate of kittens, which would be perfect. But the kittens were so little and cute, and she felt bad about using a sweet baby as the bait. What she needed was a real jerk of a cat that no one liked, and then she remembered the Jones' and how she couldn't keep that goddamn cat from using her flower bed as a litter box. And so, she went home.

Two birds. One stone.

She didn't tell John about the trail cam. She wanted to watch it alone first. She'd had to tie the cat so she'd need to edit the video to make sure he didn't see that part. But when she watched the video, it wasn't a wolf, but coyotes. "Fuck," she said.

• • •

At bedtime they were both reading when John leaned over, "I'm sorry I didn't believe you, and you're being really gracious about this. I'd be rubbing it in my face if I were you."

"Well, Snowball," she said. "I feel bad for the Joneses."

"It's not your fault," he said, "but we should tell them."

"I just hate it when people don't believe me."

"Oh, they will this time. With that mess, it's undeniable. Plus, I'll back you."

She kissed him good night, rolled over, and clicked off her bedside lamp. And in the dark, she thought about how unfair it was that she had to have proof, that she needed a scene, and a male eyewitness in order to be believed. It wasn't fair. Every part of her body felt hot.

• • •

In the morning she sent the email. She didn't send the pictures, but she told them that they could come look if they wanted to, and she told the Joneses where they could get the remains of Snowball. "I've been hearing coyotes," said reply number one. "I don't think a wolf would take a cat," said reply number two. "It needs something bigger." Maggie ground her teeth.

• • •

"I've been thinking," he said over breakfast, his suitcase that she had packed by the door. "I bet it is coyotes." She was pouring a cup of coffee, she didn't turn. "That's good, I think," he said. "You don't have to worry about coyotes. They won't come into the yard with the lights on. You can let Ernie out by himself while I'm gone."

"Why would I do that?" She was stirring her cream in slowly, still hadn't turned. She couldn't let him see the tears that had welled in her eyes.

"It'll be easier for you. You don't have to walk him in this weather."

And that's how it was, she thought. He'd been convinced, however briefly, not by her, but with something he'd seen. And then, he'd allowed himself to be talked out of it. And now, because it was inconvenient that she believed differently, he was going to gaslight her into agreeing. Or maybe it was embarrassment. Or maybe just because it was easier. She'd been here before, when she'd complained to her high school principal about her geography teacher. When she told her mom about her weird uncle. When she told her best friend about the guy that she was dating. No one had believed her. No one else had seen the danger. Everyone had said that she was exaggerating, or misunderstanding; crying wolf. She didn't really know what she was talking about, and she was going to get someone hurt jumping to conclusions like that.

● ● ●

Maggie drove Henry to the bus stop. Bigger bait, she muttered. Small things don't matter. She watched as he climbed the stairs to the bus, turned and waved as it pulled away. She was walking back to her car when she saw the Thompson girl running for the bus and waved her down. "You missed it, I'll take you," she said opening the door for the middle schooler. "There's a wolf, you know, you can't be hanging around. Why didn't your parents drive you? I told them about the wolf. Get in and get warm. I've just got to run home first," she said and then the doors locked as she accelerated, and she looked around to see if anyone saw them.

THAT PICTURE

Bobby Mathews

MAMA CAME AROUND THE corner of the house with Daddy's double-barreled shotgun socketed tight against her shoulder and sighted down it at Coach Weathers from about three feet away. Asked him point-blank how he liked it, how it felt to have a gun pointed at his head. He didn't seem like he liked it much at all. Coach went white all over, his eyes wide with fear and his mouth opening and closing like a fish pulled straight from the Cahaba River.

"Mama —" I said, but she wasn't having no noise from me.

"Be quiet, child. You why I'm here." But we all knew that anyway. She eared the hammers back on the shotgun and set her feet. The black eyes of the barrels looked like nothing and everything at the same time, an endless loop of infinity that called Coach Weathers so hard that the man couldn't look away from it. He looked like someone about to step off the ledge of a twenty-story building into the abyss, hands clenched down to hard white knuckles at his sides. Alexis stared at me, afraid to look at Mama. I looked at the ground in front of us and didn't say nothing.

Coach, he tried to say something, but no words came out. I guess about that time he was regretting that picture he put online.

Alexis Weathers wasn't no regular girl. She hated it when I said that, told me she was just like all of the other girls out there in the world, that there wasn't anything special about her that wasn't special about every other one of them. But none of them smelled like her, or hugged like her, and none of them kissed me in her bedroom the way she did while we were supposed to be studying for the trig final. She was the moon in the sky for me, and the tides of my emotions followed her every move.

I met her when we were in kindergarten. She was blonde and gray-eyed, and she wore pink shoes. She says she doesn't remember it, but I bet you somewhere deep down that she does. I followed her around the playground every day — the same as half a dozen other boys caught up in her wake — and I knew I was in love before I knew what love was, what it meant to love somebody other than yourself. I just knew that I needed to be with her. When the school year ended and we went our separate ways for the summer, I cried.

Of course, Alexis remembers *that*.

We got together finally — finally! — a hundred years later when we were sophomores. She had broken off with Scott Hayworth, and the girls in our grade fell on her like vultures on roadkill. They wanted to know what happened, what Scott had done to make her send him away. Once they got their fill of gossip, they moved away, eyes shining and happy, full with someone else's pain. Alexis stood there, unsure what to do next. She saw me coming down the hall toward her and waited. We had AP English class together, and sometimes we talked about the stuff we liked to read. She liked Sylvia Plath and Anne Sexton.

I thought they were pretty boring, but I loved watching Alexis's face when she read them aloud. I liked Hemingway okay and wondered if I might write something like him when I got old. But I didn't think too much about it. There was time. There would always be time.

"Hey," I said. I've always been big on witty talk.

She said hey back, and I asked her if she was okay. Alexis took a long look in the direction that the vulture-girls had gone and turned back to me. Tears stood in her eyes and refused to fall from the sheer force of her will. She shook her head slightly.

"No," she said finally. "I'm not. But I will be."

I walked her to class. We were both late and picked up pink tardy slips. I didn't give a shit. I took Alexis's slip from her hand and crumpled it up with mine. When the teacher wasn't looking I threw them in the trash.

● ● ●

I don't think it was personal. Coach Weathers was one of those guys who wasn't going to like any guy that Alexis dated. He warmed up to me in the winter of our junior year because I caught the touchdown that put us in the playoffs. A ball three feet in front of me. I never should have been able to catch it — wouldn't have, if the guy who was covering me hadn't shoved me hard in the back — but I stumbled and lunged and somehow caught the ball with one hand, rolled, and tucked it to my chest.

The extra point put us ahead with three seconds left on the clock. We squibbed it on the kickoff and time ran out when one of the upbacks tried a return. Two wins later, we were in the semifinals of the state tournament getting bulldozed by a team that had nine guys who were committed to play at schools from the Southeastern Conference. We didn't have a hope in hell of winning, and we knew it. But we played the game anyway, took our beating, and went back home.

Alexis didn't like football, so she didn't come to the games. Didn't matter if her Dad was the coach. Didn't matter that her boyfriend was a starter.

"It's a game for Neanderthals," she told me one time. "You're beating your brains out every day, for what?"

I didn't know how to answer her. I was young and I was fast and I was strong. I was going to live forever and not let myself get old and fat and slow. I had never been injured. I didn't know what it was like to limp around on crutches for ten weeks while the bones in my ankle knitted themselves back into place, wouldn't know that kind of pain until senior year when they carried me off the football field on a stretcher, my lower leg turned at an impossible angle that meant I'd never really run again and rarely walk without a limp.

We had so much time ahead of us. I'm still not sure where it all went.

• • •

Daddy liked Coach Weathers, and Mama and Daddy both loved Alexis almost as much as I did. But Mama never warmed up to coach at all. Our families got together every month or so. Coach said he needed to know the parents of the boy who was stealing his little girl away. Daddy laughed at him, but Mama would gather herself and go into the kitchen, wash dishes, fix a snack, whatever it took to not be in the same room with Coach Weathers.

"Does that man treat you all right?" She asked one night after coach and his wife — his *third* wife, Mama always pointed out — had left. Coach drank a few beers down with Daddy, and that same third wife had to drive coach home. Daddy himself was napping on the couch. I stood in front of the fridge, drinking the last of the orange juice from the carton.

"I guess," I said, trying to think about what Mama meant. "I mean, he doesn't cut me any slack at practice—"

"That ain't what I'm talking about." She paused from wiping down the kitchen counters that were already clean as a whistle. "Get out of that refrigerator. He don't like you being with his daughter."

"He's protective."

I didn't blame him. I was protective of Alexis, too. If anybody breathed wrong at her, I was right there with my hand balled into a bony-knuckled fist. She never needed my protection — most of the time told me to stay the hell out of whatever it was she was into — but I remained ready to tilt at any windmill she pointed at.

"You be careful around that man. Anything happens to you, we ain't got bail money for me or your Daddy."

"Yes ma'am," I said, and we didn't talk about it again.

• • •

By the time Coach Weathers took the picture that started all the trouble, I had graduated from a wheelchair to crutches to a walking boot and cane. There was never any doubt that Alexis and I would go to prom together. Even if we hadn't been inseparable, it was the Spring of our senior year and we'd made plans. I scraped every bit of savings I had and borrowed money from my parents so that I could afford the rental tux, a bright spray of flowers for Alexis, and a corsage. Alexis bought me a boutonniere for my lapel, and we looked good together. She wore a low-cut green satin gown that made her gray eyes look even more stunning. In her heels she stood nearly as tall as my shoulder. My emerald bow tie matched her dress perfectly.

You would've had to look closely to see that I was still wearing the walking boot. The cane by that point was mostly for decoration.

We took pics with Coach Weathers and his wife, everyone smiling and pleasant. Alexis and I thought we were done, readying ourselves for the car. We were going to meet some friends and all ride together in a party bus someone else's parents had rented so that we wouldn't be tempted to drink and drive after the dance. Before we could leave, coach asked for one more picture. Just for fun, he said.

He went into his bedroom and came back with a gun, a big one. I'd seen it before, Desert Eagle with brown grips and an almost sandstone finish. I always wanted to shoot that gun, and for a moment I thought coach was gonna let me. Instead he pointed the gun at my head and said don't worry it ain't loaded.

He posed with Alexis and me, big fake smiles with the gun pointing at me like he's going to blow my head off if I mess with his daughter. Like Alexis and I hadn't been messing around for two years by that time. After his wife took the photo, he laughed and dropped the magazine out of the Desert Eagle, ejected a shell from the chamber.

"Huh," he said, grinning at me with everything but his eyes. "I guess it was loaded after all."

● ● ●

And that was done. Or at least I thought it was. When the photo started showing up on social media, I tried to ignore it. Other kids tried to ask me about it, and I know some of those magpie girls that liked to hang on and hang around Alexis asked her, too. We kept our heads down. Her Daddy's dumb picture hadn't affected prom night at all, and we had three weeks of school left until graduation. Alexis was going to Vanderbilt, and I'd gotten an academic scholarship to Middle Tennessee, about 45 minutes away down I-24.

But once it got to Mama, everything changed.

She didn't say anything to me, to Daddy, to anyone. But she loaded Daddy's twelve-gauge shotgun with yellow shells she'd emptied out and filled up with rock salt and black-eyed peas to keep thieves and other nuisances out of the garden patch where she grew watermelons and strawberries every year.

"Mama," I said, my voice pleading. "Don't. Coach was just being funny."

The look in her eyes told me that she hadn't found any humor in that picture at all.

"Please," I said, "don't do nothing. Coach was just playing around."

• • •

Mama was the opposite of Coach Weathers. She wasn't playing around at all. Her knuckles were white with the strain of her anger as she pointed the shotgun, her left hand supporting the stock underneath the barrels. She eared back the hammers on the shotgun, everything so silent that we could all hear the click when the levers cocked.

She didn't come right up to coach, either. She stayed about 10 feet away, far enough that the shotgun blast wouldn't scatter much if she pulled the trigger, but not close enough for coach to lunge and grab the barrels.

"Mama," I said, "you're embarrassing me."

Mama ignored me, kept looking at coach.

"You like how it feels, gun pointed at your head?" Coach, his eyes still wide and his hands up in surrender, shook his head.

"You got something to say to my boy?"

Coach didn't speak.

"He ever hurt your daughter? Ever do one mean thing to her? He been in love with her long as he's known her, been good as gold to her and you and every goddamn body else and you point a gun at him."

Coach said *I'm sorry* low, under his breath. I could only hear him because everything else around us had gone quiet. I could see sweat rolling from his receding hairline down to the collar of his polo shirt.

"Say it like you mean it. Say it to him." Mama tilted her head toward me.

"I'm sorry," coach said. Louder this time.

"And don't you say it's all right," Mama said to me. "This man an adult. You think you grown, but you're a child. You are my child. This man ain't got no right — not one — to point no gun at you."

Coach kept his eyes on that shotgun.

"Ma'am — Missus Walker — I didn't mean any harm. I swear I didn't. Could you put the gun down, please?" Mama thought about it.

"Naw, I think I'll hold onto it. Makes me feel safe."

"Could you at least uncock it? Please. There could be an accident."

"That's right, ain't it?"

She tilted the shotgun downward at Coach's feet and pulled both triggers.

"Oops," she said.

● ● ●

Mama didn't so much as spend the night in jail. We all — even coach, once he stopped writhing on the ground and screaming — agreed that the gun went off by accident. I drove Mama home in her car, and Alexis followed her father to the hospital in my car. The rock salt and black-eyed peas were almost impossible to dig out, and coach walked pretty gingerly for the rest of the time I knew him.

Alexis and I broke up after our freshman year of college. Turns out 45 minutes is just too far away when there are classes and study groups and tailgating and parties to go to. She met someone else, and I've often wondered if Coach Weathers acted any different toward him or explained why he never took his shoes off in front of company again.

SHELIAOSOMETHING9

Cate Moyle

LAST NIGHT'S SNOWFALL DAZZLED in sunlight down Mayapple Street, luring people from their homes, shovels in hand. Not every neighbor warranted watching, but some neighborhoods invited unwelcome salutations, like this midwestern sidewalk-celebrating suburb. I hated that. At the risk of sounding like a grumpy old lady, a single woman of my age doesn't open doors unawares, and I was wary of anyone wandering on to my lawn. Even lawn three feet under. My parents had taught me vigilance, which is why I spend my first-cuppa-joe-hour casing activity along the block.

The winter-clad bulk of a next door neighbor trekked around snow piles toward my house. From my office window, I followed his weaving gait, wishing him to Jericho. As he neared the driveway, I slid open the desk drawer where my gun was stashed. The man lowered the mailbox lid and, after reaching in his coat pocket, inserted a small, padded envelope. Misdirected

"

mail again? He turned back to his own house and I exhaled. No need to worry he'd come knocking today.

I refocused on the computer screen and my online shopping. By observation and practice, internet resale sites made great fishing ponds for life story flotsam. Finding nothing of interest on Craig's List, I perused the latest auction ads on eBay for other people's junk. Nothing ostentatious. Nothing too mundane. Close-up sales photos a must.

*** ESTATE SALE ***

Costume JEWELRY

Mixed Lot includes Necklaces/Watches/Earrings/Brooches/Rings. Ranging from Vintage to Modern - Over 5 lbs of Jewelry!

SCRAPBOOKs

* Vintage scrapbook-1950s 1960s- Hollywood Movie Star Photographs, Fan Club Mementos, Cinema Ticket stubs. Well-preserved!

* 1970s Strawberry Shortcake scrapbook & album. News Clippings, loads of Pictures & Childhood Ephemera, including groovy Puffy Stickers. Super sweet!

Great for Crafters / Recycle, ReUse & Repurpose! If you have any questions, no matter how small, please ask!!! (HeaBlessed73)

Could I possibly get this lucky? I scrolled through the photos in the ad, reaching a series of scrapbook pages with slightly yellowed edges. One photo caught my eye—dad sporting hairy sideburns, mom styling in bell-bottom jeans, a little girl balancing Mickey Mouse ears. The opposing page held a Disneyland brochure. West coasters. Ideal. My mouse pointer hovered the Buy It Now button; instead, I clicked the Contact Seller link.

Okay, HeaBlessed73, I do have a question for you.

● ● ●

After several mildly successful yard sales, Heather Boyd resorted to online auctions in order to liquidate her Aunt Mary's estate. Uncomfortable Chippendale chairs—now gone. JCPenney brand oil landscapes—goodbye. She had even unloaded Uncle Bob's pickle jar of pennies. With a flush of optimism for clearing the last of the boxes out of her garage, Heather checked the current bidding first thing before breakfast. She sighed at the low interest and opened an awaiting message from eBay user SheliaOSomething9.

Hi—Regarding the Strawberry Shortcake scrapbook & album—I'm a set designer (L.A.) looking to procure material for a film production that will feature a scrapbook (it's sort of a *Ya-Ya Sisterhood* meets *The Big Chill* storyline). Anyways, the lead actress has been cast and I'm trying to match her looks. Can you tell the color of the little girl's eyes in this scrapbook?

Much thanks,

Sheila

p.s. would you guess the book's material covers the early or late 70s?

"Ooh," Heather said to no one in particular, the only other noise in the room being the final coffeepot drips. "A movie? Now, that's cool." She slippered to the fresh brew, poured a steamy mug, then settled back in front of the laptop to respond.

Hi Sheila—It is my late cousin's scrapbook and I absolutely can confirm that her eyes were gorgeous light blue! She was born in 1969, so the scrapbook covers all of the 1970s and then some. Tracey would seriously be thrilled if her scrapbook starred in a movie!! She had her own Hollywood ambitions! Let me know if you have any more questions.

Regards,

Heather (HeaBlessed73)

Heather's concentration ended with the sounds overhead of

children wrestling on the second floor. The boys were awake; time to make breakfast.

• • •

Later that morning, after shoveling snow from the sidewalk and retrieving the newspaper and mail, I returned to my office. I noticed a missed call from Inspector Perez on my cell's alert screen and muted the phone. Flicking on the faux fireplace to heat the room, I draped a Christmas afghan over my lap. My Nevada soul would never warm to these Wisconsin winters. In my childhood, the cold season meant fewer ice cubes in my parents' hi-balls and holiday lights came by way of casino rows.

As expected, the package re-directed to me by the neighbor contained a SIM card to re-furb a mobile phone for private internet access. I placed the packet on top of my to-do pile. Tossing aside the rest of the mail, junk addressed to a phony identity, I studied the messages in my ProtonMail inbox. "Interesting." I leaned back in my chair, rereading the eBay scrapbook seller's reply, *Hi Sheila—*

With a smile, I reached for my notebook. Late cousin, Tracey. 1969. Blue eyes.

So far, so good.

• • •

"Uh, not with dirty hands," Heather said to the boys hovered around a KFC bucket of chicken, the oldest attempting to remove its cover. "Go wash up. I'll call you when it's re-heated." She shooed them away.

Oven on and microwave humming, Heather slipped into her chair at the kitchen desk intending to do BillPay. She found her inbox crowded with emails regarding the lot of costume jewelry: would she separate into smaller bundles? could she post a close-up photo of the Easter egg brooch? For herself, she wondered if leaving the inquiries unanswered would help drive the auction price up. But the tug of her conscience assured she'd find the time to answer them this evening. After all, she invited questions on every posting.

She noticed two new messages from SheliaOSomething9. Opening the first, she frowned at its terseness.

Hi again—forgot to ask another strange question—whether Tracey had a part-time job?

S—

"What?" Curiosity made Heather scroll to SheliaOSomething9's earlier message to find the original 'strange' question.

Hi—It occurs to me that the scrapbook for our screenplay needs to contain material from childhood through high school, and you referred to Tracey as your "late" cousin. I assume she died? If so, my deepest sympathies. And not meaning to be insensitive, but is this scrapbook complete enough for my requirements?

Sorry, this is admittedly off-the-wall questioning because I have to nail the details—making sure the visual story in the scrapbook matches the character's narrative. The production company can pay more than your asking price if the book covers the screenplay's time span.

Much thanks,

Sheila

While reading, Heather could hear her husband upstairs directing the boys, then his footsteps on treads and behind her.

He kissed her cheek. "What's wrong?"

"Nothing. Why?"

"You're rapping that pen."

She absentmindedly noticed the ballpoint in her hand and dropped it. "Oh, just reading a fishy message from that movie person interested in the scrapbook on eBay."

"And?" Her husband helped himself to a bowl of coleslaw as he listened.

"And, they're willing to pay extra money, but she's asking some personal questions."

"About you?"

"No, questions about Tracey. Well, about the scrapbook…" Heather paused and shifted to face him. "Actually, not really asking any details that aren't already in the book." She stood. "Yeah, it's nothing."

"Well, getting a higher price for nothing sounds good to me. So does fried chicken." He pointed to the oven as an ask.

Heather smiled. "Call the boys. Let's dig in."

• • •

When the house quieted that evening, Heather responded to all her email inquiries. Despite an initial hesitation over the film-maker's line of questioning, the idea of Tracey's past taking on a whole new life appealed to her intrepid nature. Still, there was a part of her that thought this individual might be a sham. A cover story for something bigger.

Hi Sheila—these are strange questions but I can see how you are trying to match storylines. Sadly, my cousin Tracey died in a car accident at the end of her senior year. I've missed her terribly over the years—she was like a big sister to me. I'd imagined a very different future for us together. :-(

Just checked the scrapbook and it contains her prom photo. She looked so beautiful! Despite all that moussed up 80s hair, lol. I know you must think me heartless to get rid of my aunt's estate items (somedays I feel that way), but it's a necessary part of my new commitment to minimalistic living. I've scanned every photo within as a digital keepsake and I'm ready to launch their departing (Marie Kondo would approve).

Oh, and her family always lived in Sherman Oaks and we're in Glendale, so we didn't exactly live near each other, but I remember she may have worked at Dairy Queen. Most of her extracurricular time was spent on acting— she landed a walk-on TV role and starred in three high school musicals. Speaking of which, what's your film production company? What's the name of the film? Who's playing Tracey? I can't wait to see it on the big screen!

And you must be local(ish)—do you want to have a look at the scrapbook before purchasing?

Regards,

Heather (HeaBlessed73)

• • •

In order to stay vigilant at night, I usually nap during the day, but a busy afternoon had interrupted my rhythm. I sipped from a mug of tea while straightening the office. I peeked into the envelope received earlier today and removed a prepaid SIM card. Then I slid the card into a burner phone I'd purchased last year at Meijer Pharmacy. The phone gave me a private way of texting without Perez's prying oversight. Rebooted, a new cell screen came back clean. It would serve more than one identity as soon as I was ready. Meanwhile, it would wait stashed in the desk drawer.

Finishing the mug's last drop, I yawned and leaned to power down the computer, but a recent notification caught my attention in my inbox. More news on the scrapbook so I took a moment to read the response.

"Well, HeaBlessed73, that's all too perfect." I added to

my notebook under Tracey's info. Sherman Oaks CA. H.S. Yearbook—drama club. SSN. Driving age. Died late spring 1987?

A shiver overtook me. I could do southern California. Now to make sure this material comes to me. Thirty minutes passed while I edited, reconsidered, and edited again my response. This is the point to pull back, slow yet firm.

Hi—Hey, no judgment from this corner...I also live with a light footprint. Treadway Productions is the company, though, not sure I'm at liberty to reveal the project name or cast. Love your enthusiasm, but keep in mind we aren't filming Tracey's story. This will only be a prop.

I skipped the Buy It Now feature in order to double your asking price via bidding, and I can go higher if someone else comes along fishing. Looking forward to being the high bidder.

Much thanks,

Sheila

Message sent, I explored the Classmates.com website, fine tuning my search to Grant High School, Sherman Oaks, CA and to class members of 1987. The yearbook's senior photo gallery provided her last name. "Ah, there you are—Tracey *Tobbins*," I said. She gazed back at me with hopeful anticipation. I steeled myself against a tinge of guilt. It was just a bit of paperwork borrow—documentation she couldn't use anyway.

Gaining personal info must have been harder in the days of having to contact the school directly. Then again, documentation requirements were less draconian so procuring legal paperwork less of an issue. For curiosity's sake, I looked her up in the Drama Club photo. The same optimistic smile. I had auditioned, once, for the role of Maria in *West Side Story*. My father tried unsuccessfully to bribe the drama coach. Bet the dimpled Tracey would have gotten the lead.

My preoccupation was interrupted by a call notification: Inspector Perez. I looked at his contact picture and bit my lip. The two of us, a day after Jimmy The Hand was convicted, celebrating outside Luv-it Frozen Custard; he had a sweet and nervous expression holding my drippy ice cream cone. Perez was a nice guy, but I couldn't let him know my plans, and he was sharp enough to detect secrecy in my voice. Despite coming from a family of crooks, I wasn't much of a liar, at least conversationally. Now, writing a pack of lies? I could do that all day long.

Choosing the Ignore and Message option, I sent him a text describing a horrific case of laryngitis. I resisted the temptation to embellish raging fevers, and the like, since I didn't want him to call 911 on my behalf. Yeah, he was that kind of nice.

I hoped he wouldn't earn a reprimand after I disappeared. Weak moonlight barely shone on the dark snow outside the office window. Nothing but silent cold and empty dreams. Yes, I would disappear.

• • •

The car idled in the school drop-off line and, in between small forward starts, Heather read email from her iPhone. After depositing the boys at the correct zone, she parked in the emergency lane and pulled her work phone out of her purse. She quickly typed a message: subject took the bait.

• • •

Later in the office, Heather checked the eBay site and printed out the order information on the scrapbook sale. The payment came from a R.U.Cameron@treadway.com. Curious, this was not a name they'd seen yet. Who's R.U. Cameron? She forwarded the name for further inquiry.

In the big scheme, a mismatching PayPal account might not be highly suspicious, but the lead investigator told Heather to keep the conversation going. So, she drafted a message to double-check the purchaser and confirm the shipment address, in Wisconsin of all places.

• • •

First thing in the morning, I began the quest for quality forged documents. There was enough information from my notes to get a request in the works. From my file cabinet, I pulled a near empty manilla envelope sealed in plastic zip-lock. Despite the emptiness, I saved the envelope years ago, knowing the value of its contact information, "Federal Filing Specialists Inc." The outfit that provided the documents used to create my Sheila identity when entering protection.

I shook the envelope and the first items to slide out were the passport photos I had taken a few months back. Next, the letterhead I lifted the last time I'd been in the marshal's office. I laid the envelope, photos, and stationery across the desk for inspiration. Time to summon my inner bureaucrat and author a requisition for Tracey Tobbins' new passport. With that secured, I figured requesting duplicate copies of "lost" items like Tracey's birth certificate and social security card would be more easily obtained through traditional routes.

My only real meal of the day happened around eleven, usually eaten while standing at the kitchen sink, where I could immediately wash the pasta bowl. The meals I missed the most were the dinners. Lavish and noisy, with a half dozen bottles of Château Lafite Rothschild and whatever business associates my parents friended that week. It had been the only time of day I could count on my parents' best behavior. And on them getting along.

Even under a deep wave of nostalgia, it seemed a little early to use linen napkins, but I asked Alexa to play the soundtrack from *Casino Royale* and turned on the burner under my Poker Aces scented Etsy candle. Soon the house smelled like spiced cologne, warmed playing cards, with a whiff of smoky cigar. I closed my eyes and relaxed, until the flap on the kitchen pet door banged open.

"Bruce?" I called out for the unseen cat. I closed the tiny pet entry, then looked down the hall. Had he disappeared that quick? My pulse hammered.

I checked the computer to see if the outdoor cameras had captured anything. Only Bruce scampering in through the cat door—what relief. Nothing of interest after the mail delivery. I scrolled down earlier into my tasks and alerts, and noticed another message from HeaBlessed73.

"Gheeez…it's bought and paid for. Send it already, Heather," I said and banged out a response.

If it wasn't obvious, I'm the glorified stagehand and the movie's financial folks sent the money. Cameron is our production penny pincher, but if you require a higher price (due to shipping) then I'll ask for more.

Yes, I'm in Wisconsin. With the amount of film work coming to me, I've been planning a relocation to southern California for a while, but for now I'm stuck in an arctic state. Maybe by spring, I'll have lined up a couch to sleep on in L.A. (but Broyhill or not, I'm coming.)

I suppose for authenticity sake, I should visit Sherman Oaks and pick up the vibe. Then, maybe Glendale? Any must-see recommendations, Heather?

Looking forward to a much needed road trip,

Sheila

p.s. the producers are waiting on me so please ship ASAP.

● ● ●

"Okay, SheilaOSomething9 sounds defensive at follow-up questions," Heather shared with her office mate after reading the latest message from the operation's potential suspect.

"Like a guilty person," Jones replied over the top the cubical wall.

"Exactly," Heather said. She eyed the open scrapbook page and its puffy, pastel sticker of a Unicorn, posed with a rainbow. She remembered the Valentines when she'd given a package of these to Tracey. "I might miss browsing through this blast from the past. It's *like totally groovy*."

"As we say in cyber fraud, 'The better the bait, the bigger the fish.'"

"Isn't that true about all fraud?" Heather smirked and completed the requisite FBI form for the GPS tracking device she would place under the Unicorn, which she removed from the page.

The sticker used to be Scratch 'n Sniff, but after waving the tweezers past her nose, Heather couldn't detect any Tutti-Frutti scent left. She affixed a tiny GPS-enabled strip behind the Unicorn's horn, still mottled with fuzzy glitter, and adhered the sticker back onto the page. She smiled at the thought of her cousin's treasure helping to catch a ring of thieves.

Now to package the book for shipping, she left the fraud unit and headed to the Cyber Ops mail room.

Late afternoon, Heather's teammate Jones popped his head into her cubical. "That ID thief of ours originates from a Bright Prairie, Wisconsin, right?"

"Yes," she said.

He nodded. "When I ran that name through NCIC, I got a hit on a fugitive trial witness in the same locale—kind of unusual name Bright Prairie—" He looked at one of the sticky notes on his manila folder. "Fugitive is a woman by the name *Sheila* O'Sullivan. I found hits on her too—Sheila could also be using the surname O'Sheehan, or O'Shaughnessy. Contact is the U.S. Marshal's office—an Inspector Perez out of Chicago." He passed the notes to her, frowning. "Might be the WIT-SEC office."

WITSEC meant Witness Security, a secretive unit, and Heather felt leery about calling. She'd play it cool and not ask too many questions. Perez cryptically confirmed Heather's SheilaOSomething9 was under protection and asked to be informed of further contact from the fugitive. To give Perez first grabs would effectively suspend the bureau's next move. That was disappointing for a sting-operation months in the works. Unless Sheila was continuing criminal ventures while in hiding, then this might be a case of cross-purposes.

And the scrapbook had already shipped.

• • •

Tracey's scrapbook did not disappoint. Chock full of mementos, beginning with kindergarten drawings through a movie stub ticket dated May 26, 1987—*The Secret of My Success*—possibly the last she ever saw. The book provided a trove of stories to retell if the need arose. Tracey had lived a life worth documenting. The young girl had even affixed index cards labeling items with factoids and blurbs.

Removing my favorite photo, an Olan Mills portrait stamped "'82" in the corner, I mounted it in a gold 5x7 frame. Tracey was about thirteen in the photograph, and she and I resembled each other at that age. Her dad looked as studious as a professor and her mom super sweet in a blue cashmere sweater trimmed with pearls. Classic. My mother preferred plunging necklines and fake eyelashes. The look of drama—like a Kardashian.

Though, I delighted in mother's theatrical stories about her grandfather eluding the law by hiding down in the Mexican mountains. Stories that ended with a promise, "We will go there someday, Shelly, where the dahlias bloom free." I heard myself choke back a cry. Stop. No more thinking of my parents. That trail of memories would lead to the betrayal, the ambush, the shooting—everything I wanted to leave behind.

I stored the framed photo in a tote of personal items, and I couldn't wait to place Tracey's celluloid slice of Americana on my future fireplace mantel. My reverie was broken by a phone ring and a computer notification of new mail.

Perez's voicemail matched his email text.

Perez here. Figured out why you've been ghosting me.

I received an approval request on an invoice from Federal Filing Specialists, per a new passport for case number 104972-NEV. That's you.

Be in touch or we will be.

What? They invoiced? I had sent a cashier check! "Shit." All I needed was one thing. My finger gripped the side of a cold, empty coffee mug and in a flash of anger, I threw it across the room. It broke in half after impact with the bookshelf and landed in front of a printed copy of my selfie with the Inspector. "Just one last thing, Perez."

I hopped off my office chair and paced the house. Then I stomped to the front hall closet and pulled bags out. My luggage sat in the closet for months—packed, ready, like a foster kid's. All set, or so I had thought. Okay, time for a Plan B.

I sensed movement behind me, then a shadow. Bruce pressed his feline face against my shin. "Gheez. Don't worry, I have a plan for you, too," I said, rubbing the cat's cheek. At least I hoped that Wisconsonite neighborliness would prevail when I asked next door about pet sitting.

The cat pounced one of the smaller bags. Whenever settled,

I'd get a pet less prone to stalking. Maybe a chihuahua. I gathered a few last items and added them to my midnight-run luggage.

• • •

An early spring gently warmed the northern country, while the southwestern states simmered like a Mediterranean holiday. In California, Heather's change of season was marked by taking time off for family birthdays—first the twins, then her husband, and last her eldest son. A week's worth of Pisces birthdays, though it was a welcomed break from her recent career failures. The identity theft ring she wanted to hook with her lure had not been caught, but Heather hoped the Bureau's cooperation at least assisted Inspector Perez's case. Meanwhile, Agent Jones emailed he'd gotten a haul—photo albums and personal documents—from a storage unit auction. They would reboot Operation Mementos when she returned.

For her part, Heather couldn't help feeling the disappointment that she lost her cousin's materials for no net gain in the fight against crime. Even though Perez left the conversation about Sheila as "the scheme was foiled," the scrapbook hadn't yet been returned. Heather wondered if Perez was correct in his assessment, so she set a Google Alert for her cousin's name. No harm in watching for online mentions of Tracey.

And she couldn't stop thinking about the desperation that drove someone out of their identity. Hiding was hard enough. Taking on an additional persona was another difficulty. But to abandon one's past must require an overwhelming sense of hopelessness.

Heather talked herself out of making direct contact with the woman.

• • •

Shortly after her husband's birthday, Heather received a Google alert for a recent obituary sourced by the Sherman Oaks Patch website—

It is with great sadness that we announce the death of Tracey Tobbins, native of Sherman Oaks, California, who passed away last month after a highway fatality during a Wisconsin blizzard. Her family welcomes sympathy messages but has chosen to keep her memorial service private.

Heather slapped her palm on the computer desk. Un-freaking-believable! She grabbed the phone to call her husband and felt her throat tighten. Even knowing the "Tracey" in this obit was not her cousin, old wounds tore through and rendered her speechless.

Wait, had Sheila died? She read the posting again. Personal messages within the obit comments section shared her disbelief and grief.

Wow, is this referring to Tracey Tobbins, Grant High, class of '87? I mistakenly thought Tracey had died years ago. I understand the family aspect, but wonder if there's some way that old friends and former classmates can participate in her memorial? —Kathy Hill—

My condolences! I've been out of touch since high school and I'm sorry to read this news. Tracey was the nicest of all the 'popular' kids and I imagine she grew into an amazing adult. I'm back in the area now and, yes, please let us know how we can memorialize Tracey. —Val Smith—

Holy crap. Heather knew both Kathy and Val. How could she let this go unanswered? It was maddening. What kind of believable story would she have to spin to correct this? She was about

to reply to the thread of comments when she noticed an entry
signed by Sheila herself.

Having known Tracey only briefly, I can say her magnificent smile must have
always shone from a beautiful soul. We should all leave the family to grieve and
respect people's need for privacy. —SheliaO—

Even over the noise of a dozen boys playing Xbox while on sugary cake highs, Heather heard the doorbell and checked her
phone's Ring app. A delivery service woman held a parcel. Great
timing, she thought, the last birthday present had arrived.

"I got it, hon," she called to her husband, deep in the game
with the boys.

The uniformed woman stood admiring dahlias in a large
terracotta pot just outside the front door. After passing the box
to Heather, she lifted her hands in the air. "I'm unarmed if you
want to check, *Agent*."

"What—?" Heather scanned the woman's figure, detecting
no obvious bulge of a weapon. The visitor turned in a circle,
enabling a complete visual inspection.

"I know it wasn't your intention, Heather, but you complicated my relocation to Mexico." The woman smiled, "And I'm
going to need your help to fix that."

"And who?" Heather glanced at the package balanced gingerly in her hands.

A golden hue of the setting sun sparkled off the Pacific and
up the avenue, backlighting this woman on the doorstep, who
raised her sunglasses and pushed them atop her blonde hair.
"Call me, Tracey."

Heather's pulse quickened. If she didn't know better, she'd
swear this was the face of her cousin, from the baby blue eyes
down to the tiny cleft chin. But the real image of Tracey lay in
the scrapbook, which she was sure she now held. Instinctively

hugging the family memento, she considered next moves—closing the door on a wanna-be cousin or listening to a curious story from the woman before her. "Sheila?" she said.

With a contrite nod, the impostor said, "Or something like that."

THE RUMINATIONS AND CONSTERNATIONS OF A LONELY WOMAN

Jonathan Newman

I'M JUST A SINGLE mother out here looking for love. Don't I deserve that much? Ain't that what the American Dream is all about? At least part of it anyhow; they told us in school, but I never did pay no attention. But I figure I'm right: the American Dream is basically just getting whatever the hell you want and fuck everyone else. Well, what *I* want is a man. No, scratch that. What I *NEED* is a man. Some real pretty rich boy with one of them fake TV smiles and a bottomless pit of cash; one of them boys needs to get to off his butt and look after this girl. And I'm going to do whatever it takes to get me one. Don't I deserve that much in this shitty life?

I looked at my reflection in the bathroom mirror. The lighting in those gas station shitters sure wasn't flattering; I looked like I'd just crawled on out of my grave and taken a header straight into a canyon of asbestos and sawdust. There was lipstick on my teeth and mascara on my cheeks where I had been crying not ten minutes earlier. Real tears and not them fake tears what momma used before smiling and slapping me across the face whenever I got to bawling. I could summon them from deep down inside. Momma always said that I should be in the pictures, Hollywood, something like that, because I could always cry and make myself look real sad and get any person in the whole world to do what I wanted. Except for her. Momma is colder than an Eskimo's left nipple. By 'any person' I think Momma mostly meant her male friends, who had started to take a real shine to me about the time my tits started to get perky. Funny how that works ain't it? These here 'skeeter bites have been about the only currency that I've had in my adult life, and what do I got to show for it?

I gave up on my face and walked out of the bathroom. Damn if that little peckerwood wasn't standing right outside the door and I tripped over him and fell on my ass and ripped my dress all the way up to my crotch, and I spilled my purse all over the floor. I was cussing up a storm and Gene was saying "sorry momma" over and over again like a speaking clock and trying to pick up my things and I had to slap his little hands away from my Lucky Strikes and that packet of rubbers that he thought were balloon animals, and I told him to hush up. He looked at me. We looked at each other for what felt like a long time, and I saw the tears well up in them peepers like a dam fit to breach and flood the little town that lay beneath; his bottom lip took to wobbling like fresh Jell-O. Damn if he wasn't the saddest little bastard you'd ever seen.

"Momma, I…"

"Hush!"

"But Momma…"

"I said hush!" I grabbed his face, squeezing those fat little cheeks and kissing his forehead. "You hold them tears back, y'hear? I don't you wastin' none of 'em on me?"

"Momma?"

"And keep you face just like that."

"Just like what?"

"Just like you got it right now."

"How I got it, momma?"

"How you got… Like you got it right now. You look like you just seen Bambi's momma get shot."

"Someone's momma got shot?"

"No, I…" I shook my head. "Forget it. Come on."

I took Gene's hand and led the boy out to our car. It was hot that day. It must have been closing in on noon; that was the time we was waiting on. The sun was high, and I squinted up at that ribald yellow sucker and shot it my eye, and wished I had enough money to buy me some pretty sunglasses that would hide my eyes until it was time to reveal them. Like those big kind that Audrey Hepburn and those girls wore, so big that their eyes flared up like ginseng-smoking bugs. I walked back inside the gas station and the elderly proprietor looked at me as though I had goat shit in my hair.

"Ain't you gonna buy nothin'?" he said, lining his toothless gum with tobacco.

"Just needed to use the bathroom." I said.

"You don't need no gas?"

"Nope." I looked around.

Said that old fella, "This here's the last station for about thirty miles. That old Plymouth of yours sound like its fixin' to bust a lung at any second."

"Guess I'll just have to risk it," I said. "You sell sunglasses?"

"No."

"No, ma'am."

"What's that?"

"You should call me ma'am."

He scratched his face. "That your boy?" He nodded in the direction of Gene, who remained outside, leaning against the hood of my beat-up old Plymouth, and staring directly into the sun with all the understanding of a gnat.

"Yeah, he's mine," I said.

"He looks kinda' dumb."

"What?"

"He retarded?"

"No, he ain't retarded," I said. "Look, you got the time?"

"The time?"

"The time."

Regarding me with cautious eyes, the proprietor glanced at his watch. "A little before noon."

"How much is a little?"

"Why?"

"I got an appointment."

"Out here?"

"That's right?"

"You got an appointment in the middle of the desert?"

"What's the time?"

"Five minutes before."

"Obliged," I said, and turned and scuttled out into the sun, leaving that old codger standing there like a statue, juice seeping from the corner of his lips. I told Gene to get his little butt to into the car and I gunned the engine and tore out of that place like Satan himself was grabbing for my ass.

We didn't drive but two minutes up the highway; there wasn't another soul to be seen; the highway stretched on for as long as you could comprehend, and there wasn't much to spy on either side on the road: desert and rock and that hard caliche scrub that paved this part of the earth like sandpaper capable of killing a man. This was all I knew; the America where I had been born and raised, grown out of the scorched New Mexico dirt, speaking equal parts English and clumsy Mexican and not knowing nothing outside of red heat and endless sweeping nowhere. This was the gene pool where God Almighty had saw fit to drop me and tell me to find a man, a husband. I might as well have married a cactus.

I pulled over to the side of the road and killed the engine. The gas meter read close to zero, but I didn't care about that right then. It wasn't like I was going to be driving that hunk of shit home anyhow. The desert could take it for all I cared. I pulled down the mirror, looked at myself and winced. I turned to Gene in the passenger seat, and he was looking up at me with those little piglet eyes. He sure was cute. He sure did have a way of looking at you like you meant something, like you were important. It sure did feel good sometimes to be looked on like that. I almost kind of liked having him around if he wasn't so goddamned dumb.

"How do I look?" I asked.

"Real purty," he said.

"You ain't looking sad no more."

"Momma?"

"I told you to keep that sad look on your face."

"I'm sorry, momma," said Gene, and his head dropped to his chest, and didn't that just break you heart.

I clapped my hands together. "Atta boy! C'mon."

We exited the car and stood in the sun. Gene gazed up and down the road. "I don't see nothin.'"

"He'll be here," I said. "Now do like we practised."

Gene nodded and walked out into the road. He looked back at me. I nodded and smiled. He looked at the sky and I stopped smiling. It was hard to smile, always had been. I would rehearse my smiles in the mirror like some cartoon clown. They just didn't feel natural. Momma always said that it was good for a woman to smile; she said that men liked it, put them at ease, and then we could take whatever we so desired and those fat boys wouldn't be none the wiser.

A bird flew overhead, crossing the sun; it looked real black. We both watched it go. Was likely a buzzard; probably saw a dumb little pecker like Gene and figured there was going to be some good eating on this day. *Not today, bird,* I thought to myself. *Not today.* Gene scratched his stomach and then got down onto his knees and began to lie down in the middle of the road.

He squealed and bounced back up. "It's hot!"

"Of course it's hot," I said. "It's right in the sun."

"It'll burn me."

"You'll only be on it for a few seconds."

"I can't hear no engine."

"He'll be here," I said. "Now get your butt down and try to look dead."

"Yes, ma'am."

Tentatively, Eugene did return to the sizzling asphalt. He winced at the touch of it on his flesh and through his clothes, but I didn't pay him no mind. My senses was trained to the distance. I could hear me some cicadas whining in what trees there were in a dead place like this, so I had to strain to hear over them. *There it was.* The rumble of an engine.

"Eugene," I hissed. "Get down."

He did as he was told, rolling his fat carcass onto his back, and then adjusting slightly so that he was facing away from the direction of that distant engine. I ran back and hid behind the Plymouth. I mussed up my hair – not too much – and pinched myself to make sure that there was tears flowing in my eyes. I checked my dress. It was pretty low; low enough that a fella's wandering eye could easy enough catch a glimpse of tit, but not so low that he'd think me a whore or nothing. My Momma didn't raise no whores. She'd raised smart girls, that's what she always told us. You got to be smart in this world if you're born with a slit and a bush between your legs, because this game is rigged for those what have the other thing, and those bastards sure is mean as shit. So, you got to be smart. That's what I was doing. Being smart. Being smart was finding a man. Being smart wasn't having no stupid kid and being all by yourself. That wasn't no way to live in this world. I needed to be smart. I needed a man.

Oh, and didn't the finest man of them all come a-rollin' over that hill and onto the highway just like a mirage out of that there desert. I recognised that truck just from the dot it made on the horizon. I must've watched that thing drive these here roads all my life. Wasn't nothing going to fool me. But I didn't give two shits about that truck; I wanted what was inside.

It drove real close, and there was Gene's fat little body all dead and shit laying in the middle of the road like one of Earl's famous pancakes. And that truck braked real fast, and oh but didn't Bobby Sinclair himself jump out looking all worried and flustered and handsome and rich. He ran for my boy, and I ran for Bobby.

"Eugene!" I cried, and Bobby stopped and saw me.

"What's happened?" I dropped down alongside Gene and rolled him over and he kept his eyes closed.

"Talk to me, Genie!" I said and sobbed.

Bobby was with me, and I could feel his hands on my shoulders.

"What happened?" he said.

"Some car hit him."

"What car?"

"Red car."

"It just took off?"

"That's right!" I wailed.

"Talk to me, Genie! Don't leave me!"

And right on cue, Eugene did open his little eyes. "Momma."

I hugged him close and wept, and Bobby Sinclair stood over us, his cap in his hand, scratching his head and looking real perturbed by what all had just transpired.

"He alright?" said Bobby.

"I think so," I said. "Gene?"

"I'm alright," said Gene. "Just a little woozy."

"Ya'll see who was drivin'?" asked Bobby Sinclair.

"No, sir," said Gene.

"No," said I.

"What were you doin' in the middle of the road?"

"We broke down," said I. "Ran out of gas. Genie walked into the road. Bad, Genie. Bad boy. Don't you never do nothin' like that again, you hear me?"

Gene looked real sad and I could've eaten him up. "I'm sorry, momma."

"He'll need to go to the hospital," said Bobby, helping us to our feet. "He might have a concussion."

"He's fine."

"You sure?"

"Mommas know best."

"Right," said Bobby. "Sheriff station then."

"Can you drive us?"

"Er…"

"We ain't got no gas."

"I could give you some," said Bobby, and I felt a twang of sickness in my gut.

"I got plenty," Bobby was still saying. "I got an appointment, see."

"I don't feel up to drivin'," I said. "I think I'm in shock."

"You look fine."

"Why, thank you," I said, smiling at him and pouting my lips just a touch.

"That… that ain't what I mean," he stammered. "I just mean, you look well enough to drive."

"Well, I ain't."

"I got places to be."

"That ain't very gentlemanly of you, Bobby."

"You know me?"

"We live in the same town. I seen you around."

"You're from Calder?"

I nodded.

He narrowed his gaze and looked at me real hard. "Don't recognise you."

Something crawled up inside my intestines and died. "Well…" I began, but Bobby was already walking back to his truck, saying "I got plenty of gas for ya'll. Don't fret none."

"Please drive us, Bobby."

"I'm busy."

"Please. We- We ain't got no money. No… nothin.'"

He took a can from the bed of his truck and walked over to us and looked at me real suspicious like.

"I can't," he said. "I feel bad for ya'll, I sure do. But I'll fill her up for you 'fore I head off. Free of charge. I reckon that's at least something that a gentleman would do now, ain't it?"

He winked, and I forced a smile just like momma would have wanted, and it spat through my teeth, but I kept my lips closed. I hated my teeth. I didn't like men seeing my teeth. It broke the mirage, the lie, it showed them what I really was; their eyes would roll over my body with interest and a growing appetite, turning to lust, and then they'd get a gander at those gnashers and the sickness would come into their expression and the excuses would pour forth like bile and away they would go. They would leave me. They would all leave me. Bobby Sinclair was leaving me right now. He smiled that college football quarterback smile that I had seen him do since high school; the same one that had broken hearts and friendships between girlfriends and sisters; the same that he had used on me countless times, and yet that piece of shit couldn't even recognise me or remember my goddamn name. We had gone to school together. We had gone to parties together. We had lived in the same town our entire lives. And he had looked on me like a stranger from abroad.

He removed the gas cap from my Plymouth and placed the can on the ground next to it and knelt down alongside it and began to unscrew, saying, "You got a hose or someth…"

I shot him through the back of the head.

His body pitched forward and bounced off the Plymouth and then toppled onto its side and went still, arm outstretched, pointing along the empty highway like a warning against a coming tide, an onslaught.

The pistol was still in my hands. My daddy's little peckerwood .38; he sure wouldn't be missing it. I pointed over at Gene, who remained in the middle of the road with his mouth agape and his eyes fixed on the spot where the wonderful Bobby Sinclair now lay deader'n flies on crusted cowshit.

"Don't you go blubberin' on me now," I said.

He couldn't stop staring at the body.

"Hey!" I said and marched over to him and slapped him in the face. That got the little bastard's attention. "Hey," I said. "He had it comin'. Did you hear the way he spoke to your momma? He don't deserve to be your daddy."

Gene kept trying to look back at the body. I slapped him again. "Hey! Don't you be lookin' on him no more. He's dead now. He's for them buzzards yonder. They gonna have them a feast tonight, boy."

I laughed and gave my Genie a kiss on the head. "Take his wallet."

Gene stayed where he was.

"You listenin', Genie-pie? I said take his wallet." Gene waddled over to where Bobby Sinclair lay and he stood for a good while, just watching. It made me laugh to see. It sure was cute when he done something like that. I finished off what the great gentleman Bobby Sinclair had started and topped up my gas, and I fixed the cap back on the can left it at the side of the road.

Gene was still fishing through Bobby's pants.

"Goddamn it, Genie, you're takin' his wallet, not jackin' him off." I went over and did it for him. Inside were a driver's license, some family photos that weren't no good to nobody no more, and about fifty dollars. It weren't a fortune, but it was better than nothing. I could buy me some real nice sunglasses with fifty dollars. I dropped the photos in the desert.

We returned to our car and Eugene commenced his blubbering. It always happened this way. He wasn't never going to get used to this. If you want to find true love you got to be willing to do what it takes. That was what most people didn't understand. Prince Charming ain't just going to land in your lap. You got to hunt him down, put in the leg work. And even if he does, even if Prince Charming drops down right out of the goddamn sky and sits himself right on you, well, he might not be all that you'd imagined, and right then, you got to be willing to take Prince Charming out back and put one in his pretty little handsome head.

That was what my Genie didn't understand, I thought, looking on my crying son, as I tried to drive our car out of the desert and leave Bobby Sinclair's body and truck in the middle of the highway. Everyone deserves love. Even me.

Except the engine grumbled and whined and sighed and coughed itself to a silence like a dying asthmatic. Genie looked at me with eyes wetter than cat piss. I looked at the sun and sure wished I had me some sunglasses right about then.

DO DUCKLINGS FLY?

Ron Earl Phillips

THE FIRE WAS SMALL.

Marlene was tending to the boy's lunch when she saw the smoke get carried up above the yard in plumes of white, then gray with streaks of charcoal from behind the barn. She left her son sitting at the kitchen table and she raced out the door toward the rising smoke. She hollered for her husband, "Donnie Lee, Donnie Lee."

No answer came.

Near the front of the barn, Marlene grabbed a horse blanket to beat out the fire, hoping it would be enough. As she got closer, she heard raucous laughter. "Donnie…" she said. Her voice lowered because she didn't recognize it as her husband's laughter which at times could sound like the Devil's own. Less cheerful than menacing.

She rounded the corner, and saw Frank, a lubbering, thick-jowled man who was working on a lifetime of cirrhosis with a nearly empty fifth of Early Times. Marlene knew he was a drunk the day Donnie hired him, but that wasn't why she disliked him. In Frank's nearly permanent pickled state he had no filter or façade, she could see the tumblings of his feeble mind. The obvious lust when he leered at her. She had asked Donnie to fire him, or at least not have him at the house when she was there. Donnie Lee would shrug and say he was cheap labor.

Frank was red with laughter and whiskey. Marlene could see Donnie Lee with his trousers hanging off his thighs and his Johnson in his hands in an attempt to extinguish the fire.

"I don't think *his* hose is big enough," Frank said, seeing Marlene and pointing over to Donnie Lee.

"Oh, it's big enough," Donnie Lee said before seeing Marlene's face burning with irritation. Her appearance surprised him, and he stumbled back off kilter, strafing Frank with his yellow stream. Frank just laughed harder, and Marlene pushed her way toward the fire, beating it out with the horse blanket.

"The hell you doing, Donnie Lee?"

Her husband pulled up his britches, straightened up and stood direct in her face. She could smell the whiskey but didn't back down.

"Well," she said.

Donnie eased back and gave her a well-practiced grin. He was five years her senior, slim with a firm layer of natural muscle. Wearing his black hair back in a slick of pomade, charisma licked off Donnie like he was the embodiment of James Dean or Elvis Presley. Both his idols. It had worked on Marlene ten years ago when she was not much more than a teenager. It still worked on Donnie Lee's students, the girls he had seduced that Marlene wasn't supposed to know about, down at the college. Neither Donnie Lee nor Marlene were horse people, but it was a notion that he got. And when he got a notion, he was full tilt until the money, or the passion petered out.

"It weren't nothing to worry your pretty little head about.

I had it all under control" He gave Frank a glance and leaned into his faux accent. "Frank and me, we were having a little fun. Maybe it got a little out of hand. Just look at all we got done." Donnie Lee referred to the pile of still smoldering debris they had hauled out of the back of the barn.

"You could have burnt the barn down. Got yourself hurt. Burnt up *our* dreams."

Outside of giving her a son, Donnie Lee had never done anything for Marlene. He didn't share *his* dreams, even though they had been together since that little art school in Florida that Marlene begged her father to attend. It was his notion that they should get married. No wedding, no family, just a justice of the peace and a tearful phone call home to tell her mother of the *joyous* news. Her father was furious, cutting Marlene off and forbade her from coming home. She was now latched to Donnie Lee and wherever the notion would take them.

Donnie Lee's notions took them all over the country. Each destination was a failure, and the Donnie Lee that she knew left parts of himself like detritus. The slick pomade and charismatic smile couldn't hide the bitterness, the anger that was quick to flare, and quick to burn like debris pile he failed to extinguish.

Marlene could see the veneer peeling, and she started to turn away. It was too late, as a crushing hand grabbed her arm, pulling her back around to face him.

"Let go of me," she said. She didn't yell or raise her voice. She knew better.

He squeezed Marlene's arm harder, and her eyes dampened. She would not cry.

"This is my land. My barn." Though that wasn't true, they had a lease with an option to buy, and both of their names were on the agreement. "If I want to burn it all down, I will. So, you don't go raising your voice to me or tell me about *my* dreams."

Frank trying to excise himself from the confrontation,

"Donnie Lee, maybe I should get on…" His words trailed off as sobriety overtook him. The interruption was enough for Donnie Lee to loosen his grip. Marlene, feeling the tension ease and seeing Donnie Lee distraction, pulled away and loped toward the house.

The boy was sitting in the clodded dirt near the porch with a waddle of ducklings. One chirped in his hands as Marlene scooped up her son, then rushed up the stairs and through the door, throwing the door shut. She needed to get the keys to the car, get away to her girlfriend's while things cooled down, but they weren't on the hook.

"Stay," she told the boy as she set him down on a chair just inside the kitchen. Marlene ran to the bedroom, thinking she had left the keys in her purse. She had and shouldered the purse when she heard the back door open.

"Junior, what are you doing?" She heard Donnie Lee yell, but it wasn't inside the house.

She saw through the kitchen door, Donnie Lee raised up the boy by one arm, teetering him atop the porch railing.

"Do you want to see if you can fly?"

"Donnie Lee, don't you do it."

Marlene had grabbed the .22 rifle from behind the door as she stepped out onto the porch. The one Donnie Lee kept handy to shoot scavengers. It was her rifle that her uncle had given to her when she was young. Marlene took to shooting and was a good aim, even winning a regional tournament in junior high school. She knew this rifle and now she had it aimed at Donnie Lee.

Donnie Lee startled, and the boy crashed into the dirt below. "I didn't mean…"

Marlene pushed past Donnie Lee focused only on the cries of her son. The boy flopped in the dirt with tears turning to crusting mud. She tried to sit him upright to examine him for injury.

The boy let out a horrific howl. She heard Donnie Lee step off the stairs, and she turned, grabbing the rifle.

"Marlene… Is he, okay?"

"I think he broke a bone."

Marlene's cheeks were red with anger and her eyes burned with tears. She aimed the rifle toward Donnie Lee.

"What are you going to do? Shoot me?"

"Just get back, Donnie Lee. I need to take him to a doctor."

"Not without me. It was an accident, Marlene. I just wanted to scare him. He was throwing ducklings in the air. It was…"

An accident. She knew. She had many accidents over the years. He always came back with sweet talk trying to put out fires the only way he knew how.

"No," she said. "We're going." She thrusted the barrel of the rifle at Donnie Lee.

"It's not even loaded."

Marlene flipped the rifle in her hands, gripping the barrel like a bat and swung the butt of the .22 into Donnie Lee's groin. He grunted, collapsed to his knees, and puked up the whiskey he had drank with Frank.

"I know. I took the cartridge out."

Marlene gathered up her wailing son, got into her beat up car, and never came back.

MIRROR IMAGE

Lori Robbins

REBECCA WASN'T DEAD. I'D have known if she was. Twins are like that. But no one listened to me, because no one, other than my missing sister, could understand how lost I felt after she disappeared. And so I set out to find her.

The police were no help, and neither was Carrie Ann, our former foster mother. She stopped answering my phone calls, but I didn't give up. She was the last person to see Rebecca.

I drove to the edge of town, to the last house on the street, and rang the bell. "Carrie Ann! I know you're inside."

She opened the door, but only as far as the chain lock allowed. "Do us both a favor and forget about Rebecca. It's time to move on with your life."

"How can I forget her, when every time I look in the mirror I see her face?"

"You're an adult now. Not my responsibility." She slammed the door shut.

I'm sorry now I ever told Carrie Ann anything. She'd never

understood our relationship when we were together and had even less sympathy after Rebecca vanished.

• • •

The first step was easy enough. Flight 2112 left Des Moines International Airport and landed on time at JFK. A good omen. I collected my backpack from the overhead rack and headed to Rebecca's apartment. I knew no one in New York City and had no idea where I was going to spend the night. A sensible person would have secured a place to stay before making the trip. I used to be that sensible person. But after Rebecca went missing, reason and logic lost their hold over my actions. If I wanted to find my sister, I'd have to be more like her and less like the cautious, careful person I'd always been.

Going to her apartment was more than a starting point for my quest. It was a birthday present of sorts. For me and for her. To commemorate a quarter century of life that we'd mostly spent together.

Weary from the flight, the Air Train, and the subway, I stopped by a corner café and ordered a large coffee. The woman behind the register didn't look up. "Name?"

I don't know what made me answer as I did. "Rebecca."

She did a double take. "Oh my God, Rebecca! When did you get back? Where have you been."

It hadn't been my intention to impersonate my beloved sister. I swear, it was more an accident than a plan. I bowed my head and whispered, "It's a long story. I'm so sorry, but it's too painful to discuss. I honestly don't remember most of it."

She ignored the growing line of impatient, caffeine-starved customers behind me. "You mean, like amnesia?"

"Yes." I bit my lip. "You seem really nice. Are we friends?"

Her eyes filled with tears. "I can't believe this. Yes, we're friends. I'm Emma. Listen, girl, we're best friends!"

I examined her. She was definitely lying. Rebecca didn't have best friends, other than me. But I didn't challenge her relationship with my sister, as I was on rather shaky ground myself. Instead, I lifted my shoulders in a helpless gesture. "I can't find my keys. Any ideas about how I can get into my apartment?"

She wiped her eyes with the back of her hand. Most unhygienic. My sister would never be friends with a slob like her. She sniffled and said, "I'll tell Marty. He'll let you in."

I rubbed my forehead and pretended to think. "How do I know Marty?"

She texted a quick message. "You poor thing. Honey, he's the super. Marty will take care of you. I'll try to get off work early. Help you out. And don't you worry about paying. I'll take care of it."

I grabbed the coffee. "Thanks so much. But I need to get home. I'm really tired from all I've been through. Maybe later."

● ● ●

Marty met me in front of the building. We walked up four flights of stairs and stopped at a door that had a wreath of dried flowers and ribbons hanging from the top. The colorful circle very nearly made me cry. It bore the unmistakable stamp of my sister's sure hand. She was the creative one. I was more pragmatic. Better with numbers and analytics than people or art.

The super pulled a heavy keyring from his belt and opened the door to Rebecca's apartment. I stood in the doorway and didn't let him inside.

Marty wasn't happy. Perhaps the long climb had made him grumpy. He detached three keys and handed them to me. "I'm gonna leave these here for you. Make copies and get them back to me no later than tomorrow. If I gotta call a locksmith, it's gonna cost you."

He seemed unaware of Rebecca's absence. I smiled at him. "This is going to sound completely crazy, but when was the last time you saw me? I've had an accident and I'm trying to get back my memory of what happened. Do you have any idea where I might have gone while I was away?"

His eyes grew wide. "No kidding! That's really something." He squinted as he examined my face. "Can't really say the last time I saw you. Sorry I can't be more exact. I got a lot of buildings. A lot of tenants."

I handed him a ten-dollar bill, closed the door, and entered Rebecca's last known home.

The apartment, a single room studio, was disturbing in its emptiness. The sofa bed was open, but there were no sheets or pillows on it. The walls were bare, with faint outlines of where pictures used to be. Three plants had dropped their withered brown leaves and the stems were naked and dead. No laptop. No electronics at all. Not even a toaster. In the closet, a line of mismatched clothes hangers hung empty, but my sister's scent lingered in the musty air.

An envelope on the kitchen counter had my name on it. My heart throbbed with painful intensity as I undid the flap. The note inside said: *Stop following me.*

• • •

I filed that note with the other two. It was the shortest one Rebecca had written me, but I didn't hold it against her. And I didn't stop searching. I haven't yet caught her. But I will. She'll never escape me. After all, I know her as well as I know myself.

FOR THE BEST

J. Rohr

FEET ON FIRE SHE shuffled into the house. She kicked off her shoes and peeled off sweaty socks. Stepping inside, the shag carpeting felt fantastic. It offered the soft touch her burning feet needed. She risked a smile, though the energy it ate up almost put her to sleep. Leaning against the wall, she took a deep breath.

"What do you make of it, Professor?"

"I don't know. All I can say is, it's not of this world."

Raising an eyebrow, she went into the living room. No lights except for the glow from the tube tv. She found her kid on the couch snoozing. The television blathered on, some black and white sci-fi from yesteryear. The way the glow spilled onto her boy, she thought about taking a picture. Unfortunately, she still couldn't find her camera. Misplaced along with so many other pieces of her life, she sighed heavily. The memory would have to do.

Snack wrappers and crushed coke cans littered the coffee table. Shaking her head, she began clearing the teenager's mess.

Regardless of the workday, Mom shift started as soon as she walked in the house. Twelve hours shuttling slop around a diner didn't matter. Hell, Mom shift was 24/7—always on call—but she liked to think the boy was getting old enough to give her breaks.

"No rest for the weary," she murmured.

Her hand hesitated. Under a candy bar wrapper, she spotted her son's notebook. He carried it with him everywhere, always scratching at pages with a pencil. The glimpses she caught now and again suggested drawings, but the boy made a serious effort to keep it out of sight. He never let her get any real sense of the images inside. This seemed like an opportunity to see for once.

"Now, Claudia," she thought. "Don't be a snoop. Your mother was a snoop and it pissed you off to no end."

She sucked on her teeth. One peek couldn't hurt. Claudia turned the notebook around, flipped it open with a finger, and eyed the first page that fell into view.

The hair went up on the back of her neck. Her son grunted. He shifted a bit, but mostly stayed on his side with his back to her. Still, she closed the notebook quickly and slipped out of the room.

In the kitchen, she stood in the dark. The drawing flashed through her mind. Claudia shivered, dropping trash on the floor.

"Professor, what're your thoughts?"

"At the risk of sounding unscientific, these beings are monsters."

Claudia went to her bedroom. There she closed the door, sat on the edge of the bed, and dialed the phone. The click of the rotary dial conjured the sense of long nails ticking down her spine. The line rang three times. Claudia chewed her lip.

"Hullo?" a sleepy voice answered.

"Hi, May," Claudia said. "Is this a bad time?"

"No," May replied groggily. "It's never a bad time. I'm always up for a chat."

"Okay," Claudia huffed. "It's just been a really long day."

"Lemme listen," May said.

"Fuck-all, I just wanna slide down to Charlie's, over on Lincoln Ave., and get a tall, cold martini with those blue cheese olives."

"That does sound tempting," May said. "But then what happens?"

"The usual," Claudia sighed. "One turns to four, and I'm falling out the door."

"You really need to write country music."

"Yeah, maybe, but I'm not a fan of redneck blues. It'd be hard writing music I don't even wanna hear."

The ladies laughed. Claudia felt a tear roll down her cheek. She wiped it away.

"Rough day at work?" May asked, sounding more awake.

"Work is work," Claudia said. "It's—"

She heard thumping footsteps in the hall. May asked her to go on. Claudia listened. The footsteps passed. She heard the soft click of her boy's bedroom door being shut. Realizing she held her breath, Claudia inhaled sharply.

"Is it Henry?" May asked.

"I just worry about him," Claudia said. "What kind of person he's growing up into, ya know?"

"Every mother does," May said. "But you're a good mom."

"I like to think so, although, what if that's not enough?"

"What do you mean?"

"I," she hesitated to say it out loud. Shaking her head, she set the notion aside for the thousandth time. Then she said, "I just worry."

"Well then," May said. "The only thing you can do is keep an eye on him."

● ● ●

Walking to work, Claudia paused by a telephone pole. She noticed two new fliers tacked to it. One for a missing dog, the other for a cat. Six total papered the pole, all asking for anyone to be on the lookout for lost pets. Claudia frowned.

She recalled seeing a coyote the other evening. She wondered if those poor critters got eaten. Still, she made a mental note of the animals in question.

Work amounted to the same soul crushing nonsense as always. Customers gnawed at her sanity, while her boss did little to help. Every other guy thought her professional politeness indicated a craving for their cocks she did not possess. Yet, the manager, as usual, simply rolled his eyes at her complaints – "Maybe if you leaned into it, you'd get bigger tips." And although her coworkers commiserated with Claudia to a degree, it always seemed to her like they were really just waiting for their chance to talk; their problems more important than hers. As such, she spent most of the day feeling alone, waiting for the chance to leave.

During lunch, she sat at the counter reading a newspaper some customer left behind. One article reported odd break-ins lately. A perpetrator snuck into houses but didn't appear to take anything. One victim, after being awakened by the sound of footsteps, reported hearing a click like a camera shutter, leading police to suspect some type of pervert peeping tom. Though the victim caught a glimpse of the intruder the description sounded like any gangly teen, even Claudia's boy Henry.

After ten hours, the diner mostly empty, her manager magnanimously allowed her to leave. Claudia punched out and started the walk home. Along the way, she passed the telephone pole again. She noticed another fresh flier. This one for a terrier named Terry.

Arriving home, she found the front door unlocked. More importantly, she saw blood on the doorknob.

"Henry?" she called, hurrying inside.

"In the kitchen, Ma."

Claudia rushed there. A trail of blood lined the linoleum. It led to Henry standing at the sink, wincing as he washed his hand. Claudia practically leapt across the room.

Beside her boy, she gasped.

"What happened?"

"Nothing," Henry said.

"This is not nothing," Claudia said.

His hand looked chewed up. Blood poured into the sink. The holes in his hand washed clean then red welled out again in seconds.

Claudia gently laid a hand on Henry's back.

"Baby, what happened?"

"It's no big deal," Henry said. "I got bit by a dog."

"Oh my god," Claudia grimaced. "We need to take you to the hospital."

"Don't freak out Ma."

"You could have rabies."

"I don't have rabies."

"Oh, so you're a doctor now?"

Henry's shoulders slumped. He glanced her way. The way he glared made her stomach twist. It didn't just cut, it pushed her away.

"You're overreacting," Henry said.

"I'm your mother," Claudia replied. "I'm supposed to overreact."

She told him to stay by the sink. She would go next door to ask about borrowing the neighbor's car. Old Mrs. Goosman only ever drover hers on Sundays anyway. It being Tuesday, Claudia knew it'd be available.

Henry protested, but she ignored him. It took barely five minutes to get the keys. Claudia hurried back. Seeing blood on the carpet, she followed a fresh trail to Henry's room. She found him locking his closet.

"What the hell are you doing?" Claudia said. "We gotta go."

Grabbing towels out of the hall closet, she wrapped up his hand. Half dragging him, Claudia pulled Henry out to the car. Then she carted her sullen boy to the hospital.

There, a doctor asked questions. He wanted to know about the animal that bit Henry.

"It was a dog," Henry said. "I don't really remember much else."

"Well, without the animal," the doctor said. "We can't be sure if you have rabies. So, just to be safe, you'll have to get injections."

"How much is that going to cost?" Claudia asked.

The doctor told her. Her face tightened. Before the doctor said anything about necessity, she told him to get started. She said she knew enough already having had a cousin who died from rabies.

"Really?" Henry said. "I didn't know that."

"Well, it's not a pleasant memory," Claudia said.

"What was it like? Did you see him die?"

She squinted at her sixteen-year-old son. He looked around as though unsure what he did wrong.

"It's very horrible," the doctor chimed in. "You don't want it to happen to you."

Henry nodded. His gaze seemed miles away. Claudia touched his shoulder, and Henry flinched.

"Sorry," she said. "What were you thinking about?"

"We can't afford all this," Henry said. "But I don't wanna get in trouble."

"For what?" she asked. "Honey, I'm not at all mad at you for getting hurt."

"Yeah, but after the dog bit me," Henry hesitated. "I stomped it."

"To death?" the doctor said looking disgusted.

"Yeah."

"That's a natural reaction," Claudia said quickly. "A vicious animal attacked my son and he defended himself."

"Indeed," the doctor folded his arms across his chest. "Where's the body? We still need to dissect its brain."

Henry told them where to find the terrier. Something flashed in the back of Claudia's mind.

"A little brown and white terrier?" she asked.

"How'd you know?" Henry said.

"Lucky guess," she said, not mentioning the flier.

Henry asked if he could watch them dissect the dead dog's brain. Claudia told him no and felt a wave of relief when the doctor agreed. Henry huffed in displeasure. Claudia promised to buy him ice cream later. He still moaned as if a dissection ranked higher than rocky road.

Three hours later they left the hospital. Henry stared out the passenger side. Claudia considered ways to clean the carpet. She thought about making a thin paste with cold water and salt but figured she might still need a vinegar solution since, by now, the blood was probably dry. She didn't look forward to cleaning drops all the way down the hall to Henry's room.

Claudia furrowed her brow.

"Hey honey?"

"Yeah, Ma?"

"Why do you have a padlock on your closet door?"

• • •

"Privacy?" May chuckled. "Why can I not stop thinking there's a gross reason behind that?"

Claudia handed her a glass of sweet tea. She remarked on growing boys naturally having certain appetites. May interjected girls had the same. Then both recounted their own experiences as teenagers in need of *that* kind of privacy.

"Oh god," Claudia cringed. "Now I'm scared to walk into a room."

"Because he might be jerking off?" May snickered.

"I do not want to talk about my son like that," Claudia said. "But yes."

She couldn't help smirking. These type of situations, though somewhat inevitable, never really occurred to her. At least, they seemed too far down the line to consider. When she first got pregnant, so many worries ate up her attention. Finally holding her baby boy, every conceivable issue hit her at once, and the resulting panic attack almost got her locked up in the psych ward. When doctors reluctantly let her go, Claudia had learned to make it through everything by tackling one obstacle at a time, learning never to set her eyes too far down the line. Although, that said, sometimes she wondered if limiting her foresight is how she didn't notice her husband packing to leave until he was already gone. It worried her what else she may have missed along the way.

May rattled the ice in her glass.

"You know what'd make this drink glorious?" she said.

"Bourbon," Claudia said.

"Strawberries," May frowned. "And screw you because now I want bourbon."

"Sorry."

"No worries," May said. "So, where is the little chicken choker?"

"I dunno. Probably walking around the woods. He loves hiking out there. Oh! maybe he'll be a forest ranger one day."

"Maybe," May leaned forward. "You know, I can pick a lock."

"Since when?"

"Since I fell in love with Percocet and the pharmacy wouldn't give me anymore."

"Dark times," Claudia raised her drink.

"Dark times," May concurred and they clinked glasses. "I

just know you've been worrying about your boy a lot, and if you wanted to peek in that closet…"

She trailed off, though the implication remained clear. It felt like snooping. So, Claudia shook head.

"I am not turning into my mother," she said. "Hell, that's half the reason I quit drinking."

"Fair enough," May said. "However, what if there's a loophole?"

Claudia raised an eyebrow. May offered her alternative. Though Claudia didn't want to snoop, May seemed free to do as she pleased. Perhaps she could do some reconnaissance. Henry would never know, and Claudia didn't have to get any details. May would then only mention something if it seemed weird.

"Okay," Claudia nodded. "Ugh, I feel like an asshole, but yeah—do it."

May clapped her hands. Rubbing them together gleefully, she went hunting for paper clips. Finding a pair, she deftly crimped and bent one into a tension wrench then fashioned the other into a makeshift rake.

Claudia told her to be quick. The situation upset her stomach. May hurried down the hall, while she went to the front room window to act as lookout. The last thing she wanted was Henry catching them in the act.

After a few minutes, Claudia called out, "How's it going?"

"Claudia?"

"Yeah?"

"I think you need to see this."

She didn't like the sound of May's voice. Still, Claudia didn't hesitate. She went down the hall.

In Henry's room she found May sitting on the bed. At her feet, a cardboard box. She held several photos. May looked sick.

Claudia clenched her jaw and went inside. She looked down into the box. Inside she saw her missing camera, several short stacks of photos, notebooks, and a pile of small bones. In addition, two knives, a hammer, and some twine.

Claudia bent down. She plucked out a pile of photos. Each appeared to feature images of animals in various states of dissection. She recognized several from the missing pet fliers.

She almost smiled. Though gruesome, the photos were good. Clear, capturing every gory detail, and vibrantly colored. The hideousness leapt off the photo. She half expected to see the exposed dog heart beating. Claudia dreamed of being a photographer before life sent her down a different path. She almost smiled because it seemed she passed that shutterbug skill onto her son. Unfortunately, that odd pride couldn't undo her disgust.

"Where would he even get these developed?" May asked. "I mean, someone would report this, right?"

"He's in a club at school," Claudia said. "He probably developed them himself."

She picked up a different set of pictures. May started examining a notebook. She made it through a few pages before throwing it back in the box.

"It's like a slasher drew a porno," May said. "Have you seen any of this?"

"No," Claudia said. "Henry is very private."

"Because he knows this is fucked up."

Claudia looked down at her friend. She felt a reflexive need to defend her baby boy. Yet, the words wouldn't come out. Instead, she stared down in silence for a second then went back to the photos.

"This explains the twine," she said, holding one out to May.

It showed the remains of a cat. Twine secured parts of the animal to a T-shaped form made of plywood. The result created a sort of scarecrow out of cat pieces. The background suggested the totem might be out in the woods somewhere.

May pushed the picture away. Unable to stomach anymore,

she left the room. Claudia carefully put everything back in the box. Then she carried it out to the kitchen. May paced, fanning herself with her hand.

"I don't know how you're so calm," May said. "I am freaking out."

"I suppose I'm in shock," Claudia said.

She opened one of the notebooks. The first page she saw featured an auger drilling into an anus. Blood gushed everywhere. The screaming face featured a lot of great detail. Henry really captured the expression of terror.

Some photos fell out onto the floor. Claudia picked them up.

"What're those?" May said. "Impaled Pomeranians?"

Claudia looked at the pictures. Her face tightened. She set them back in the notebook and put them both into the box.

"I think you should go," Claudia said.

"You shouldn't deal with this alone," May said. "I'm here for whatever you need."

Not true, Claudia thought, since she knew May would never get her a bottle of booze. Still, she appreciated the sentiment. Her friend meant well.

It took some prodding, but Claudia convinced May to leave. She sold the notion on the idea it'd be best if Henry didn't feel confronted. At the very least, he might explain himself more to his mother alone. A part of Claudia secretly hoped a reason existed for all this that didn't end in a horror show.

Reluctantly, May left. Though she insisted Claudia call with details of how things went as soon as possible. Agreeing to, Claudia shut the front door.

She went back to the box. She retrieved the photos that fell on the floor earlier. All taken at night, several featured people asleep in their beds. One showed a startled man in his pajamas squinting, trying to penetrate the dark. The article she read the other day came to mind.

Claudia picked up a pile of the animal photos. She realized they actually went in a kind of order. The first few featured the animal on the street or in someone's yard. Cycling through them led to the vivid gruesome dissections and finally the totems.

She looked back at the sleeping people.

"This is how the hunt starts."

• • •

She laid everything out on the kitchen table. As such, when Henry got home Claudia confronted him with his box of horrors, its contents laid out undeniable. Henry pretended not to know what it was. Claudia cut off that avenue. Then he tried to steer the conversation into an argument about privacy. She shot that down too, prevented another deflection, and eventually, without an escape, Henry fell silent.

"What are you going to do?" he asked softly.

"We are going to get you some help."

"From who?"

"I don't exactly know," Claudia said. "But honey, it's 1986. They can fix all kinds of things they couldn't before."

She took hold of his hand. She touched his cheek. He gazed at her with lifeless eyes.

"I love you," she said.

"I'm going to my room," he walked away.

"Okay."

She watched Henry leave. The gangly young man never seemed so alien to her. It broke her heart not being able to see him as her baby boy anymore.

Furiously, Claudia put everything back in the box. Carrying it outside, she stormed out back to the patio. Grabbing some lighter fluid from the garage, she hosed down the contents. As if the box were to blame, Claudia set it ablaze. She hoped never to see anything like it ever again.

That night, she tossed and turned like a tumble weed. Yet, she made zero progress towards slumber. Her mind kept racing over a thousand nightmares inspired by that goddamn box. The worst of which featured her little boy creeping through houses, hammering skulls and slitting throats then capturing snapshots of the dead and dying. Newspapers dubbing him the Click-click Killer because of the last sound his victims heard.

"Why couldn't it just be porn?" Claudia said.

Somewhere around two a.m., she heard faint footsteps creeping down the hall. She figured Henry must be restless as well. It sounded like he went into the kitchen. Claudia assumed he wanted a late-night snack. She decided to join him. Maybe they could talk about things, clear the air a bit.

Slipping into a robe, she went towards the kitchen. The lights not on caused her brow to furrow. She flipped the switch as she entered the room.

Henry stood in the middle of the kitchen holding a butcher's knife. He stood frozen like a deer in headlights. He and Claudia stared at one another. He appeared to be in midstride as though leaving the room.

"Are you making a sandwich?" Claudia asked.

"Yes."

"In the dark?"

"I didn't want to wake you."

Though the light couldn't reach her room, Claudia nodded. She feigned a yawn.

"Put the dishes in the machine when you're done," she said.

"Okay, Ma."

She backed out of the room. In her bedroom, Claudia closed and locked the door. She spent the rest of the night awake.

• • •

"Can I call you Claudia?"

"That depends, can I call you Pat?"

"Well, maybe Dr. Pat. Things shouldn't get too casual."

The balding psychiatrist chuckled. Claudia forced a smile. He picked up a folder. Flipping through the contents he found a page covered in handwritten notes.

"So," Dr. Pat said. "I've seen your son, Henry, a few times now."

"Yes, I'm really anxious to hear what's going on," Claudia said.

Henry never shared anything with her anymore. Not that he was ever what one might call chatty, but recently, he might as well have been mute. It got to the point even Claudia stopped trying to talk to him. They now lived together in silence save for the television's nonsense.

"To the extent I can share our discussions," Dr. Pat said. "Henry is a very charming young man. After talking with him, I've come to agree with some of the things he's said."

"Such as?" Claudia said.

"His opinion of his problem," Dr. Pat said. "He and I, for the most part, see eye to eye on that. It's actually kind of refreshing having a patient who is so self-aware."

"So, he does agree he has a problem."

"Oh yes," Dr. Pat nodded. "Children of alcoholics often do."

"I'm sorry," Claudia leaned away from the desk. "What's that got to do with anything?"

"A great deal," Dr. Pat said.

"Plus, I've been sober for six years."

"And that's commendable," Dr. Pat said. "But I feel your problems have had an effect on your son."

Claudia narrowed her gaze. She ground her teeth. In the back of her mind, she immediately thought about how much money she poured into this man's pocket.

"Please explain to me," Claudia said. "How my drinking made my son murder animals."

"About that," Dr. Pat said, knocking on the desk with his class ring. "Henry says you misunderstood an art project."

"An art project?" Claudia scoffed. "If you saw those photos—"

"Which you burned," Dr. Pat interrupted.

"Yes, but if you saw them—"

"And why did you burn them?"

"They were horrifying," Claudia said. "I suppose I wasn't thinking clearly."

"Had you been drinking?"

"No, and I don't appreciate that accusation."

"It's not an accusation," Dr. Pat held up his hands. "It's just a question. Do you usually react this way to questions? With hostility and suspicion?"

Claudia snorted angrily. She knew the route this led down. She considered calling May. She'd be able to confirm everything, but Claudia doubted doctor dumbass would consider another recovering addict a credible source.

"It's okay if you fell off the wagon," Dr. Pat said.

"I did not *fall off* the wagon," Claudia rolled her eyes to the ceiling.

"I'm just saying you look a little worse for wear."

She chuckled. Claudia placed a hand over her eyes. Anger burned the tears out of her sockets.

She knew she looked like a wreck. That stemmed from sleepless nights jumping awake at the slightest creak. The increasingly crushing strain of turning around to find her son standing silently on the other side of the room staring at her. The toxic reality of a creeping certainty eating her alive. Namely, the solid suspicion her son planned to kill her.

"I don't doubt Henry has a violent imagination," Dr. Pat said.

"But there's nothing wrong with that, especially for a young man. Masculine fantasies often involve violence."

"We're done," Claudia said.

She rose and left. Dr. Pat called after her, but Claudia didn't hear a word he said. Though she did reply by giving him the finger on the way out.

• • •

For weeks, Claudia expressed her concerns to whoever listened. Co-workers and customers became well versed in her worries. Her Henry's depression seemed worse every day, and she worried like any good mother would. Even a cashier at the grocery got an earful. That seed planted Claudia started the next step in her plan.

Making dinner, she prepared one of Henry's favorites. Growing up, he used to insist on watching her make a whole roasted Athenian chicken. He always giggled when she spatch-cocked the bird. The sound of bones snapping delighted him so absolutely. She hated how hindsight tainted the memory.

Claudia mixed up olive oil, garlic, lemon juice, oregano, salt, and pepper in a bowl. After coating the bird, she left it in the fridge to marinate for a few hours. Then she got in the car and drove to Charlie's over on Lincoln Ave.

Taking her old spot at the end of the bar, Claudia ordered a Shirley temple. Sipping the non-alcoholic beverage, she waited. About an hour later someone walking by doubled back.

"Claudia?"

"Hi Davey," she said.

"Holy shit," Davey said sitting beside her. "I haven't seen you in forever. What've you been up to?"

"Living the dream," Claudia said.

They reminisced for a few minutes. He informed her about

all the regulars she left behind. It felt good hearing about folks who used to be a fixture in her life. They were never the best people, but they were good friends. For her own part, Claudia mostly shared the strain of raising her son.

"He's a troubled boy," she said. "He's depressed all the time. I worry about him, Davey, I really do."

"How can you not?" Davey said. "You were always a good mom."

"I like to think so," Claudia said.

She drained her beverage. Davey adjusted his flat cap. Leaning in, he lowered his voice.

"By the by," he said. "Don't take this the wrong way, but I heard you quit drinkin'."

"I did."

"So, should you be in a place like this?"

Claudia shrugged. The risk existed, though, unfortunately, just living with her son involved worse chances than being in this dive.

"I've been having trouble sleeping," she said. "Sleeping pills just don't cut it, so I figured this always knocked me out."

"Hey," Davey said scooting closer. "If you need some knock-out drops, I'm your man."

"I half remember May mentioning that."

They went out to his car. From the trunk he produced several sacks of pills. After examining them for a minute, Davey offered her a handful of what he called the last quaaludes in the country.

"These things are priceless since they stopped making 'em last year," he smirked. "But for you, I'm happy to help a friend."

"Thanks," Claudia said. "I gotta get home before my kid, but I'll be back if I need more sleep."

"I don't doubt it," Davey waved as she headed away. "Sure I'll see you around."

Back home, Claudia got busy making lemonade. Henry

loved lemonade. She made a simple syrup on the stovetop then squeezed juice out of a dozen lemons. She mixed it sweet then crushed up the quaaludes and dumped them in the pitcher.

She put the chicken in the oven. As the appetizing aroma filled the air, she heard the front door open. Henry coming home from school, no doubt. He went straight to his room, while Claudia made mashed potatoes with the skins on just the way Henry liked. A dollop of sour cream and plenty of butter really brought it to life.

Around six, they sat down at the kitchen table together. They ate in silence. Henry devoured his dinner and drained two tall glasses of lemonade. It didn't take long before his eyelids started sagging.

He looked at his mother with a curious expression.

"I'm not right," Henry said.

"You should go to bed," Claudia said.

He narrowed his gaze. She tensed. Then he nodded, and yawning, headed for bed.

Claudia waited a half hour as planned. Certain the boy must be asleep, she got razorblades from the garage then slipped silently into Henry's room.

He looked so peaceful passed out. Claudia used to watch him slumber as a child. He used to fall asleep looking through the encyclopedia. There were still dog-eared pages wherever the books contained anatomy diagrams.

Taking a deep breath, Claudia took hold of her son's wrist. She opened his arm from elbow to palm with a razor. Blood poured out almost immediately. Henry stirred.

Claudia placed a hand on his forehead.

"Hush baby," she petted his face. "It's for the best."

Softly, she sang a lullaby that always worked on him as a baby. Around the chorus, she opened his other arm. Blood waterfalled off the bed.

Claudia wiped off the razorblade then pressed it between Henry's fingers to get his prints on it. She let it fall from his hand naturally. It disappeared in the deluge staining his sheets.

Shortly thereafter, Henry stopped breathing. Claudia sucked in a shaky breath. She went out into the living room. Sitting down on the couch, Claudia turned off the lamp. Alone in the dark, she nodded.

"It's for the best."

WOODPECKERS

Jessica Slee

SHE DOESN'T PAY IT much attention when the kid comes in that morning, asking to speak to her, to report something he'd seen. Dermody had caught him once drawing graffiti on the side of a vacant mini-mart but let him go with a warning, and now she guesses that gives her an air of sympathy and consideration that she really wishes she didn't have to humor.

Her partner intercedes before the kid can make it to Dermody's desk and guides him forward instead. Bless him, Dermody thinks. Even as her attention is drawn to the conversation just beginning to take shape at the head of the room, her jaw twinges with the phantom pain of a mostly-healed bruise.

The eavesdropping is a habit she wishes she could break. She has enough work to deal with without adding conjecture and gossip on top of it.

"I told you, I know what I saw," the kid is telling her partner, Detective Morrigan. He has a notepad open, and takes down every word, nodding with a professional, detached interest.

"I saw somebody throwing a rifle into the river, down by the docks."

"A rifle," Morrigan repeats. "You didn't see them use it?"

The kid shrugs. "I wasn't about to go closer! But I stayed to watch."

"Why?" Morrigan asks.

"There was something off about it."

Morrigan continues the interrogation, asking what the person looked like and what time of day it was. Together, they learn that the kid didn't get a good enough look at their face to tell their gender, but they were broad-shouldered and wore a big hat that covered their hair, and a long brown overcoat and a patterned scarf on top of that. All new-looking. It had been late the night before, after dusk, but not so late the cicadas started chirping. Morrigan writes down 7:30pm.

"Something off about it," Dermody echoes, wandering over. "What do you mean by that?"

The kid fidgets, twisting his fingers together. The tips of his shoes are pointed in towards one another, his posture unsteady.

"They stayed too," he says at last. "They watched it sink."

Something occurs to her, then. "Hey, what were *you* doing down there?"

The kid freezes, looks guilty. After so many years, she's developed a good sense of when someone is lying and when they aren't. Some people are better at it than others. It's a learned skill.

"If I go for a visit, I won't find some new murals on the side of a warehouse or something, will I?"

The kid shakes his head, his eyes too wide. Dermody shoos him away with one hand. The kid stumbles out the door, pauses just outside the threshold. He stops to glance back, watching. It makes Dermody feel a little perturbed.

"Suppose we go take a look, then," Morrigan says.

Dermody nods. "I suppose we should."

• • •

Dermody throws the first punch. There's a cheer from the crowd, gathered around the ring painted into the cracked concrete floor. It makes her blood sing, makes it a little easier to find a rhythm. The other woman is off to a sluggish start, but she's got a smile on her face. She'll get there, soon enough.

They circle one another, and her opponent throws a wild haymaker, like she doesn't know how to punch right. She's got enthusiasm but no technique.

Dermody ducks and responds with a punch of her own, to show her how it's done. There are more than a few people in the crowd tonight she knows have never been here before. All women, here to take out some unspoken grievances or outrage, to indulge in some fantastical new form of self-expression. Once, that was her, and although she couldn't say who had been the first to meet her in the ring she is grateful for the gift that they have given her.

It feels good when the back of her knuckles crack across a stranger's eyebrow. The light from a streetlight washes over the ground, and when she blinks the sweat from her eyes it makes the world look like an oil painting. The crowd cheers. She strikes again, emboldened, aiming for the ribs. She thinks she can draw out her opponent's ire. It is where she most wants to be hit, herself.

Her opponent wears what looks like a bandana tied around the upper half of her face, with jagged holes cut into the fabric for her eyes. It looks hastily made. Even now Dermody cannot help herself from making these tiny observations, even as she dodges the next punch. The other woman has injuries, too, cuts and scrapes from before Dermody had ever gotten her hands on her. Maybe from falling on the ground, or a particularly over-zealous challenger in an earlier fight. She's taking most of the hits, too, not even bothering to dodge. Sometimes it's like that. She understands.

She found this place in the course of an investigation. She should've shuttered it, like the dive bars without a license or the shops that stock contraband goods. Instead, out of some morbid curiosity, she chose something different. It wasn't what she was expecting. In fact, it gave her a new appreciation for the violence inherent to so many of her cases, kept her mind sharp, helped with her self-control.

The other woman throws herself forward with a scream. Dermody puts her fists up, blocking the first of several punches, then feints and lets herself be hit, square in the chest. The breath is knocked from her lungs, but she manages a wheezing laugh once it clears.

She lets this go on for a moment, blocking attacks and receiving a few glancing blows, none as direct as the first. Once she is satisfied, once she notices her opponent slowing down, breathing heavily from the effort, she draws back one fist and brings it crashing forward.

She has a gift to give, too.

● ● ●

The two of them make their way from their car towards the first of the warehouses, stomping across the mud. The ground slopes in a steep angle away from the parking lot, and the warehouses spread out in a wide arc opposite from the river, such that it is impossible to hear the noise from a group unloading equipment from one building just at the edge of their sightline, past a copse of tall, sparse trees.

The birds are louder, clinging to the branches, shrieking like they're competing for an award.

"It's a collared dove," Morrigan says with interest, glancing up and pausing their trek. "Awfully rare for this area. I wouldn't have expected to see any here. What a sight."

Dermody blinks into the sunlight; there is nothing spectacular to her about the plain creatures. All birds look alike to her. Two wings, a beak, feathers. And these are a mottled gray, without a drop of color.

"What a sight, indeed," Dermody echoes. She stalks off towards one of the warehouses, looking down instead of at the trees, like her partner continues to do. She is careful of the ground—any prints will show in the mud, and they do not want to efface any evidence that might have been left behind. Dermody finds nothing at first, and as they continue to wander the banks of the river, stopping to observe the interior and exterior of each building, Morrigan points out interesting tidbits about the wildlife and the geography.

On one of the buildings they find a mural in-progress, nothing more than a few curls of white and some jagged black lines. It isn't clear by looking at it what the kid was going for, if it is indeed his work, but Dermody merely sighs and continues on.

There is nothing out of the ordinary in the first four warehouses, each a vision of oxidized corrugated metal and peeling rust-colored paint. Their path towards the last unsearched warehouse takes them closer to the water, where a few fishermen are spread out along the riverbank, close enough for professional solidarity but far enough away to avoid each other's company. She'll have to ask them later what they've seen.

Another noise draws her attention up, towards the heavy boughs of a tree. "Look, more birds," she says.

Above, almost too high to see, a woodpecker jams its head repeatedly into the bark.

"A common bird." Still, Morrigan regards it with clear appreciation. "There's more over there, in those trees." There are at least three or four, each ignorant of everything an inch further away from their necks. She spots them by the splash of red feathers across the head of each bird.

"One warehouse left," Dermody says. The constant drill of beaks against bark produces a noise that Dermody alternatively finds grating and reassuring.

"If we find anything at all." Morrigan continues to look around, but his attention is drawn, even moreso than his partner, towards the wildlife roosting in the boughs.

"You really like these creatures, huh?" Dermody asks. She'd assumed the bird-themed calendar on Morrigan's desk was some kitschy gift, something he kept out of obligation or used for necessity, not choice. It'd been there all year, and another before that, but the conversation had just never come up. And besides, there was plenty her partner didn't know about her.

"I started birding when I was young. I used to go on the weekends, with my folks, to some of the larger national parks, but things have been too busy around here to take off like that for awhile," he says, shrugging his shoulders. "It's not just about finding one that's rare, or photographing every variety of a specific type. It's about watching something fly. Isn't that a marvel?"

"Sure," Dermody agrees blandly. At the entrance to the warehouse, she finds the door ever so slightly loose. Wheeling it the rest of the way open, it squeaks on its casters. The interior is dark and stuffy; bits of straw at the threshold cling to the mud on her shoes. There is a heavy sourness to the air, and although the space is full of crates, Dermody feels herself stepping forward, strongly aware that the sounds have stopped. Morrigan moves ahead of her, checking behind each stack of crates and boxes dispassionately. He disappears from sight, and a few moments pass before Dermody hears him call out.

"You should see this." He sounds grim, and as Dermody approaches she looks over Morrigan's shoulder to see some strange discoloration stretching across the wooden slats.

A pool of blood spreads from the bottom of the crate down and across the floor, large enough that whatever it came from, barring a miracle, must certainly be dead. It's nearly completely dried, but still shiny in places towards the middle, sloped in an oblong arch like the shoreline of a shallow pond. Then her attention catches on the long stalks of dried grass and clumps of dirt in places across the floor, and considers a dozen different explanations for what had happened there possibly only the day before.

"I'll call it in," Morrigan is saying. "We'll secure the scene—get statements from the fishermen...how many do you remember seeing at the riverbank? Five? And we'll have to get forensics out here immediately. It'll be a mess, after all the rain, but they've worked greater miracles with less."

"Yes," Dermody says. More uprooted grasses litter the ground further away, and she studies the symmetry to the shapes, considering whether the effect looks staged, like a painting, or more like a work of random entropy.

When they leave the warehouse to greet the arriving technicians, the sun is close to setting and the riverbank is empty of any presence but the renewed chirping in the trees above.

• • •

"A body was pulled from the river this morning," Detective Morrigan says, in a quiet moment after they'd returned to the riverbank to interview the fishermen. "Gunshot wound in the center of the chest. Medical Examiner's office still has him, so we don't know yet which killed him—the gunshot or the drowning."

"Near the industrial sector?"

"Close enough. We'll see if it matches the blood found at the warehouse yesterday. If so..." As he trails off, his shoulders rise and then fall.

"What would you like to do?" Dermody asks.

"If we can identify the man, we can get closer to the motive." He makes another attempt at a shrug. "What we saw in the warehouse was messy, careless. It could have been planned, or it could have just been opportune. So many things in life are disordered, but violence is rather simple."

Dermody rubs the edge of her jaw as she pieces together her thoughts. The image, of so much blood against the smooth concrete floor, remains firmly rooted in her mind. The CSIs had mentioned the amount and placement of the blood was all wrong for a knife, but perfectly in line with a bullet.

If Morrigan notices her discomfort, he doesn't mention it. "Maybe by the time we're done here they'll have cleared the body for us to see."

The woods are not silent, and they try not to add to the disturbance as they move from one encampment to the next, interviewing the groups of commercial fishermen and older hobbyists simply enjoying their mornings, gaining little. Most know one another, and seem to react to the news of a weapon and a murder with the appropriate amount of surprise. It's common, they say, for people to linger by the riverside. It had been such a peaceful place.

They're finishing up talking to a small group; Dermody asks the questions while Morrigan once more dutifully takes down each statement. A few others remain close, those they've already spoken to, curious to hear more, and a loner just out of sight, moving behind the trees but keeping a distant watch.

"Who's next?" Dermody asks. "There's some others we missed down by the clearing."

"No, I want to talk to whoever's up there, first. You see them?"

"They've been watching us this whole time, you know," Dermody says.

"Well, then they should know the dance." Morrigan raises a hand and waves. "Hey, you!"

The indivudual goes abruptly still, and when Morrigan shouts again their long legs turn and they run, past the trees and down the hillside.

The ground is much more solid without the rain. As they give chase, shouting, Dermody calls to her partner, familiar adrenaline fueling her breaths. "So much for the interview, huh?"

"Just get them!"

Their target's path seems chosen at random, their gait uneven, and although Dermody is fit, Morrigan is much faster. He soon overtakes them and tackles them to the ground. She arrives to see Morrigan putting cuffs on a young woman, with choppy blond hair and a deep-set scowl.

She has no fishing gear or similar supplies with her, her clothes appear brand new, and she refuses to speak a single word as they return together to the station.

It is Dermody who gets the call that the body is ready for viewing, so they leave their newest suspect there as the ink dries on the paperwork. Any questioning will simply have to wait.

● ● ●

Arranged before them is a corpse—young, male, bloated from water. An entry wound from a gunshot—Dermody estimates courtesy of the rifle the kid saw—exists about six inches below the throat.

"No bullet was found," the ME tells them, "so we can't match ballistics. Likewise, no foreign DNA appears anywhere on the body, no drugs in their system. We have an ID, too. Contract worker at the warehouses. I pulled what little information on him I could find for you. It's not much—wasn't very social, didn't have any local family. But I thought you would like to know that the blood is indeed a match."

"Time of death?" Morrigan prompts.

"Somewhere between six and nine PM, two nights prior."

The rest of the body has been cleaned up. The few marks around the forehead and arms are inconclusive—the scrapes could just as easily have come from rocks and the current as they could have been another sign of injury or evidence of a struggle.

"What do you make of it?" Dermody asks. Morrigan is still staring at the body, his expression encouraging; her partner often has better instincts about things like that.

"I'm trying to picture it, how it must've been at the warehouse. The body all laid out like that."

Dermody tilts her head to the side as she does the same, absorbs the stillness of the room. As soon as she puts thoughts into words, she feels a little foolish. "It was wild and uncaring. Like some animal thing."

"Animals don't carry rifles."

"Yeah, but they hunt, and they wait, and they build, and they strike. I think that's the angle we should take with the suspect. I think that's what we're looking for—someone indulging an animal instinct."

"That's just shifting responsibility. An animal can be savage, sure, but they aren't cruel for cruelty's sake. The person that did this was indulging an inclination for violence. The highest levels of it, in fact," Morrigan says, unconvinced.

"So tell me. Why do men commit violence?" Dermody asks.

"Hatred, mostly."

"Mostly?" A sound of amusement sticks in her throat. "What else?"

"Easy. For the approval of other men." He pauses, considering. "Although, we do have a woman currently in custody. We shouldn't assume. Why do *women* commit violence?"

"You tell me," Dermody says coolly.

Morrigan talks like he's reading from a checklist. "Revenge. Rage. Desperation. And so on. These cases typically draw less attention, less scrutiny. But these things take time. Practice."

"Hm. Not easy to come by."

"What do you think?" Morrigan asks her.

The word *rage* still echoes in her mind. Next is *attention*. "I think we should speak to our suspect."

● ● ●

Their suspect, a Davina Ravindahl, aged thirty-nine, waits in one of the holding rooms; according to one of the rookies, she'd been completely silent and calm as a cucumber. They decide to let her wait a little longer while they assemble a file of everything the ME was able to discover.

Morrigan is absently stirring his second cup of coffee when he asks, "Did you do anything fun over the weekend?"

Dermody freezes, her next exhale caught in her throat before she recovers and says smoothly, "No, I'm afraid I didn't really have the time."

"That's too bad."

"Did you go..." She waves a hand, struggling to remember what her partner had called that hobby of his. "...Birdwatching?"

"No. Thought about it, but in the end I stayed in. I have plans for next week, though. Volunteer work. You're always welcome to join."

She gives a noncommittal hum, unwilling to say more. She cannot imagine her virtuous partner keeping a secret like hers. Cannot imagine him seeking out thrills a little too dangerous for someone in their line of work.

"Ready to go?" Morrigan jerks a thumb towards the holding room. "Mind if I take the lead?"

He receives another hum in response. A minute later finds them inside a bright square box, walls freshly painted white, with a long metal table and three chairs, one occupied. While the bullpen they'd left smells like burnt coffee, to her nose this room is almost antiseptic. The suspect sits, wrists bound to the table. Her face and sleeves are still streaked with dirt from her tumble in the woods, a bruise against the back of her head, but her eyes are alert and her zipped-up jacket looks otherwise without wear, the color the same light blue as an unpolluted sky.

Morrigan sets the opening, dropping a series of photographs onto the table and spreading them out, most focusing on the bloody warehouse floor.

"You ever shoot a gun before, Ms. Ravindahl?" Morrigan asks her.

"I don't know how," she says. Her gaze is drawn to the first photograph, taken overhead of the oblong pool of dark blood. "This is a disturbing image."

"Quite so." Morrigan slides the photograph to the side to make room for the next. Taken from a distance, it encompasses nearly the entire room. The next, a smear on a packing crate. The next, a smudge of dirt with an impression of a heel.

He coughs. Ravindahl finally looks up.

"Tell us what you were doing two nights ago."

"I was alone for most of the time," she says, then tenses, as if aware how it sounds. "But I went to the corner store."

"What for?"

Her voice turns acerbic as for the first time a crack appears in her otherwise bland veneer. "Milk and bread. What else?"

"And what time was that?"

"I have no idea. My credit card statement would say."

"Why'd you run?"

"You ran after *me*."

"I remember it a little differently." Morrigan pushes another photograph forward, a driver's license photo of the victim. "Do you know this person?"

"Who?" Ravindahl leans forward, eyebrows furrowed. "They don't look familiar."

There's unforthcoming, and then there's whatever this woman is pretending to be. It's only the strange glint in her eye and her remarkable composure that has Dermody convinced there's something more to her than what she has shown them so far. Most suspects crumble under the pressure or get caught up in a lie, but above all else, Ravindahl seems so certain—both that she will not falter under any questioning and that they will find no evidence in her guilt.

"Do you go to the river often?"

"There's a bridge, a few miles up. The little park next to it—I like to go there sometimes. Great view of the city, very peaceful."

"Why were you *there* in the first place?" Dermody interrupts. She places her closed fists on the table and leans forward.

Ravindahl pauses. At first, she seems taken aback when she hears Dermody's voice. "Rubbernecking," is the answer she gives. "I wanted to see something cool."

Morrigan all but throws his hands up, missing the strange look that comes over Ravindahl's face. There's a shadow of a bruise across the knuckles of Dermody's right hand, and Ravindahl's eyes seek it out where her fists remain planted on the table. Then, any variance in her expression is carefully bricked over, just as it'd been before.

"You can't keep me here forever," she says at last.

"You have some scrapes on your arms," Morrigan continues. "How'd they get there?"

"Tripped in the woods," is the answer. "Right before you cuffed me."

They're getting nothing, and what had seemed like such an easy catch now has Morrigan scowling at the shadow of defeat.

"You don't even have an alibi. You were at the right place at the right time. You just sit tight while we get some more paperwork in order. Shouldn't take too long."

He rocks back on his feet, his frown deepening. The look of performative derision isn't as convincing as he wants it to be; Morrigan has never played the bad cop well. Still, Dermody backs him up, copying his expression as once more their suspect seems entirely unaffected by anything her partner has said. Then, she looks over, and Ravindahl's entire expression shifts into something hard and deliberate. Dermody falters, suddenly uncertain.

Outside, the sun streams through the windows, the blinds casting long shadows across the worn beige carpeting. Morrigan has a look about him, like he's itching to talk but doesn't want to start a conversation. Dermody recalls the body, lying against the cold metal table, and the person they'd just left, as ordinary in appearance as they come. "Do you really think she's the kind of person who would do something like that?

Morrigan immediately launches into another speech. "She's suspicious. It's so convenient—her being there, that cavalier attitude, the scrapes, no alibi. I don't like any of what she said. It's a shame we have so little to work with. If the ME could pull any DNA from the body, it'd be different..."

"The marks on her arms," Dermody says. "Do you buy that line about falling over in the woods?"

"I know you somehow manage to cut yourself slicing vegetables all the time, but I don't think most people are so prone to routine accidents."

A flush creeps up Dermody's neck. Somehow, she still feels watched, even from outside the interrogation room. "She's right. We can't keep her here for much longer. Without more concrete evidence, we're going to have to let her go."

She knows how common it is for those responsible to return

to the scene of their crimes. So far, there is nothing personal to tie this woman to the one who has died. No cameras by the warehouses, except for those on the roads at the larger intersections a mile to either side. Plenty of routes to avoid detection. Then, Dermody realizes she hadn't answered a single question directly, only weaved around their remarks. She has nothing but her own intuition, to say that Ravindahl was involved.

And now, she is unable to hide the truth from herself, that there is something about Ravindahl that is familiar to her. She has seen this person before. And she knows, in a disastrous finish, that the other woman has recognized her as well.

She knows the marks on her arms, the barely-healed bruise on the side of her head. Dermody had been the one to put them there.

• • •

Her opponent falters but does not go down. Dermody gives her a moment to recover as she decides whether to charge forward or circle around. Her fist burns from a punch she hasn't even thrown yet.

Dermody steps forward, planting herself firmly before delivering a blow right below her ribcage. The other woman jerks to the side, coughing. A mouthful of blood spatters against the concrete, and under the streetlights it almost looks gold.

As Dermody prepares for the next hit, her opponent's head snaps up. She is met with eyes full of such feral glee that, for the first time, she feels unmatched. She hesitates for the barest of seconds.

This time, instead of the punch connecting, her opponent grabs at her fists and they grapple in their struggle for victory. No ground is gained or lost, and she is reminded of Jacob, wrestling with the angel. Which is she, again? The prophet, or the angel? Pain blooms against her injured side as her opponent bears down against her, and Dermody's pulse strikes in her ears like a hammer against steel.

Is that how this started?

One day, there will be a last time she will go to the fight club. There was a first time, after all, so there must be a last.

Her struggle is rewarded, and with one powerful shove Dermody pitches her to the floor. There is a mottled bruise, just barely visible at the collar of her shirt, below her right shoulder. Dermody aims for it and punches. Once, twice.

The roar of the crowd crests as Dermody seizes her at the base of her neck, lifts.

And bashes her head against the ground repeatedly, like a feral animal, like she had no choice at all.

• • •

Dermody is the one to call it a few hours later, after all procedures have ran their course and any immediate avenues have been searched and found hollow. One of the other officers is sent to release her, and the two detectives stand together against one wall.

"She has no alibi. Any profile, she would fit it," is all that Morrigan can say. "I don't understand why you're so intent to let her go."

How can she say that she believes that if they charge her, Ravindahl will simply implicate her as their alibi for that night, and then no matter what happens in the case her entire reputation would be hanging by a shoelace. She knows that someone inexperienced, shooting a rifle, would develop an impact bruise in the exact same place on their chest as Dermody's opponent in the ring that night. She'd covered it up with something new. It would be indistinguishable, now.

She had asked her partner if Ravindahl seemed the sort to do something so violent. She can say with quiet confidence that, while convenient, the choice of victim and choice of location had very little to do with the act. As to her appearance in the ring, it was done for the attention.

She never asked that kid why he paints abstract constellations and quotes across brick walls and the pillars of bridges. Because he must. Because he didn't know what he'd do with himself if he didn't.

An officer marches Ravindahl through a side hallway, and Dermody peers at her through the wall of dappled glass paneling that divides them.

There will be a press conference to announce the discovered body, and they will have to report their lack of suspects, their lack of formal leads. There will be a different crowd, watching her and waiting for deliverance. What would Ravindahl do with that attention?

The paneling ends, and there is nothing but air separating the groups. Ravindahl raises her unbound hands to rub at the edge of one wrist. Morrigan stalks off to grab another cup of coffee.

"Maybe we'll see each other again," Ravindahl says.

"For your sake," Dermody tells her, "you should hope not."

She will not admit to her own misconduct, but she can supply a different station with an anonymous tip of her own, and see that place stamped out. She does not know what the lack of justice in this case will do to her tomorrow.

As Ravindahl turns to leave, her face is in profile. That healing bruise, against the back of her neck, reminds Dermody suddenly of the splash of red on the birds by the river. Could a woodpecker ever fell a tree?

Ravindahl steps outside, to bright sunshine and the persistent noise from the street. Then the door closes, and she is gone.

THERE ARE MANY WOLVES

Rob D. Smith

THE SOFTBALL THROWN TO Melanie Cook at home plate was coming in low as she needed. Too high and the St. Anthanasius field lights would hamper her vision. The runner from third had a full head of steam barreling right at her. Going to be tight. The woman got down in the red dirt a little too early and Cook snagged the ball in her leather mitt tagging her foot before she slid into the plate.

"Out!"

The last out of the last inning and the last ball game of the night. Rhinos 8 and the Trojanettes 4. Cook shook some of the losing team's hands then got her gear out of the dugout. No sore feelings in their league so far. She put her aluminum bat in the bag last and half-zipped it up on the gray wooden bleachers. Kelly and Lisa wanted to buy her a beer at the concession stand but Cook couldn't get deep in the cheap beer tonight. She was on call all night. The women from both teams hung around the bleacher with plastic cups of beer talking to their boyfriends and husbands.

As Cook passed by the Trojanette side of the field on the way to her car in the parking lot, a booming voice called out. "Cook. You couldn't let my girl have one run?"

She turned to the policeman in uniform with his hand on his nightstick. "Her run wouldn't have made a difference."

"Why you let her score," he laughed. "It didn't matter."

"Everything matters to me, Tommy."

He jiggled his cuff holster on his belt. "Lucky I'm on break or I'd arrest you for harassment."

She waved him off and headed to her Plymouth Duster. Changing into jeans, a t-shirt and a blue bomber jacket behind her opened car door mostly hidden in the dark. The pager Mother Underground gave her chirped and vibrated across the dusty dash of her car. The message gave her the go code for tonight's mission. Goose pimples rose on her arm. She stowed her softball bag in the back seat and slammed the door. The old car drifted out of the well-lit parking lot of St. A's onto the dark streets of Okolona.

● ● ●

It was after eleven when she parked in front of the yellow brick ranch-style house on Michael Drive. The street came to a dead-end three houses down. A lonely basketball pole without a net bent a little to the left stood sentry. Not a lot of houses had any lights on. This was a working-class neighborhood and they all had to get up early to head to the GE Appliance Park or the Ford Plant. God willing, she could get her job done without much ruckus.

She double-checked the Despain's address with the xeroxes in the manila envelope, placed the envelope above in the sun visor, and got out. Just in case, she leaned back in the window and grabbed her softball bat out of the bag. Halfway up the gravel driveway, the metal storm door creaked open. The person in the door seam was in shadow but had a womanly shape. Cook walked cautiously up the concrete porch steps.

"Penny?"

Just a nod. Cook said, "Are you ready to go?"

The woman opened the door and stepped onto the porch with a suitcase in one hand and an orange-headed little girl holding her other hand. The girl had a backpack strapped on. Her wide eyes probing the night found Cook then her bat.

"Are we going to play baseball?"

"Not tonight, honey." Cook hoisted her up in her free arm and looked at Penny. Bruises laced her swollen cheeks. Her left eye was frighteningly red from a broken blood vessel. Her gaze cast downwards. Soul beaten more than the body. Cook was afraid to touch her.

"You can do this Penny. Just one step at a time." She walked down the steps giving a head movement for her to follow. She took a step but still held onto the metal storm door. Stretching her arm further she crept to the edge of the steps which was a good sign until she let go of the door. It whacked shut like a gunshot in the night.

Cook tucked the bat under her arm. She reached out her hand and when Penny took it, she almost yanked her down the steps but instead calmly reeled her down. Slow was smooth and smooth was fast. They had to go now. Now, now, now. A light flicked on in a front room. A yell from inside followed shortly after. The trio of women wasn't moving fast enough. More lights came on inside the house. Something crashed and the front door swung off its hinges crashing into the yellow brick.

A rangy man with striped boxer shorts and a t-shirt too short for him stood in a wide stance at the door. He flicked the porch and walk-light on. His head held rings of curly red hair. The stance was extra wide because he was still drunk. Cook smelled the beer stench across the yard. He barked and somehow made it down the porch steps without tripping. Cutting across the yard, he would intercept them before they reached her car. She handed Leah over to a trembling Penny.

"Get in the car. I'll be right there."

Penny hugged her daughter close but didn't move as she stared at her charging husband. "But Derek…"

Cook bumped her with her hip. "Go!"

The battered mom hustled down the gravel driveway with her daughter. Cook unsheathed the bat out from under her arm like a samurai. Three steps into the yard, she cocked the bat on her shoulder in a two-handed grip, took one longer step, and swung the metal bat into his right lower shin. Ping! The follow-through on the swing took Derek's leg far behind him tripping him face-first in the dying fall grass. Arms splayed out in front. His nose took the brunt of the fall.

Penny shouted from the car. "Don't hurt him."

Misplaced concern always bothered Cook on these missions. She cocked the bat on her shoulder again as she walked upon the fallen man. He had rolled onto his back bleeding badly from his two nostrils. White t-shirt dotted with blood.

"Who the fuck are you?"

"I'm a bitch with a bat."

Derek started to push off the ground and she chopped her bat into his left hand. A howl from the bottom of his soul came out of his mouth. Some fingers were broken and possibly a knuckle. Penny left the side of the car until Cook jabbed a finger at her to stop. More lights blinked on at the neighboring houses. A door opened behind her across the street.

"Are you done?" she asked the whimpering bully. He didn't

respond so she cocked her bat back on her shoulder. Holding his injured hand close to his body, he scuttled back.

She turned heel for the car. "Get in and buckle up Penny."

The wife was wide-eyed and wringing her shirt but she got in the car. Cook rounded the front of the car and saw a man in a robe with a large beer belly poking out on the porch across the street. He stammered some words she couldn't make out. The rush of escaping adrenaline flushed through her ears. Her bat went back in her softball bag in the back seat.

"Hey. Don't ignore me. You can't go beating up on people around here. I'm calling the cops."

Cook leaned against the car and faced him. A cigarette would be divine right now but she quit three months ago. "How many times did you call the cops on your buddy Derek?"

Some other neighbors had come outside to see the commotion. The man on the porch stayed where he was and put his hands on his hips. "What goes on between a man and his wife is none of my business."

"See, I'm different. I take care of business." She spoke to the gathering crowd. "A bunch of deaf and blind people in this neighborhood. But suddenly a man gets what's coming to him and the Lord has healed your afflictions."

The crowd shied back to their houses a little. They weren't ones to get involved just wanted to watch the car wreck on their front lawns.

"Okay smart mouth. I'm calling the cops." He took out his cordless phone and extended the antenna.

"Go ahead. But when I get out and I will get out, I'll come back and pay you a visit."

"You don't scare me, little girl."

She kicked off the car and he fumbled the phone in his hands. It fell into the well-manicured shrubs next to the porch. She smiled as the man scrambled down the steps to dig out his phone. Quickly getting in the car, she buckled up and gave a warm look to little Leah.

"Okay, honey. We're off."

The Plymouth Duster barked rubber on the asphalt and left this rotten on the inside apple of a neighborhood behind them.

• • •

They rode down Briscoe Lane mostly silent in the dark. Cook felt the eyes of the little girl on her though. A little smile set her at ease. A glance and she saw Penny staring blankly out the window. Shock most likely.

"Leah, you like comic books?"

The girl whispered yes. Cook said, "Open my glove box. There are some comic books in there. Spider-man and the X-men. Penny, there's a flashlight in there too so she can read."

The simple task broke the mother's trance. She trained the flashlight beam on the comic book pages as the car passed Highview Park on their left. Empty softball fields, basketball, and tennis courts. One lone car sitting in the rear of the park near the woods. If she had a guess the teens inside were smoking weed and listening to Zeppelin. She swiftly put the park in their rearview lights. The backroads were the best way to the Mother Underground farm.

She would have to guide them across the well-lit and traveled Old Shepherdsville Road before hitting another dark side road. She had transported several women and children to the farm with little interference but she could never relax until they made it there. The Goldilocks Rule was in effect. Drive fast but not too fast and everyone would get there in one piece. Leah had climbed down to the floorboard between her mother's feet holding the flashlight and flipping through pages of heroes battling villains. Cook relaxed a little. Until she looked at the mother.

Every female passenger was a mirror to her. Reflecting how she used to be. She had come far these last five years. No one could call it growth but it sure wasn't the slow death she had expected from the events leading her to work with the Underground. Jeanette Graham the Mother of the secret non-profit saw potential in Cook. They developed skills she never knew she could possess to protect other women even if it was too late to protect her daughter Kristin. Saving mothers, sisters, and daughters at all costs.

"Why did you have to hurt Derek?" The question broke her thoughts.

Looking down at the little girl who she knew was listening, she said, "Some men only understand pain."

"But you didn't even warn him first. Just started swinging."

Cook gripped the steering wheel. "You got a lot of warnings from him, didn't you? Did those warnings ever stop what came next?"

The mother's chin dropped to her chest. "No. I don't reckon it did. But it just didn't seem fair is all. You with a bat."

Cook huffed but didn't respond. Her foot just pushed a little more on the gas pedal. The missions involving daughters always raised the heat in her. They came upon the intersection with Old Shep and took a left at the stop sign. Three miles on this bright road and then they could jump back in the shadows until they reached the Underground farm. She settled down into the posted speed limit and steered the car into the right lane.

They passed a Druthers restaurant, TuneUp 2000, and other service stations as they made great time. Only a couple of cars passed by them going in the other direction. Their side of the road was empty. They were all by their lonesome until they weren't. A muscular police patrol came out of nowhere lights flashing and pumping its siren shrill twice. A disembodied voice spoke from the heavens.

"Pullover!"

Cook guided the car slowly into the Real Deal Liquor Store parking lot. One of the businesses along this stretch still had its neon open sign lit. Penny picked Leah up off the floor. The little girl wasn't scared but her mother was.

"They're going to take us back. Jeanette promised me..."

"Look at me." Penny's head spun around looking for the next threat. The next punch. "Look at me. I'm here to keep Mother Underground's promise. Trust me."

A door slammed and you could hear the heavy footsteps on the asphalt approach. She told Penny to stay quiet and let her do all the talking. Everything would be fine. In her head, she was calculating what hiding holes she could race her car to before the cop got back to his car and gave pursuit. None were close enough.

The bright light of a long flashlight showed in her window almost blinding her but she could still see his right hand resting on the pistol at his waist. "License and registration...ah Cook."

She blinked her eyes from the light as Tommy dropped the flashlight. He crouched down to her level. "You beat the holy Hell out of that guy tonight. I got the 10-16 call a little bit ago. Witnesses said a yellow Plymouth Duster."

"By witness, you mean fat guy in a robe?"

"He wasn't a fan of yours. I'm going to need you to step out of the car. You ladies sit tight."

Cook got out after the policeman gave her some room. His hand still resting on his gun. Once again, she craved some nicotine to take the edge off. He slid his long Mag-lite back into the holder on his belt. She was tall but Tommy stood a head and a half over her with a wide frame.

"Nice job on her husband. Fucked his shin up probably fractured. Broke some fingers. Was all the violence necessary?"

She squinted at the law enforcement officer's dumb question.

"Okay. I saw the bruises on her face plus the bad eye. And yes, we've been called multiple times to their address but you can't go taking a bat to every crisis. Smarter not harder." He tapped his head with two fingers. "The Underground works better in the shadows."

The Underground survived because they had allies in law enforcement, the judicial system, and political offices. The ugly truth was everyone had a mother, sister, or daughter with some experience with domestic abuse.

"Can we go now?"

"I'll radio this quadrant is clear. But next time don't cause a ruckus. Okay?"

As she climbed back into her car, she said, "You have my word."

She shut the door as she heard him use profanity laced with her name. A huge smile spread across her face. Making a cop cuss was the best. Penny shook and fidgeted like a chihuahua. Cook placed a gentle hand on her and then brought it down to rest on Leah's head.

"Okay ladies. Time to get rolling again."

Penny asked, "Just like that?"

"I told you I keep promises." She revved the engine and kicked gravel out of the liquor store parking lot with a little girl giggling beside her and hopefully a large cop swearing again.

• • •

Thirty minutes later they were just outside the Jefferson County line crossing into Bullitt County. Leah had become drowsy after all the excitement from the policeman pulling them over. Cook gave her a blanket she had in the back seat and the girl drifted off to sleep. Her mother didn't sleep but she didn't speak to Cook either. She wasn't at rest and she wasn't at peace. Her decision had unmoored her and she didn't have a firm hand to steer the rudder anymore.

The battered wife did sniffle a little and when she wasn't morose, she sighed a lot. After one-to-many sighs, Cook turned on the radio to a soft rock channel. Mother could counsel this woman when they reached the shelter. Or Dana or Suzy. Ones with a background in social work and therapy. Her skill set was extraction or protection. Sure, the Underground had softened her rough edges but she didn't have it in her to give what was missing. She certainly carried empathy in her. It was just easier to share the rage.

"What's it like?"

The question like a dart. "The farm is pretty relaxed. Calming."

"I've never been on a farm before."

"They have some gardens and even a hen house but I wouldn't call it a working farm. Just enough to keep the residents fed."

The blanket had slipped and Cook picked it up trying to cover the sleeping girl. Penny tucked the blanket in tight and her hand brushed Cook's. She flinched bringing her hand back to the steering wheel. The woman smoothed her daughter's hair.

"You don't like me much, do you?"

"I like you fine. And your little girl."

"Leah's hard not to love." She kissed her daughter's head.

"There are other girls at the farm her age to play with. She'll have a good time."

Cook heard a sniffle and the woman began to tear up into a full-blown crying jag. This was why she preferred to be the silent type. Just deliver them to the farm and let the others sort them out. Most of the active Sisters lived on the grounds but not her. She had a small apartment near the strip of Frankfort Ave. She could ride her bike or visit a bakery. Disappear into all the people shopping and eating. Just enough white noise of society to keep her from thinking too much about her loss.

Cook slowed down to an unmarked gravel driveway and turned left onto it. The tires rolled and popped the gravel loose. About two hundred yards in they came to an ornate wrought iron gate between two creek rock columns. A high pinewood fence ran as far as the eye could see down both sides of the columns. There were bright floodlights at the top of the columns haloing Cook's car. She turned the radio off and put the car in park. A woman with a shotgun appeared on the other side of the fence.

Cook swung open the door and stood up. "Hey, Stacy. I got two for Mother."

"Copy that Cook. We've been waiting for you." The sentry unlocked the gates and spread them wide for the car to pass through. As Cook went past she stuck her hand out the window and Stacy hi-fived it.

Inside the gate, the winding driveway was paved and smoothed with black asphalt. Penny had stopped crying but she was still sniffling a little bit as Cook drove into the circle by the main house. As soon as she parked, the woman moaned.

"I can't do this alone. Not without someone to take care of me."

"Like Derek took care of you?"

"I'm not strong like you."

Cook chuckled. She turned off the car and started to laugh harder. "You were right earlier when you said I didn't like you. I don't."

"You don't have to be cruel."

Her voice rising. "I hate you because once a long time ago I was exactly like you. Beaten, lost, weak. And worst alone. Saying the same thing. I can't do this. No one will love me."

"You were never like me."

Cook nodded. "I'm a Sister of the Underground now. But we all come from the same desolate place. You can do this. You aren't alone. Not here." She put a soft arm across the woman's shoulders and pulled her closer with the little girl between them until their heads touched.

A portly woman with a natural afro came out of the house and down the big steps towards their car. A tall woman wearing clothes too big for her lithe frame followed beside her. Cook let go of the woman.

"The short one's Mother and the stick is CiCi. They'll take great care of you but remember you have to do all the heavy lifting yourself. You got a daughter who needs you. More than I'll ever have."

The newest member of the Underground hoisted her daughter and got out of the car without thanks. CiCi was waiting and took her daughter from her arms into hers. Penny got her suitcase and Leah's backpack out of her backseat without making any eye contact with Cook. Mother had snuck up to her driver's side door and placed a hand on her forearm startling her.

"Tough one tonight, kiddo?"

"Nothing a little batting practice couldn't help."

"I meant with the little girl." She kneaded her forearm gently. "Did you tell her about your daughter?"

She hung her head. Now finding it hard to meet anyone's eyes, especially Mother's. Her daughter's death was her secret engine. Lost to a wolf Cook let into their home because she needed a man and Kristin a father. Mother patted her arm and stood up.

"When you start sharing, you'll finish healing."

"If I ever heal up, I won't be of any use to the Underground."

Mother huffed out some air and grinned. "Alright. This is where I tell you I'm worried about you and you say don't worry about me then you tear ass on outta here because you think you're a female Clint Eastwood in a Western."

Vaya con Dios, Mother."

She spun her wheels and listened to Mother's sonorous laugh behind her. Penny and Leah would be safe here and hopefully thrive. The thoughts of Leah running and playing with all the other girls on the farm might be enough to stave off the bad dreams tonight. About the wolf who ate her heart.

THE BOOK OF RUTH

Mary Thorson

KIRTLAND, OH. 1989

THE FIRST THING DOLLY noticed about her daughter was not the hole in her tooth, but her hair. It went all the way to the tops of her thighs. She could have tucked it into her back pockets. Clementine, or Tiny, as they called her until just before she left them, stood on the front porch with her stringy, long brown hair and her khaki skirt that went down to her shoes and her white shirt that buttoned all the way up, making Dolly pull at the skin of her own neck. She hadn't seen her daughter in two years. It was not without trying. The florescent porch light turned her daughter's pale skin a shade of blue.

"Hello, mother."

Tiny's voice sounded deeper. Dolly wondered if female voices did that between ages 18 and 20. Dolly wondered if her daughter started smoking. She stepped forward and put her daughter's face in her hands, coming very close because she couldn't help herself. Tiny went stiff but didn't pull away, and Dolly could feel her daughter's jaw clench against her palms. She found more differences. Slight changes around her daughter's eyes and mouth-- her lips seemed thinner. She had more spots now, light and dark, dotting her cheeks and nose and forehead. A very dark one had developed in the middle of her chin. Dolly brought her daughter closer and buried her face into Tiny's neck. She breathed her in until she thought she would faint. She smelled different, almost antiseptic, but underneath there was something familiar. Maybe Tiny was sweating or producing oils on her skin in order to make it easier to slip from her mother's boney hands, but Dolly knew that smell and her grip was strong.

Finally, Tiny put her hands up to her mother's arms—not moving them away, but a warning.

"Is it okay if I stay here? I don't know for how long. Is that okay?"

Dolly laughed and at that moment the wind came, blowing some of Tiny's hair into her mouth. She pulled it out. That was when Dolly saw the small black hole in her daughter's canine, eroding the edge and slowly splitting the tooth apart.

"Tiny, baby, of course it is. This is your home. We've been waiting for you to come home."

"It's Ruth, actually." Tiny let her arms fall as her mother kept holding her. Tiny attempted to back up.

"Oh, still?"

"Still, yes."

Before she left them, before the hole, she asked her parents to call her Ruth.

"I'm not a miner's daughter, I'm God's daughter," she had said at dinner. Dolly knew her daughter thought this was clever. Her father laughed, but Dolly also knew then that the fracture between them had worsened. Grown deeper while she wasn't looking.

"I think I'll stick with Clementine, Tiny," her father said. Dolly didn't say anything, trying to commit herself to not using a name at all.

"I lie at the feet of *Him*, like Ruth."

"That's enough of that talk," her father said. Dolly continued her silence and two weeks later, Ruth was gone.

"That's fine," Dolly said, smiling. She brought her daughter into the house and locked the door behind her, as if that had stopped her before. Tiny stood in the middle of the living room, surveying the things around her. Dolly wondered what had changed, if anything, since she left.

"Do you want anything to eat? Or do you want to put your things away?" It was a stupid question, Tiny didn't have anything with her, and she lifted her empty hands in demonstration.

"That's alright, everything is in your room."

"My room?"

"Of course. All your clothes, your records, books, whatever. It's all still there."

"Oh," Tiny said.

• • •

Tiny was their only child, and Dolly thought this was why Tiny didn't sleep in her own room until high school. When she was young, still just a toddler, it was easy to let her stay in their bed. Don pretended and put up a show of annoyance, but when he realized no one was watching, that it was just the three of them in that little house, he let her in-between them and everybody slept better. When she got older, she tried harder at sleeping alone. She would start off in her own bed, but then, sometime during the night, she would end up outside their open door, waiting in the dark to be invited.

Then, it seemed like it happened in one night, she became

doggedly possessive of her space. The room that had been decorated the same since she was three; a pink flowered quilt, plain white walls, baskets of toys and things on shelves—transformed into something else, something older. Tiny grew in there, alone. And despite that she no longer came to their door at night, Dolly kept it open, always waiting. Dolly started having trouble sleeping.

• • •

"How about I make you a sandwich? We have some cold cuts in the fridge, and some mayo."

"Did you paint in here?" Tiny asked.

"Of course not," Dolly lied.

"I remember it different."

"I'm going to make us some sandwiches. I have some iced tea, too. Would you like some?" Dolly asked but was really saying: *please please stay, I'll keep it all the same for you, please.*

"Does it have caffeine?"

"No, I don't think so," Dolly said, but she didn't really know. After Tiny left, she kept up the things she wanted for a few months. No caffeine or booze in the house, the Bible stayed out on the coffee table. She kept working on the cross stitch of a passage from the book of Ruth: *Do not urge me to leave you or to return from following you. For where you go I will go, and where you lodge I will lodge. Your people shall be my people, and your God my God.* She meant it as a kind of plea to her daughter, but it was not taken. After some time, her husband brought home some beer and they had it at dinner. Then the Bible was put away.

"I'll just have some water."

"Sure."

She pulled out an old cup from the cabinet. It had a kissing Donald and Daisy on it with hearts floating up that were almost scratched away. When she finished making the sandwiches she set the cup with the image facing towards her daughter, hoping to incite a comment. Tiny didn't notice. It had been her favorite cup, even in high school. The only thing she'd wash herself if it was dirty. Dolly watched her throat move as she drink, her cheeks slightly puffing in and out with each gulp. Tiny finished it all at once.

"Do you want some more?"

"Yes, please." She pushed the glass toward her mother and then left her hand out. The palm was calloused and looked much harder than it had, but then again, Dolly couldn't really remember her hands before, all she could think of was the way they were when Tiny was a baby. Of course, they had grown and hardened since then. She picked up the cup and went over to the sink. Behind her, her daughter moved. She couldn't see what she was doing, but Tiny was shifting or stirring, quietly, as if she was trying not to be heard. Dolly turned around and saw her daughter scraping the skin away from her thumb nail. She stretched it until it bled and then put her whole thumb in her mouth and sucked it like an infant—something she had never done. Tiny caught her mother staring and dropped it then wiped it against her cheek.

"Where is he?"

Dolly brought over the glass and set it in front of her daughter as she sat down across from her, again. Tiny's eyes were trained on her, peering through thin slits with her hands in her lap.

"He's still at work, should be home in about an hour." Dolly rubbed her palm against the table as she said, "Oh, he'll be so happy to see you." She wished she could have held her daughter's hand to keep her thumb out of her mouth, but she kept them to herself.

• • •

When they had gone to the Lundgren farm a few weeks after Tiny left, she was kept away, or maybe she kept herself away. They had waited because Don had said she'd come back when she realized how good she had it at home. When everything wasn't being done for her. Dolly didn't think so, and finally Don relented. Dolly went to the door alone. It was a big white farmhouse with a long, dirty porch, and she stepped around the pieces of a broken chair spread out on the floorboards. She pressed her finger down on the doorbell, but nothing happened so she knocked. She heard hard footsteps coming and she looked at Don sitting in the car in the driveway. He was watching her.

"Who's there?" The voice was low and strong on the other side of the door. If it had been any louder it might have caused a slight vibration in Dolly's chest.

"Hello?"

"Who's there?"

"This is Dolly Miller. I'm Clementine's mother."

Then the door opened and he stepped out onto the porch. Jeff Lundgren was fat and Dolly hadn't expected that. His hair was long and slicked back, showing off how it was receding away from his forehead. His skin was pockmarked and shiny, and he was tall, but very fat. He stepped forward, coming too close. She looked, again, to Don in the car and he finally got out. The man didn't even blink when the car door shut. Instead he put his hand forward, the tips of his fingers almost grazing her stomach. She sucked in deeply.

"My name's Jeff." He kept still.

She took her hand out of her glove and backed up in order to put it in his.

"Dolly Miller. Like I said, I'm Clementine's mom."

"Clementine?"

"We're here for our daughter," Don said, coming up behind Dolly.

Jeff let go of Dolly's hand and extended his to Don. Don eyed it before shaking it hard.

"That's a good grip, Mister…"

"Miller. You know, the same as Clementine."

"I'm sorry, as I was just about to tell your wife, I don't have anybody here by that name."

"You do, we know you do. She told us about you before she left. About this." Her voice was too high. In the house behind him she imagined many women dressed all the same. Their hair back in a single braid. And when she thought of Tiny in there, she thought of her when she was seven and had learned how to braid, braiding everything she found.

"I'm sorry, ma'am, I'm being honest."

"Ruth, what about a Ruth?" Don asked with his eyes closed.

"Ah." Jeff smiled and winked—a trick, then. "Ruth. Ruth is staying with us, me and my wife and children, and others like her who want to get closer to God."

"Sure," Don said.

"Can we see her? Can you send her out?"

"I can't make her do anything she doesn't want to."

"That's some horseshit if I ever heard. I know people like you; con artists, cheats. You can convince weaker people to do anything you want."

"Don," Dolly said.

"Get my daughter you piece of shit or I'll come in there myself." Don brustled up closer and taller, and Dolly saw he had the same gut Jeff had. She had no clue when he had gotten so big.

"Now, sir, Ruth is a strong adult. Not so weak as you think. She can leave whenever she wants. We love her and respect her here, which is something she says she was missing in her life. But, if you continue to trespass or attempt to gain entry to my home, I'm afraid I'll have to call the police."

"The police? I should be calling them on you for kidnapping!"

"Ruth came here to us in search of help and home. And, I'm sure I don't have to remind you, but she ain't no kid."

Don went forward to hit him, but Dolly grabbed onto his arm and he almost lifted her off the ground.

"Don! Stop, this isn't going to help anything."

Jeff flinched then and Don put his arm down. He stormed back to the car and Jeff watched before he turned back to Dolly, suddenly smiling, as if he had been the whole time.

"I'll let Ruth know that you all came by." He went back in house and slammed the door.

Dolly stood alone on the porch for a moment. It was quiet even though she strained to hear behind the walls. She listened for her daughter's voice but heard nothing.

• • •

Dolly stared at her daughter across the table, willing her to smile in the little way she used to when she was trying to keep her happiness contained. But she only rolled her eyes.

"Right," Tiny said. "I'm sure he'll be."

"He will be. He's missed you so much. We both have."

Tiny looked at the ground. This was making her uncomfortable.

"Are you okay? Are you tired?"

"I'm fine."

The phone rang, sounding unbearably loud. Tiny's eyes grew wide.

"I'm not here, okay? Please don't tell anyone I'm here."

"Okay, baby. I'm sure it's just a telemarketer."

Dolly thought her daughter was going to cry. Tiny started biting around the inside of her mouth. Dolly wanted to stay with her and smooth her very long hair. The phone rang at least ten times before she finally tore herself from the kitchen table and picked it up.

"Hello?"

There was a click, and then silence, and then the dial tone came. She hung up and walked back to the table.

"Who did you think it would be?" Dolly asked her daughter.

"Nobody." Tiny began picking up the crumbs around her sandwich with her index finger.

"You can tell me."

"I don't live here. I don't know who calls."

After the visit to the farm, Dolly and Don went to the police station. The officer they talked to, Dolly couldn't remember his name after he told it to her, said they'd had troubles with Jeff Lundgren before. Gunshots going off at the house, theft, trespassing. They'd talked to him several times, and he always backed down.

"Backed down from what?" Don asked.

"His threats, or whatever he calls them. His prophesizing."

"His what?"

"He says he can talk to God directly, and he gives instructions to all his followers as if he himself were Jesus Christ. Never heard of Jesus needing all that money, or all that company."

Dolly thought she might get sick.

"The women especially get sucked in by him. They're all in love with him, worship him, sleep with him, do whatever he wants. He hangs up a sheet in the woods and hides behind it while they dance naked out there in the dark," this he whispered, leaning closer to Don. "One of them, not his wife, came up and slapped one of my deputies in the face last time we went over there. They guard him like dogs. He's lucky we didn't take her in. Figured she's not exactly in her right mind, if you get me. None of them are, over there."

"What about our daughter?" Don asked through his teeth.

"Ah, my mouth, no one needs to hear that. Really, it's a shame, I'm sorry about that, but there's nothing we can do. She's over 18, sir. Just pray she'll wake up and see that man for what he is."

Dolly wanted to explain to this man how impossible that was. Tiny was joyful, but so naïve. She took things on their face and held them there always. She had never asked about made up things because she never questioned them. Once, she found her Christmas presents in the back of Dolly's closet. She was staring right at the pink plastic sled she had asked for after seeing it at the mall, and all she said was, "oh!" Quickly, Dolly said "sometimes he has to drop off presents ahead of time, if he's in the neighborhood." Her daughter kept smiling, and responded with, "I know that, mom." Though, of course, she didn't know.

• • •

Tiny ate the sandwich slowly. She was not starving and this almost disappointed Dolly. She took small bites and chewed them for too long before taking another. Dolly could hear her daughter swallow. The hole in her daughter's tooth showed itself only once or twice while she ate and Dolly thought maybe this was why it was taking so long. Tiny had to be careful because her teeth were rotting.

The phone rang again, but the air in the room had changed and as if watching cracking glass Dolly was braced for the break in silence, this time. She grabbed the phone off the hook in the middle of the second ring, but instead of saying "hello," she just watched her daughter's face. The person on the other end was quiet. Dolly heard them part their lips and push them back together and swallow. Then they hung up.

"Mom?" Tiny asked, softly.

"Yes, baby?"

"He's so angry."

"Did he do something to you?"

"He wouldn't," Tiny said, but she said it to herself. She looked at the red skin she'd scratched away at her thumb and Dolly could tell her daughter wasn't breathing.

"Am I different now?" Tiny asked.

"Of course not," Dolly said, lying again.

"He loves us all, even those children—it just had to be."

The front door swung open and shut inside of a second and both women held their breath.

Don said, "Someone just standing in the middle of the road out there, high as a goddam kite, wouldn't move when I got close and I almost had to drive up on the grass getting around them."

He came into the kitchen and Dolly couldn't see his face, but she could hear the way his body went when he saw his daughter at the table.

"Tiny," he said.

"Ruth," Dolly said. "Please."

Don swallowed and then squared his shoulders.

"Sure. Ruth."

"Hi, dad."

"Hi."

"Come sit down, Don."

"Are you home, now?" Don asked.

"For now," Tiny said.

He came to the table, to the chair next to his daughter, and he pulled it out so he was sitting in the middle of the kitchen, far away from both of them.

"When you're done here, are you going back there?"

"Don, we don't need to figure this out yet," Dolly said.

"No. I can't." When Tiny said it, something caught in her throat and there was a break in her voice. Don ran his hand down his face and then put his hands on his knees as he got up.

He was getting older and Dolly hadn't noticed. She wondered if it was a shock to Tiny, but her daughter wasn't watching.

"Well, then, we won't talk about it in this house. When you're here, you won't talk about it. Understand me?"

Tiny stared at him, almost glaring, before she nodded.

"Good. I'm sure your mother told you, everything's as it was in your room."

"Yes," Tiny said. "Thank you. I'm tired, do you mind if I go to bed, mother?"

"Do whatever you like," Don said.

"Are you sure you don't want to talk more?" Dolly asked.

"She said she's tired."

"Don, Jesus Christ." Dolly whipped around and narrowed her eyes at him.

Don opened his mouth and then shut it.

"Now, do you want to tell me something, Ruth?" Dolly asked.

Tiny stood and shook her head.

"I'm tired, is it alright if I just go to bed?"

"Sure. Maybe tomorrow we can call the dentist, too, yeah?" Don asked

There was a moment where it seemed as if her daughter wanted to jump out of her own skin, and Dolly desperately wanted to keep her all together.

"That's fine, baby. Okay," Dolly said.

Tiny left and Dolly heard her room door shut softly. She had never shut it like that, before. She was reckless with the way she would close it, always too excited, and she moved part of the frame out of place over time. That part was still off. Alone in the kitchen, Dolly went over to the sink to wash her daughter's dishes for the first time in two years. She scrubbed them with her hands instead of the sponge, touching all the parts her daughter touched. Outside the kitchen window, she saw someone walking slowly up the sidewalk, past their house. She did not know them. She turned her back to the window and leaned against the sink. She was waiting for the phone to ring—she felt it coming through the hairs on her arms. She rushed to it, snatching it off the hook and then letting it drop on the floor. It twisted around like a snake on the tile and when she heard the dial tone beeping, she shut off the lights and walked down the hallway into her own bedroom. Don was awake in the dark, she could tell, but she didn't speak to him. She took off her clothes and crawled into bed, keeping a distance of inches of cold sheets between them. After a while of listening for movement from her daughter's room on the other side of the wall, and hearing nothing but the silence that had been there before, her body relaxed and she drifted off to sleep.

It was still dark when she woke up, and she had the sense that she had just been having a very vivid dream, but she couldn't remember it. She was about to turn over and put her arm around her husband when she saw a shadow on the wall next to her bed. It shifted slightly, but didn't get bigger or smaller, just swayed. She watched it for a little while until she couldn't bare it anymore and shut her eyes. She shut them tightly, hoping her daughter couldn't see her face from where she stood in the doorway. Dolly breathed slow and shallow, trying to listen for her daughter's breath, but she couldn't hear it. Maybe, her daughter wasn't there at all, but Dolly didn't want to know. She kept her eyes closed and did not sleep well.

SOME THINGS NEVER CHANGE

Julie Tollefson

FLICKERS OF LIGHTNING WRITHED between and around black, anvil-topped clouds at least a hundred miles south of where I stood on a sandstone bluff over the Cimarron River. I'd forgotten the sheer power of early June storms here in southwest Kansas. Electric with anticipation. Dark and dangerous.

I inhaled deeply, the scents of sagebrush and cattle, of heat and dust. Of childhood. Of home.

Behind me, a battered Ford pickup truck shimmied down the sandy Overlook access road and parked between my 4Runner and a Dodge Durango marked with the shield and motto of the Harman County Sheriff's Office. The truck's cab door swung open, and a tall and lanky man stepped out, all cowboy boots and blue jeans and close-cropped hair. But it was the nose, crooked and too big for the thin face, that made my breath catch in my throat. It had been twenty-five years, but I'd know that nose anywhere.

"Zeke." My voice did not shake, but I couldn't say the same

for my hands. Zeke Parsons. *My* Zeke. The strength of his jaw-line and his intense hazel eyes were as familiar as the day I'd left Harman County. And him.

He gave me a long appraising once over, as if he couldn't decide how to approach me. With a nod, he settled on something halfway between formal and familiar. "Jenny. Glad you're here."

Far below us at the base of the Overlook, a wrecker winched a twisted hunk of metal out of a sand pit, an abandoned quarry long filled with water and known to generations of Harman County youth as *the* place to party. A hunched figure stood at the edge of the pit, now pumped nearly dry save for a sludge that had accumulated for decades in its depths. The mud and muck released their hold on the junked car with a wet, sucking sound.

My stomach turned over.

"How did they find her?" I asked.

Zeke hesitated. "Kid went missing last week. He and his buddies had been camping, drinking down there."

Some things never changed. Memories from that long ago night came to me in fragments, like half-remembered postcards from a distant relative's travels. I couldn't allow myself to accept the truth that we had all been there, and not one of us had known.

"The kid's friends passed out," he continued, "and when they woke up the next day, he was gone. They freaked, convinced he'd drowned. So search and rescue drained the pit."

And found Heather, tangled in the ruins of the rusted heap of metal now strapped to the back of a trailer.

The figure at the edge of the pit raised his head and saw us silhouetted against the skyline. I couldn't make out his features from this distance, but I knew who it had to be. He trudged toward the trail that wound up the side of the bluff and a few minutes later Frank Robertson Junior, FJ to his friends, appeared.

"Jen." Heather's older brother pulled his shoulders back and spread his feet wide. He still sported the unmistakable swagger of his youth, when he'd been like a brother to me, too. We'd sat side by side on beach towels beside the pit and chugged beer and downed cheap bourbon from the bottle. We'd joked about the damnation and hellfire to come if his daddy, the sheriff, caught him.

Now he'd taken his daddy's place on the county payroll.

"Zeke called."

His eyes flicked to his friend. "That right."

He even sounded like his father. Frank Senior had used the same tone the night he caught me smoking pot under the visitors' bleachers at the high school football stadium. *Your daddy would roll over in his grave if he knew what his girl was up to.* He'd snatched the joint out of my hand and obliterated it under the heel of his cowboy boot.

That same harsh Robertson judgment had crushed Heather's spirit. I'd been at her side dozens of times when Frank Senior went full cop mode on his daughter. Once, he pulled her over for speeding, sixty-five in a fifty-five, and shouted at her by the side of the road for fifteen minutes about the "optics" of the sheriff's daughter running wild, while I sat in the passenger seat and chewed my thumbnail.

When he finally let us go, Heather mashed the accelerator to the floor, her fingers wrapped so tight around the steering wheel her knuckles glowed white. As the needle hit eighty-five, she released a high-pitched scream that hurt my ears. *God I wish he could just be my dad, just one time. Why does he always have to be sheriff?*

The night she disappeared, I'd celebrated. I thought she'd finally broken free.

I'm getting out of here, Jen, she'd whispered. Her eyes flashed in the firelight, her hair damp from skinny dipping in the old quarry and skin flushed from too much alcohol. "Hey

Man Nice Shot" blasted from someone's car stereo. *And I'm not coming back.*

I'd held that image of her, happy and determined and carefree, close for twenty-five years.

"You have some nerve, showing up here after all this time." FJ's fists clenched at his side.

"After that night, there didn't seem much for me here any more."

Zeke flinched as if I'd struck him. FJ spat in the dirt at his feet, stomped to the Durango, and left me and Zeke alone in the wind.

Zeke's eyes, when they met mine, were dark pits of hurt and resentment and anger. Like FJ's fists, his jaw clenched and unclenched as he wrestled with how to respond. His nice-guy nature won out. "We're meeting at the tavern tonight. You'd be welcome."

● ● ●

Stepping into Tom's Tavern — a small, dark shack on a sandy road outside city limits — was like entering a life-sized time capsule stuffed with all the smells and sounds of high school. Spilled beer. Greasy nachos. Perfume, hair gel, and that godawful body wash the younger generation soaked in. Underlying it all a faint whiff of vomit and sweat.

The same framed newspaper stories hung on the walls. The same string of Christmas lights blinked behind the bar. The same eponymous Tom, owner of the tavern, tended bar and no doubt still pretended not to recognize underage drinkers with their fake IDs slouched in the darkest corners.

And the noise, a turned-up-to-eleven wall of unrelenting babble as everyone in the tight, hot space shouted to make themselves heard over everyone else.

I couldn't breathe.

Coming here had been a mistake. I pivoted toward the door but hadn't gone two steps before I heard a shrill soprano call my name. I bit my lip, weighed my options, then turned and threaded through the crush of bodies to the round table tucked in the back corner that had been "ours" throughout senior year of high school. FJ sat in his usual place, chair rocked back against the wall, his once-football-hard body gone soft. Beside him, his wife Belinda still wore too much makeup but now it caked in the frown lines around her mouth. Silver threaded Zeke's black hair.

The only face that hadn't changed was Heather's, eternally eighteen and smiling at me from a cardboard cutout in the chair to FJ's left. The seat on the other side of Heather, rightfully Mitch's, vacant.

I sat next to Zeke, who had yet to glance my way. Still pissed about this afternoon. Maybe I would be, too, in his place.

"Jenny McClane. I thought we'd never see you again." A tiny, insincere smile played at the corner of Belinda's dark red lips. Long blonde hair cascaded over one shoulder, and a perfectly manicured finger rested on FJ's forearm, a predator marking her territory. She'd set her sights on him sophomore year and married him two years after graduation. That they were still together surely owed more to her determination to be Mrs. Frank Robertson Junior than to a true tale of high school sweethearts destined to be together forever.

I snagged a clean mug from the center of the table and filled it from one of the pitchers.

"We see your name in the paper all the time." Belinda's eyes glittered in the half-dark of the bar. "Investigative reporter."

She made my job sound dirty.

Across the table, Cardboard Heather smiled at me. *Don't let her get to you.*

I shouldn't have come, I told her. *I want to remember you the way you were. I want to remember* us *the way we were, to hold on to the perfection of that summer.*

Her smile never wavered. *Oh, Jen, it was never perfect.*

"You're smiling," Zeke murmured, for my ears only.

"Remembering." I nodded at Heather's picture. "Can you imagine what she would have thought of this?"

His mouth crooked up at the corner, too, and made my heart flutter in a way it hadn't in years. "She would have been the first to call bullshit."

Belinda glared at us.

"She thinks we're talking about her." I bumped shoulders with him and the heat of the contact seared my flesh. Every molecule in my body strained toward him.

"Some things never change," he said. His thigh pressed mine. A shiver of desire and possibility enveloped us. "She always thinks everyone is talking about her."

The noise level in the bar dropped abruptly, as if a hundred people inhaled together and by unspoken agreement held their breath. Everyone's attention, even Belinda's, shifted to the front of the bar. I swiveled in my seat.

A rectangle of early evening sunlight backlit a figure at the open door. The light shrank as the door closed, and the figure resolved into the one other person I'd both hoped and dreaded to see this weekend. Mitch, Heather's boyfriend.

FJ made a sound deep in his throat that might have been a growl. I glanced back. He flushed a brilliant scarlet. In that moment, he was the spitting image of Frank Senior on the cusp of exploding in fury.

Before I could work out what was happening, Mitch shouldered past me and slapped his hands flat on the table, sending a basket of fries skittering over the edge. "You bastard. After all these years, you found her and you didn't have the decency to tell me yourself."

FJ rocked forward. When he rose to his feet, his chair clattered sideways and knocked Cardboard Heather to the floor. "Get out of my sight before I have you locked up, you fucking waste of space."

"I stayed quiet all these years. I thought that's what *she* wanted." Tears coursed down Mitch's cheeks and pooled on the table, mixing with spilled salt and spattered grease. "But she didn't run away, not from me, not from you. She was always there, waiting. We both failed her."

FJ bounded around the table and seized two fistfulls of Mitch's shirt and bent Mitch backward over the table. "You. Don't. Belong. Here."

Mitch didn't blink. "But you, you just fucking moved on, like it was nothing. Like *she* was nothing." Then he turned his head to the side, toward Cardboard Heather. The poster listed sideways against the wall, one corner crumpled where it had crashed to the floor. A harsh burble of laughter rumbled deep in his chest, grew louder, and burst into the open. Jarring. Wrong. As suddenly as it began, his laughter dissolved into a sob.

FJ yanked him upright and shoved him toward the exit. "You're drunk. If I catch you on the road tonight, I'll make you sorry."

Mitch staggered, caught himself on a high-backed barstool, and looked at each of us in turn before locking on FJ again. "What did I ever do besides love your sister?"

• • •

I caught up with Mitch as he began to swing up into his truck, a beatup dark blue piece of junk that, like its owner, had seen better days. It came to me with a start that it was the same truck he'd driven in high school. Then, it had been brand new and spotless. Now, road dust clung to it, dents and scratches marred the paint, and the driver's side quarter panel had been replaced with a rusted out white piece obviously picked up at the salvage yard. It was hard to reconcile the Mitch of my memories — proud, young, in love — with the broken, drunk man who rested his forehead against the truck's frame.

"They fought that night." Mitch flicked his eyes toward the bar.

"They always fought."

"This time was different. *She* was different."

I bit my lip to stop the truth from escaping.

He climbed into his truck. "I'm not saying he could have saved her, but he knew and I think his daddy knew. Thought he was protecting him by not asking the right questions. That fucked up family. FJ's spent his whole adult life trying to live up to his old man's expectations, and Belinda's always at his side propping him up when he stumbles."

• • •

I stared after Mitch's receding taillights trying to make sense of what he'd said.

That night, the night that changed everything, tiki torches burned in a circle in the sand around the pit. We'd spread our beach towels and passed around strawberry wine and whiskey filched from our parents' stashes. Joints passed from hand to hand, Alanis Morissette and Garbage on a car stereo.

The suggestion—a midnight skinny dip—rippled from group to group. Every party at the sand pit ended with at least half of us in the water, despite constant dire warnings about the unseen threats that lurked below.

We flirted with danger but never believed it would touch us. We were invincible. Young and optimistic and utterly naive.

That night, while the others dared and double-dared each other to swim farther out or hold their breath longer, Zeke took my hand and led me away from the circle of light to a clear patch of sand among clumps of sagebrush and yucca. I remembered the sky, a blanket of glitter that stretched from horizon to horizon, and a red plastic cup full of cherry vodka and Coke. Bliss.

The tavern door opened, and Zeke, FJ, and Belinda stepped out. FJ saw me waiting and swerved, Cardboard Heather cradled against his side, toward a big silver Chevy truck. But Belinda, a little wobbly in her high heels, made straight for me.

"Don't believe everything you hear," she said, her voice sharp. "Especially if it comes from Mitch. FJ is a good man. A good sheriff. He would have done anything for Heather, and I *will* do anything for him. It just about killed him when she disappeared. He shouldn't have to suffer again."

"Mitch is grieving, too."

She snorted, very un-Belinda-like. "Mitch spent the last twenty-five years trying to drink himself into an early grave. Alternates between wild accusations and drunken confessions. What you saw tonight, it's what we've all been living with since that night."

"He just wants answers. He deserves them. We all do."

"The rest of us have made peace with what happened. We're your *friends*, not the subject of one of your exposés."

Zeke and I were quiet after she left. Across the road, a lone coyote broke into a high, mournful wail. The sound lingered in the heavy air, then another returned the call and another until the night vibrated with their song.

Zeke reached into his back pocket and brought out a flask-sized bottle of cherry vodka. "A toast to the follies of youth? Sorry I don't have any Coke."

"Oh my god. I haven't touched that stuff since high school."

He took a sip and handed it to me. I hesitated, then took a sip and grimaced. It tasted like cough syrup. "Awful."

"Yeah." He capped the bottle, shoved it back into his pocket, and grinned. I reminded myself I'd come for Heather, not him. That's what I'd told myself during the long drive across the state, during the few minutes at the Overlook as we watched the wrecker remove the car that had trapped Heather under twenty feet of water, for the last few hours as we sat thighs touching under the table. But then Zeke traced his thumb along my jawline. The stubble of his chin brushed against my cheek, and my knees and resolve weakened.

But when I closed my eyes, I saw not Zeke, but Heather. Not Cardboard Heather, but the Heather of that night, flushed and damp and happy.

Reluctantly, I pulled away.

"Regardless of what Belinda says, Mitch is right about unanswered questions."

"Nothing you ask now will change anything."

Maybe not, but my reporter's brain couldn't stop churning.

"Someone suggested Heather left on her own. Do you remember who?"

Zeke's hands dropped to his pockets. He regarded me with a sadness that tore my soul.

"Did anyone ask *how* she left town? Bus? Train? Her car was still parked at the sand pit the next day."

He sighed and looked away. "Belinda was right. This isn't a story you can investigate. She went for a swim and she got caught in a rusted wreck no one knew was at the bottom of the pit."

"The thing I don't understand is that everyone just accepted that she'd left, but this kid this week, the first thing they do is drain the sand pit? Why didn't Frank Senior drain the pit? Why didn't he ask *me* what I knew?"

"Would you have told him?"

I'm going to Colorado, Jen. I'm going to find a job and every morning when I wake up, I'll see mountains and trees and anything but a cornfield. Promise you won't tell Dad or FJ. They'd kill me if they knew.

No, I would never have broken my promise to her, not as long as I believed she was alive.

Still. "Why was FJ so angry with Mitch after all these years if he thought she left on her own?"

Zeke kicked away from my 4Runner. "You're like a dog with a bone, Jen. I'm sure that's great when you're chasing a story, but it's not so great for those of us who just want to be your friend."

The Garden Motel, an old-fashioned, family-owned Harman County institution, was dark when I returned. All guest rooms opened directly onto the parking lot, which tonight held only two other cars.

I locked my door and secured the chain then lay in the dark examining the facts as I knew them one by one. After Heather disappeared, I had been happy she got away but angry she'd left without me. Knowing what I knew now, though, I forced myself to remember details I'd kept buried all these years.

Heather's hand in mine, pulling me away from the bonfire. *I can't stand it here one more second. They're killing me. Staying here is literally killing me. I'm suffocating in that house. Dad. FJ. I can't breathe.*

Three months, Heather. Then we'll both be out of here forever.

I'll be dead in three months.

You're drunk. Everything will look better in the morning.

A final squeeze of her hand.

* * *

A long yellow streak appeared in the corner of my room, stretched down from the ceiling like a stalagtite. It snaked slowly across the TV stand and microwave, past the vanity, to the wall between the bedroom and bath. A truck — its lights were too far off the ground to be a car — idled outside my room, high beams on.

Asshole.

I rolled onto my side, back to the window, and shut my eyes tight.

The truck's engine revved, then revved again.

I rolled back and grabbed my phone from the night stand. Before I could decide who to call or why, tires squealed and the truck raced toward the building. I dove off the side of the bed farthest from the window, pulled sheets and pillow with me, and threw my arms over my head. Tires screeched, a clang of metal on metal, then a growl as the truck reversed and sped away.

What the hell.

I leapt to my feet and grabbed my keys. The chain on the door stuck until a hard jab and a string of profanity jolted it loose. I spilled into the parking lot in time to see taillights wink around the corner at the end of the street. A piece of the wrought iron trellis that supported the awning outside the room lay smashed across the hood of my 4Runner. I yanked it off and let it fall to the side. A moment later, hands tight on the wheel, I raced in the direction I'd seen the lights disappear. I'd driven only a block before I saw them again. I smashed the accelerator.

I almost caught him. The truck swerved onto River Road. I followed, past the turn for the sand pit. My 4Runner fishtailed around an S-curve, my dash lighting up in warning. When I hit the next straightaway, I stomped the accelerator again.

The curve just before the Overlook crossroads took me by surprise. I stood on the brake hard as the 4Runner skidded across a shallow ditch and narrowly missed a fencepost separating the road from a cow pasture. I took a deep breath, then wrenched the SUV back onto the road.

Straight ahead, a single beam of light cut through the night sky. I slammed to a halt.

A pickup truck lay upside down half a football field's length away in the pasture between the road and the Overlook. I ran toward it, grateful for the full moon that lit the way. Pieces of metal and glass sparkled like confetti and traced a trail of destruction across the sand. The pickup had been flying when it missed the turn.

Halfway there, I slowed, caution and common sense catching up after the surge of adrenaline. I was reluctant to get closer. I didn't want to know who drove this truck or why they'd led me on this chase or where they were now or what had happened to them.

Then I saw the glow of a rusted white quarter panel, mismatched to the truck's dark body.

The driver's door hung open and the cab was empty. I scanned the dunes around the wreckage for any signs of life, for any shape that seemed out of place, but an almost complete silence enveloped the prairie. Nothing moved.

Confusion clouded my thoughts.

It was Mitch's truck, no doubt, but what had he wanted at the motel? Why run away from me? I turned back toward the wreck, suddenly sure that I'd missed something. If he'd been running away, how had I managed to stay so close? It had taken me awhile to get out the door, to grab my keys, to tug the trellis off my 4Runner. He could have made a clean getaway if all he wanted to do was scare me.

I ran my hand over the truck's front bumper. Mitch's truck had suffered massive damage, the bed and cab twisted and mangled. But the one thing it didn't have was a trellis-sized dent in its bumper.

Mitch hadn't led me here. Someone else had wanted me to find this. To find him. And that someone was still out here.

The wind picked up, and lightning flickered in the southwest. A rumble of thunder rolled across the sand. For the first time in my life, the vastness of the prairie made me feel small and vulnerable.

I broke into a run.

I was seconds away from the safety of my SUV when a pair of headlights snapped on, blinding me. For the second time tonight, an engine raced. Only here, cut off from my SUV and with nothing but sand and scrubby brush in every direction, I had nowhere to hide.

The truck surged forward. I turned and dashed deeper into the field. I cut right, then back left. The headlights kept pace and changed trajectory with me. I chanced a glance over my shoulder. The truck gained on me, but I sensed the driver was holding back. Taunting me. My toe caught on a devil's claw stem, and I pitched forward, righting myself a hair's breadth before I tumbled into the waiting swords of a yucca. I stumbled on. The dune sand shifted under my feet. Every step forward felt cartoonishly exaggerated and slow.

I topped a dune and slid down the other side.

The truck roared over the dune behind me and skidded sideways on the downhill slope, the driver no longer in the mood for games. It was almost upon me, and I had no options.

In desperation, I faced the truck. I felt the heat of its engine bearing down on me. Then I twisted to the side, rolled, and waited for six thousand pounds of metal to crush me into the sand.

The pain never came.

The driver tried to spin the truck around but lost traction in the sand. The truck spun wildly and, for a fraction of a second as it passed by, the moon and the dashboard lights combined to give me a clear glimpse of the driver. Long blonde hair. Dark lipstick framing a mouth open in a perfect O.

Brake lights flared too late and the truck's engine whined. It hung in the air, suspended between past and future. And then it disappeared, followed a few seconds later by the crunch of metal on rock as the truck driven by Belinda Robertson plunged thirty-five hundred feet to the bottom of the Overlook.

• • •

I leaned against my SUV. The sky had begun to lighten, sunrise not far away. Behind me, Harman County deputies photographed Mitch's truck from every angle, sifted through wreckage, sketched the scene. At the bottom of the Overlook, a team from the Kansas Highway Patrol investigated the second crash. Ambulances waited to take the bodies away.

A dozen yards away, FJ sat behind the wheel of his Harman County Sheriff's Office Durango, a broken man. He'd barely spoken to me. Under different circumstances, I'd have felt sorry for him, but two people — my friend and his wife — were dead. It was time to face the truth.

Heather's death had been an accident. She'd swum out too far or dived too deep. She'd found the danger our parents had warned us about, a true monster beneath the surface. But the two deaths here, tonight, were different. I knew it. FJ knew it.

Zeke handed me a travel cup of coffee. He'd come when I called. Of course he had. Some things never change. I took the coffee to the Durango and passed it through the window. "We need to talk."

FJ looked at me with dry, red eyes, as if he'd run out of tears. "She thought she was protecting me." He mumbled more to the coffee cup than to me.

I swallowed my disgust. "She warned me off asking questions about the night Heather died. She said you'd all moved on. But I don't think you'd moved on at all. I think Heather's disappearance haunted you every day of the past twenty-five years."

FJ stared off into nothingness. "My dad was so mad. Furious that we'd gone to the party. Furious when she didn't come home. Furious that I hadn't protected her. Unrelentingly furious. Then Belinda stepped in, spun a wild lie about how she saw Heather walk away from the bonfire on her own. She took the heat off me and I was…grateful."

I waited another moment, but that was all he had to offer. I shook my head and turned my back on him.

● ● ●

A few hours later, I stood on a small rise a dozen yards away from the graveside to say my goodbyes. Every bit of my body ached, but the pain was nothing compared to my emotional turmoil as I thought about the damage done, the secrets and the fear, the selfishness and ambition. The lies. My heart ached.

In the green tent, Cardboard Heather beamed out at the gathered mourners from an easel beside the casket that held her bones. I saw Zeke in profile among the mourners and for one fleeting moment I felt again the brush of his lips against mine last night and *that* night. Cherry vodka kisses and the promise of what might have been.

As I began the long walk to my car, a voice carried to me across the graves of Harman County's dead. "May she finally rest in peace."

PETTY ON THE OUTSKIRTS OF SIN AND CAPITAL

Ilyn Welch

IN KEELY'S SILVER MERCEDES camper van, we headed to Jurupa Valley for a welfare check on Tia, Keely's trans elder. Tia was struggling with the scum of a shifty boyfriend named Lyle who wouldn't leave her house.

"He's been stealing from her," Keely said.

Keely had once stolen from me. My wallet. That's how we hit it off.

I followed her around a Barnes & Noble when she attempted to shoplift an Eckhart Tolle audiobook. Store clerks stopped her at the exit, where she relinquished the item.

Then olive-skinned, raven-haired Keely invited me into the swanky van—its grill coated with smashed bugs—for mind-blowing sex. The surprises continued post-climax when she removed a bright-red butt plug from her posterior ("One of many guilty pleasures"). After she kicked me out of her vehicle and drove off, I felt euphoric but physically different. Lighter, as in pickpocketed. I swooned when she turned up at my house, handing over the wallet, conning my mom out of $100 as reward (I will make it up to you one day, Mom).

A note tucked in the wallet had me quickly packing a bag and booking to meet her down the road, beginning our whirlwind romance.

"Getting off at Euclid. It's more scenic, and I want to fill the tank."

After a stop at Shell, Keely steered south, passing sore-thumb warehouses among ranch land.

Beyond a regional airport she hung a left, then right at a countrified road. I pointed at a building complex, sign identifying the California Institution for Women.

"See, Tiger, we are sightseeing," Keely said. "A couple of Manson Family members reside there."

The road went perpendicular, where stood a nature preserve.

"Cucamonga Creek Wetlands. Can we stop, take a look?" I said.

"Let's keep it in mind." Keely pointed east. "We can stay the night along the river trail, closer to Tia's place."

We moved through sterile housing developments in a new bedroom community. Those city limits abruptly cut off, with spacious horse properties unfolding. I spotted horses, goats, chickens, turkeys.

"Welcome to Jurupa Valley."

"What street does she live on?"

"Wineville Avenue," Keely answered. "About a century ago, this general area used to be called Wineville, because…who knows? Grapes and a winery? Anyway, something notorious happened, and the name changed."

A Riverside County sheriff cruiser idled by, its driver studying us and the van.

"What happened in Wineville?"

"The unspeakable. I can't go there now. Look it up one day, but be prepared for horror."

Keely pulled the van into an ample driveway of a simple ranch house with a stoop, surrounded by scrappy land aplenty, remnants of a stable out back and an intact chicken coop. A horn honk prompted the screen door to open.

"Hey, Tia!" called Keely.

Tia wore a full apron over mom jeans and a short-sleeved polka-dot blouse, tennis shoes, hair in a neat wash and set. I was amused to see her sneak a marshmallow from the apron pocket, taking a bite.

"I'm so glad to see you, Keely dear," Tia said as we exited the van. "And who's this?"

"Officially I'm Ofelia, but please call me Tiger."

"Well, aren't you the cat's meow! Good catch, Keely."

Keely embraced Tia. "I know. You're a good catch too, my queen." She lowered her voice. "Where's the scumbag mooch?"

Tia spoke softly too. "Gaming in the back room. Jeez, I wish he'd leave." She turned to me. "Lyle's like a vampire I should never've invited inside. He's gonna suck me and my bank account dry."

Tia shuffled past a neat living room to a bright kitchen.

Out the front door I noticed the cruiser go by again.

I whispered to Keely. "Why can't she get the fuzz to boot him out?"

"You are too sweet and innocent! Law mentality around here is wild west: men are men, and women must shut the fuck up. Nothing in between."

In the kitchen, cutlery clinked against ceramic plates. "Come sit for a cold supper."

Keely pulled me toward a nook table set for three. A stack of white bread, platter of cold cuts, bowl of potato salad and condiments were all ready for a spin on a lazy Susan.

We three sat, verbally silent for a few minutes as some food went down the hatch.

"Tia?"

"Yes, Tiger."

"How did you first get tangled with this man?"

"I'd seen Lyle at the neighborhood center's ice cream socials. Couldn't miss him and his coke-bottle glasses. One occasion he weren't there. When I came home, he'd broken into the house, and was watching a porno on the sofa."

Tia spooned more potato salad onto our plates.

"I know I shoulda been mad. But I felt sorry for him, let him stay, started to take care of him. But once I bought him a more attractive pair of eyeglasses, he really started to take advantage."

She sipped some ice tea, cubes jangling.

"And he turned mean."

I noticed bruises on Tia's arms, looked at Keely who was looking back at me, lips pursed in anger, a silent understanding between us.

"Oh, shit, we got intruders." Lyle stood in the doorway, thick but trendy glasses atop his nose, greasy wife beater over pasty skin and dumb tattoos. Wide black shorts, hem above white tube socks and flip flops. "And I think they're reeeeaal girls! Right, Tranny Granny?"

Tia's face crushed.

"That's disrespectful." Keely stood, staring him down. "Apologize."

"Mmmkay. Soooorrreee." Lyle grabbed a bread slice, stuffed half into his pie hole, rude chewing revealing hollow spaces among teeth. Scratching a stubbly scalp, he swung the fridge open, nibbling the bread crust, grabbing a Coors. "Whatever."

When Lyle went back to gaming, Keely turned to Tia, her face stern.

"Does he have a spare set of glasses?"

"Just the coke bottles." Tia rose, pulling out a drawer. "Here."

Keely put them in her jacket pocket. "Is he still huffing?"

"Cans o' spray paint in the utility cabinet."

"I'll need a couple cans, a case of beer, and a few folding lawn chairs." Keely moved to the back room, towards Lyle, motioning me along. "I promise to return them."

"Anything you need, dear."

Keely rapped twice, then barged into darkness. The computer monitor made Lyle's skin glow blue. I stayed in the hall, not wanting to step on the mess of clothes and food wrappers on the floor. Keely marched right behind him, flicking his skull.

Lyle yanked out earbuds. "What the fug?"

"You wanna party at the river tonight? Just us three?"

Lyle's face went from shitass to pleasantly surprised. "Hell yeah!"

"Be ready in 30, for sunset."

• • •

Keely and I equipped the van with the chairs and vice, in addition to the ever-present supply of BDSM sex toys in the vehicle cabinets, where she hid Lyle's old pair of glasses. She had tossed a few items, including the butt plug ("It's clean.") with a strap attached, into the paper bag holding the spray paint and a quart-size Ziploc.

"Have fun." Tia waved from the porch, eating another marshmallow.

Minutes later, Keely pulled into a vast regional-park lot.

"Yippee! Finally hanging with some real women!" Lyle said from the passenger seat. I was sitting on the back bench. "How'd you come to score this machine?"

"Oh, I've got my magic ways," Keely said, backing into a spot close to a dirt trail. "Lyle, you take the beer. Tiger will haul the chairs."

Holding the bag, she led us downward to a sandy shore, the

river flowing southwest under arches of an old bridge decorated with graffiti. "Midweek is a good time to partake. We have the place to ourselves tonight."

We stripped to underwear, while Lyle only removed flip flops and socks.

Keely set up the chairs in the middle part of the stream, knee deep. When Lyle relaxed on the webbed seat, she handed him a beer, the Ziploc and a can of spray paint.

"I'll be seeing stars."

Keely's teeth flashed in the late-afternoon light as she sunk a mesh bag with more beer cans into the water, hooking the straps onto the metal chair arm.

Flanking Lyle, we nursed our drinks while he pounded several. At dusk, he cracked open the paint, spraying contents into the plastic bag, inhaling. His head lolled back, a residue of institutional gray around his nose and mouth.

Keely hustled to shore, retrieving the sack full of toys and more paint cans. "Cuff him." She handed me a steel Smith & Wesson restraint. "You hang onto the key."

I clicked one on a wrist, using the body slackness of his inebriation to wrangle and connect both arms at his back. I balanced him on the chair so he wouldn't submerge.

Keely yanked the top off another paint can, and sprayed Lyle's designer lenses opaque.

Gurgles came from his throat.

Keely gagged Lyle's mouth with the butt plug, securing the strap to the back of his head. She roughly grabbed the crook of an arm. "Get up, fucker."

His almost inhuman sounds were muffled. Keely forced him toward shore and put her sweat pants and shoes on fast. "Tiger, get Tia's chairs. Tie the beer bag on a branch closer to shore for someone else to find. Also pass me the paper sack."

I tugged on my pants and Van's slip-ons, and gathered Lyle's shoes and socks.

From the bag, Keely took out a rigid dildo, poking it at Lyle's back, using the balls as handle. "I like Smith & Wesson products." She winked at me. "Go forward quietly or I'll waste you here and no one will care." To me. "Walk in front, ready the side door."

Keely pushed a sobbing, breathy Lyle up the trail, rolling him into the van back space. Tears streaked over the gray pigment on his face. Keely zip tied his ankles together, and slammed the door. "I'd put a bag over his head, but I don't want him asphyxiated."

The van rambled west, reversing the route we took to Jurupa Valley. Keely steered into Cucamonga Creek Wetlands. "Told ya I'd keep it in mind. It's perfect, frequented mostly by birding nerds."

"I'd like to be a birding nerd." I tickled her ribs.

"Me too!" She beamed at me. "When this is OVER," she shouted over her shoulder toward Lyle who moaned, "we'll get some binoculars."

The small lot was desolate, hidden from the rural road by thriving native marsh plants. Keely slid the side open, kicking Lyle in the butt. "Time to get out again, asshole." She undid the foot restraint. "Time for a serious talk." She rolled him out, letting him fall on the asphalt. "Tiger, bring the Maglite."

We both raised him on his feet, trudging well into the preserve. Our footstep sounds were diminished against amphibian communications. Keely stopped us at a flat spot near a short slope leading to a good-sized pond. She shook Lyle, pushing him to the ground. "Crisscross."

His lower limbs complied, torso vibrating, sobs quiet.

Keely gestured at the flashlight. Its illumination picked up some eyes along the water's edge.

She found a rock, throwing it long and hard, eliciting a fine splash. "Now for that important talk. The topic being, I want you to stay away from Tia. To never, ever visit, show up, or trespass her property again."

She grabbed a thick stick, tapping his shoulder, then launched it into the water.

"Without prescription glasses—you're welcome, by the way, on behalf of my Tia—you are as blind as a bat, correct? Nod your confirmation."

Lyle's head moved vertically, the circular hard-latex base jutting from his lips pooling with spit.

"So, you are at our mercy. I can lethally shoot you in that cranium, weigh you down with rocks, and roll you into a watery nature grave. Or you can agree to forever stay away from Tia and permanently move out of Jurupa Valley tonight. I'm going to temporarily take out the gag, and you speak your choice. It better be a promise. Don't bother screaming. Frogs don't give a shit."

Keely took a napkin from her pocket, using it to help extract the dripping butt plug. As Lyle gasped, copious strings of saliva shone. I wretched with disgust.

She set the plug on dry ground, then nudged the dildo-as-gun at his ear. "Say it."

Lyle coughed at length.

Keely leaned to the pond, scooped water in her cupped palms, dripping it over his lips.

"I promise." He sputtered more.

"To do as I say?"

"Yes."

"Excellent." Keely splashed more water onto his face. She plunged the butt plug in the pond, returning it to Lyle's suffering mouth, readjusting the strap. She helped him stand. Undoing his fly and yanking his shorts and skivvies down, she slapped his back. "Looks like you pissed yourself already, but go again before we hit the road."

After dragging him back into the van, he slept all the way on the 15 North, stirring a bit on Pearblossom Highway.

Around twilight, Keely found an Antelope Valley optometrist office. She left the van running.

Settling him on an outdoor waiting bench, she dumped his socks and flip flops onto his lap. "Tiger, from the toy cabinet, will you get the…" Keely mouthed the word *glasses*, making a circle with her thumb and index finger around her eye. When I handed them over, she put them on the concrete ground, stomped each lens useless, putting them also on Lyle's lap. She stuffed a few hundred dollar bills into a wet pocket. "That should get you a basic pair of glasses. Take off the handcuffs, please." As Keely held the dildo gun to his forehead, I unrestrained his wrists.

"Get in the vehicle, baby. And Lyle, be as still as a statue till you don't hear the engine. My piece is aimed on you." She yanked out the gag, backing away.

● ● ●

"I know a great Mexican breakfast joint nearby," Keely told me, driving through the desert, sun rising. "Then we can score some binoculars at the state park gift shop, and go birding on the buttes!"

"What about Tia?"

"She's okay now, and I'll make sure she stays that way."

TELL ME NO LIES

Holly West

MY AUNT PATSY GOT a gun for Christmas. It was a .38 special with a pink grip, finished in matte black.

Uncle Ray leaned forward in his recliner as she opened it. "I know you asked for one of those Louis Vuitton bags, honey. But with me being away so much, I thought you could use this."

"It's just what I wanted, Ray." Aunt Patsy smiled as she lifted the gun from its molded foam nest, but there was disappointment in her eyes. It was obvious she was lying, but I didn't know why—a gun was so much cooler than some dumb purse, even if it was pink.

Uncle Ray beamed. "I'll take you out back after dinner. Show you how to use it." He turned to me. "What about you, Janelle? You want some shooting lessons, too?"

Hell yes, I did. I was about to say so when Mom said, "No, Ray."

"C'mon now, Melanie." He winked at me. Gross. "You let this girl get a tattoo but you won't let her learn to shoot? She's a country girl for God's sake. Oughta at least know how to fire a weapon."

I turned my arm over so the tiny, black-ink bird on my wrist didn't show. Mom hadn't exactly *let* me get it. I'd lied about my age so the guy at the tattoo shop would agree to do it and paid for it with cash I'd stolen from Mom's top dresser drawer. That was six months ago and she was still mad.

I wondered if she'd rat me out to my aunt and uncle, but she only said, "Not gonna happen, Ray."

The last thing I wanted to do was spend any time alone with my skeevy uncle, but I didn't want to pass up the chance to go shooting. "Yeah, c'mon Mom. I'll be safe, I promise."

"Out of the question."

I pouted. "Everyone I know has shot a gun but me." I had no idea if it was true, but it didn't matter.

"What did I tell you about lying, Janelle?"

Mom handed me a garbage bag and told me to gather up the torn paper and ribbons while she and Aunt Patsy finished dinner. When we were alone, Uncle Ray sidled up close. I smelled the booze on his breath from downing spiked eggnog all afternoon. "I'm glad Melanie and Patsy made up. We needed more beautiful women in this family. 'Course, you'd be prettier if you smiled more often."

Ugh. Like I gave a shit about what he thought.

He continued as though I'd asked him for his opinion. "And why'd you cut your hair so short? You had such pretty long hair when you were a kid." He shook his head. "Tattoos, shaved heads, dressing like boys… I don't get why girls today don't want to look good."

I touched my recently shaved head, enjoying the way it felt. Like velvet. But I still had my heart set on a shooting lesson, so I let his comments slide. "You think you can get Mom to let you teach me to shoot?"

"Sure, I can." He gave me another wink. What a perve.

I took the bag to the kitchen. "I can't believe he got me a gun," Aunt Patsy said as I walked in. "And a pink one, no less. He knows I hate pink."

"Yeah, pink sucks," I said.

"Maybe you can return it," Mom said.

"Or maybe I should just shoot the bastard and get it over with." Aunt Patsy smiled half-heartedly. "Don't worry, I'll divorce him before I shoot him. He's not worth going to jail over."

While they were occupied with dinner, I snuck a sip from Mom's wine glass. It wasn't my first stolen drink of the day and I was beginning to feel tipsy. With any luck, I'd be able to sneak outside later to smoke the blunt I had in my pocket.

It was shaping up to be a crappy Christmas, just like I'd predicted. I told Mom I didn't want to spend it here, but she'd recently reconciled with Aunt Patsy, so she felt obligated. I begged her to let me go to my best friend's house instead, but of course she said no. It wasn't fair. Just because she felt guilty for refusing to speak to her sister for thirteen years didn't mean that I did.

Mom opened the oven to check on something. "Face it, Patsy," she said. "If you haven't divorced him yet, you never will." She closed the oven door and focused on me. "Janelle, did you take some of my wine?"

"Ew, no, gross."

This time, Mom let the lie slide, probably because she needed a drink of her own. She rolled her eyes and moved the glass out of my reach.

She was right about Aunt Patsy divorcing Uncle Ray, though. Everyone knew he played around. It was a small town and people talked, which was one of the reasons I couldn't wait to get out of this stupid place.

But what would she do if she left him? Mom said all she'd ever done was take care of the house and raise my cousins Toby and

Ray Jr. while Uncle Ray made a fortune developing real estate. "He controls the money," Mom told me. "Promise me, if you ever get married, you'll keep your own bank account."

She didn't have to worry because I was never getting married. But if I ever did, I wouldn't let my spouse get away with that bullshit.

My cousins were now both married and living out of state with kids of their own and, according to Mom, rarely came home to visit. Aside from Mom and me, Aunt Patsy had no other family, which is probably why she reached out to Mom six months ago, saying they should bury the hatchet.

"Janelle," Aunt Patsy said, interrupting my thoughts, "will you tell Ray dinner's ready, please?"

The four of us ate in the family room at a table for six. Still too big, but the formal dining room table seated twelve, leaving eight empty chairs to remind Aunt Patsy that her sons and grandchildren weren't coming. Didn't matter—Aunt Patsy had spared no effort in decorating their McMansion for the holidays. When Mom commented on the display, she told us she'd spent years collecting Christmas decorations, making their home a star attraction in the El Dorado Hills Holiday House Tour.

I liked the small, two-bedroom house we lived in a lot better. It took Mom ten years to save up the down payment, but she did it. Uncle Ray had custom-built this home, but it was a cheap knock-off of an Italian villa full of ridiculously ornate furniture and cheugy wall art. Grotesque.

When Uncle Ray's cell phone rang, Aunt Patsy frowned. "Really, Ray? At Christmas dinner?"

He glanced at the screen. "Sorry, honey, I've got to take this."

He left the room and Aunt Patsy seemed to crumble. "It's that woman. He doesn't bother to hide it anymore."

Mom reached across the table and touched her wrist. "Leave him, Patsy. Make an appointment with a lawyer. You're a beautiful, intelligent woman and there's no reason you can't make a new start. Put all that experience you've got entertaining to use and start an event planning company. Or do some catering. You'd be so good at that."

"Easy for you to say, Melanie. You managed to get your degree and work full-time all while raising Janelle by yourself. I don't know how you did it."

"You think it's been easy? It's not. But you're right, I'm doing it, and you can, too. And it will be so much easier for you with the boys grown up now."

Hearing Mom say this, it made me feel guilty for the trouble I caused her over the years. I rubbed my tattoo. Maybe I'd get a job over the summer so I could pay her back. I'd stop lying, too. And I'd quit skipping class so she wouldn't have to take off work to meet with the principal.

Aunt Patsy said, "Do you know the reason the boys never come home for holidays?"

Mom chewed and swallowed. "I assumed Kelly and Robin preferred to spend it at their own homes."

Aunt Patsy shook her head. "Two weeks ago, I called Toby and told him I wanted my whole family together for Christmas. He said no. Turns out, Ray cornered Kelly when they visited two years ago and told her he wanted to sleep with her." She lowered her voice, as if speaking to herself. "What kind of disgusting person does such a thing?"

"Was it that much of a surprise? Ray tried to bed me when I was seventeen years old, for Christ's sake. You forgave him and let him kick us out of the house."

This was news to me. "We lived here?"

"Your grandparents weren't happy when I got pregnant with you," Mom sighed. "You know that, of course. But Patsy and Ray agreed to take us in for a while, until I refused Ray's advances. I never told you because it didn't seem appropriate."

"You'll always hold that against me, won't you?" Aunt Patsy asked.

"I don't think you understand how rough Janelle and I had it after we moved out. It took a long time for me to get over it."

"I've been as good a sister as I know how to be, Melanie. I'm sorry that hasn't been enough for you. What Ray did was terrible, but I had two boys of my own to think about—I didn't want to take them away from their father."

I hated when adults talked like this in front of me. It's not as if I could solve their problems. I had enough of my own.

Aunt Patsy didn't notice my discomfort. "I'm not perfect and I never expected Ray to be perfect, either. But now, my daughters-in-law refuse to set foot in my house." Her face scrunched up as she started to cry. "I feel like I've lost my family."

Mom's expression softened. "You haven't lost the boys. And Kelly and Robin love you, you know that. But you can't expect them to spend time in this house with Ray."

Uncle Ray sauntered back in and glanced at all of us before resting his eyes on Aunt Patsy. "Looks like I missed something interesting," he said. "What've you been chattering about?"

Aunt Patsy tapped the table next to his plate. "Who was that on the phone?"

"Jack wants to discuss a project in Tahoe tomorrow morning. I asked if it could wait until next week, but he insisted. I'll be going up later tonight, probably be gone a couple of days."

"It's *Christmas*."

"Honey, you know how business is." He winked at me. "Sorry, kid, I'll have to give you a rain check on that shooting lesson."

Now I was mad. Not only did I have to spend Christmas in this stupid, ugly house, I wasn't going to get my shooting lesson.

"You're lying, Ray." Aunt Patsy said. "Tell me who was on the phone."

"You're disappointed," he said, his tone sharp. "I understand that but it's no reason to be rude in front of our guests."

Mom's eyes pleaded with Aunt Patsy. *Stand up to him*, they said. *Tell him to get out.*

Aunt Patsy's own eyes glittered with tears. Her headshake was almost imperceptible. She wasn't going to leave him, not ever. It didn't matter how many shitty things he did, how many holidays he skipped, how many women he hit on. She was going to stay.

"You're right, Ray," she finally said. "Janelle, Melanie, I apologize." Then she stood up, dropped her napkin on the table, and ran upstairs.

As I watched my aunt take the stairs two at a time, I thought about it. Maybe there was something I could do to help.

• • •

I knocked on the door to Aunt Patsy's craft room and she told me to come in. I found her slumped on an ottoman with a square of quilting fabric in her hands.

"Are you all right?" I asked, closing the door behind me.

Aunt Patsy blew her nose into the fabric. "I'm fine. I'm so sorry I ruined everybody's Christmas."

"It's okay. Mom's downstairs, cleaning up. I told her I'd check on you."

"I appreciate that, honey. I hope you're not upset by anything we said. Adults are sometimes more childish than kids."

"I'm not upset." I stepped further into the room. "Not about that, anyway."

"Is something wrong?"

I'd practiced what I was going to say in the bathroom before coming up. "I'm not sure if I should tell you. It might make things worse."

"Janelle, if something's bothering you, you shouldn't keep it bottled up inside. Sit down and tell me."

I sat on the stool in front of the sewing machine. "You have to promise not to tell Mom."

"Of course."

"Today, when I was cleaning up the wrapping paper with Uncle Ray... he... well, he touched me."

Aunt Patsy's face went white. "What do you mean, he touched you?"

"I was bending over to pick up paper and he touched my butt. I thought it was an accident, but when I turned around, he told me I had a pretty smile and he caressed my cheek."

I wasn't sure how far to go with my story. The only experience I had with boys was from watching TV or the movies. It had to be believable, but it also had to be bad enough that Aunt Patsy would do something.

"It was super weird," I continued. I wasn't lying, exactly. Uncle Ray had made me feel uncomfortable. This was just tweaking the truth a little. "I thought maybe he was just trying to be nice. But then he put his hands on my arms and asked if I'd ever been held by a man."

Aunt Patsy put her hand to her mouth and shook her head, incredulous. "Oh, honey. Please tell me he stopped there."

I hung my head. It would be better if I could shed a few tears, but those were hard to fake. "After that, he put his hand on my breast. Then, he tried to kiss me. I blocked him with the garbage bag and went to find you and Mom."

"Oh my god." Aunt Patsy was shaking. She stood and hugged me close. "That goddamn bastard. I'm not going to let him get away with this." She was quiet for a moment, thinking. Then she said, "You go downstairs now and tell your Mom to take you home. Tell her I'll call her later."

I went downstairs like she said, pleased with myself because

I thought I'd finally convinced Aunt Patsy to leave Uncle Ray. Our family would be happier without him. Mom could have her sister back and I wouldn't have to spend any more lousy Christmas's at their house.

In the kitchen, Mom was wrapping up the remaining beef tenderloin. "How's Patsy doing?" she asked.

"I think she'll be all right."

"I hope so. But I swear, Janelle, this is the last holiday we're spending with them. I should've never brought you here."

"It's okay, Mom. I'm pretty sure she's going to leave him."

"I wish I had your faith."

We both winced when we heard the first gunshot. "That sounded like it came from upstairs," Mom said.

I thought so, too. But before I could respond, I heard Uncle Ray shouting. "—always knew you were stupid Patsy but I never knew you were a goddammed idiot. How many times have I told you never to point a gun at anything you don't want to shoot?"

Uncle Ray entered the kitchen holding the pink gun by the barrel. Patsy followed, looking more defiant than contrite. Had she tried to shoot him?

"Janelle told me what you did," Aunt Patsy said. "I want you out of this house, now."

Mom looked from Aunt Patsy to me, eyebrows raised. "What did Janelle tell you?"

"I don't know what you're talking about," Uncle Ray said. He waved the gun's butt in Aunt Patsy's direction before setting it on the counter. "But I'll be damned if I let you talk to me this way."

"Get. Out. Of. My. House."

"Your house?" Uncle Ray laughed. "You're joking. *I* built this house. *I* paid for it and every stick of furniture inside of it. This is *my* house."

Aunt Patsy snatched the gun off the counter and pointed it at Uncle Ray. "You need to leave. Now."

"Really, Patsy? You're going to shoot me?"

She slid the gun's hammer back. "If that's what it takes."

"Get out of here, Janelle." Mom's voice was firm, but I didn't move. "Now! Go into the bathroom, shut the door, and don't come out until I say so."

Mom was going to kill me when she found out what I'd done. She'd warned me repeatedly not to tell lies and I finally understood why. I hurried toward the foyer and hid behind one of the twelve-foot columns flanking the house's foyer.

"Put down the gun, Patsy," Mom pleaded. "Shooting him won't solve anything."

"Listen to Melanie." I heard fear in Uncle Ray's voice. "We'll work this out, I promise, honey."

"He touched Janelle." Aunt Patsy's voice was flat and icy. "He's a pedophile piece of shit."

"The hell are you talking about?" Uncle Ray said. "I never laid a hand on her!"

I peeked out from behind the column, but a wall blocked my line of sight. I slipped into the dining room, where I could see what was going on without being seen myself.

Mom charged at Uncle Ray, pummeling his chest with her fists. "You fucking bastard, how could you? She's only fourteen! You fucking keep your hands off my daughter!"

I was scared now. Mom was much smaller than Uncle Ray, but she was strong. She looked like she was trying to kill him with her bare hands. But Uncle Ray fought back, connecting his fist to Mom's jaw. Stunned, she stumbled backwards onto the floor.

I ran toward her. "Mom!"

She scrambled toward me. "Get out of here, Janelle! Get my keys and get in the car!"

Aunt Patsy took advantage of her clear sight line. She aimed the gun at Uncle Ray and pulled the trigger. But instead of a bang, there was a click. Uncle Ray stood still for a moment, incredulous. Then he rushed Aunt Patsy knocked her against the kitchen island. The gun clattered onto the floor. She reached for it, but he kicked it away and pinned her to the floor so she couldn't move.

"I'm calling the cops, you stupid bitch."

He shifted his position so that his knee was on her neck. He raised himself up to take his phone out of his pants pocket and Aunt Patsy wriggled beneath him, her arms flailing, trying to push him off.

Mom lunged at him. "Get off her, Ray! She can't breathe!" He elbowed Mom in the stomach. She doubled over for a second before she picked up the gun. She tried to hit him with its butt, but he backhanded her and the gun skittered across the floor.

The gun landed at my feet, and I picked it up. Uncle Ray didn't see me coming. I struck him over the head, over and over again, until my arm went numb. Aunt Patsy rolled out from under him and Mom tried to pull me away. Only then did I see the blood on my hands.

Mom gently took the gun from me. Aunt Patsy knelt beside Ray, feeling for a pulse. Then she looked up at Mom and me and shook her head. She put her hand across her mouth.

Mom fell back against the kitchen counter. "Jesus, Patsy… how are we going to explain this?"

Patsy stood and took a deep breath. "Go home. This is my mess to clean up."

"I won't let you," Mom said. They locked eyes, silently communicating.

We were a family again. Mom and Aunt Patsy gathered around me, and we hugged. Then, we put our heads together and came up with one last lie.

SINCE I FELL FOR YOU

Michael Wiley

AS THE ARIZONA SUN set, Missy Denners swam laps in the pool at the Siesta Motel. The chlorine stung the tender welt on her shoulder where Marcel Beauvien had struck her—and then they'd both frozen as if stunned by what they saw in each other's eyes. Now, the first pain passed, and she welcomed the slow throb and the liquid nest.

When she tired of swimming, she lay on a deck chair in the dry heat. Tito Puente played "Teach Me Tonight" on the speakers at the empty poolside bar. Two men came from the motel and climbed into the pool. They were nineteen or twenty—three or four years younger than Missy. One, deeply tanned, had a tattoo of a gray wolf extending from his back over his left shoulder and onto his arm. The other, pale, looked soft and vulnerable. They saw Missy watching and returned her gaze.

Missy looked up at the sky. The first bright stars shined through the dark.

Why shouldn't I? she wondered. After all, her cheating,

thieving moron of a husband was dead. But she went back to her room alone.

She showered, then put on jeans, a button-up cotton shirt, and black boots. She checked her dead husband's weapons. Two nine-millimeter pistols and a Remington hunting rifle. She zipped them into a duffel.

She took the bag with her when she left the room. The men from the pool approached on the concrete breezeway. They wore shorts and sandals. The pale one had on a sun-bleached oxford cloth shirt. The other's tattoo stretched a paw out of the sleeve of a red T-shirt. The tattooed one grinned. The pale one said, "Hi there."

They told her they were vacationing from Tulsa. They were going to the poolside bar for drinks. Did Missy want to join them?

Missy liked the pale one's drawl. "Just one drink," she said.

They sat at a table, under strings of Christmas lights. The men drank tequila, Missy a vodka tonic. They laughed, the three of them, as if nothing in the world mattered more than sitting by a pool on a hot dry night under a star-speckled sky. They were young, their laughter seemed to say, and if their noise bothered the couple at the other end of the bar, the couple could go back to their room where the sound of air conditioning would drown out the music of life. Still, Missy pressed her feet against her duffel bag of weapons.

"What are you doing in Tucson?" the pale one asked.

"Hunting down a French gunrunner," Missy said.

The tattooed one said, "Ha"—too loudly, as if to indulge her for a joke that wasn't quite funny.

Missy said. "He killed my husband."

"Yeah, *right*," the pale one said, and then they all laughed together.

The tattooed one winked, "You're just another assassin hanging out at a motel pool?"

She smiled. "The water steadies my nerves." She held her hands out, steady, to show how calm she was.

"Well, you've got great strokes," he said.

Missy rolled her eyes.

The pale one grinned. "He can't help himself."

"That explains the wolf," Missy said.

The tattooed man peeled back the sleeve of his T-shirt to show more of the animal's extended paw. "What's wrong with the wolf?"

The pale one said, "Tell us about yourself."

"I'm exactly what I look like," Missy said. Which was easier than saying, *My cheating, thieving moron of a husband double-crossed Marcel Beauvien. Beauvien killed him, and now I'm going after him because if I don't, he'll kill me too.*

The tattooed man gestured at Missy's duffel bag. "You always carry your luggage with you?"

She drank from her vodka tonic. "I like to keep my guns close."

Both men laughed.

Three tequilas later, the tattooed man leaned on an elbow and gazed at Missy. "Want to come back to my room?"

She smiled. "I'm a grieving widow."

"I'll help you grieve."

"I'm carrying a bag of guns."

He laughed. "You said."

She shook her head. "Not tonight."

"Other plans?"

"I'm afraid so."

• • •

She left them at the motel bar at midnight. The late-night air had cooled, but she sweated as she lugged the duffel a mile to Speedway Boulevard. She carried seven hundred dollars in cash, her weapons, and ammunition. She waved away the first three taxis, clean cars glistening under the streetlights, and flagged the fourth, a bruised old Nissan.

She climbed in, settled low in the back seat, and said, "The border."

The driver smelled like the car looked. He stayed at the curb. "Where on the border?"

"We'll talk about that while we drive," she said.

"This time of night, it'll cost a hundred fifty."

"No," she said. "It'll cost three hundred. But we can talk about that too."

The car tunneled through the dark, the windows open. The driver wanted to talk, but Missy had no interest in listening, so after explaining what she wanted, she turned inward. She'd ridden like this on trips to swim meets when she was a teenager. She would put on headphones and play music. Then, as the other girls napped or gossiped, she would disappear into herself. She was five foot three, and the other girls nicknamed her *The Beast* because of how she stared down competitors before beating them in the pool. Now the driver turned on the radio—Etta James singing "Since I Fell For You"—and Missy sank into the seat and drifted into visions of chlorinated water splashing and splashing and splashing.

When the taxi reached Nogales, the driver left the highway, and they drove into the rough, scrub- and cactus-covered hills west of town. The roadside businesses gave way to little dark houses, the houses to long stretches of dusty land where the road cut through rises and seemed to float over gulches.

The driver turned onto a badly paved road. They climbed over the hills, zigzagging toward the border.

The driver said, "You got balls, *chica*. Maybe no brains, but you got balls."

He turned onto a dirt road. They'd passed no businesses or houses for ten minutes or more, but now Missy saw lights ahead. "Where are we?" she asked.

The driver said, "I drive you where you tell me, but you don't get to tell me how to take you there."

They passed through an open gate. A man stood in the dark on one side, a guard of some sort. He did nothing to stop the car, showed no sign he even saw it, and the driver sped through.

As they neared the lights, Missy saw two mobile homes and a clapboard house. Cars and beat-up pickup trucks were parked behind the house. Between the mobile homes, thirty or forty men stood in a circle. Some wore bandanas, others baseball caps or cowboy hats. Spotlights, mounted on wooden posts, shined inward.

"What's this?" Missy asked.

The driver stopped the car. "The money?"

She shook her head, her eyes on the circle of men. "Not until I cross the border."

"You want to cross, give me the money."

She did.

"Stay in the car or come," the driver said. "Better if you stay."

She grabbed her duffel and followed him toward the crowd. The still night air smelled of salt, sweat, and blood. A dog barked somewhere, metal rattled against metal, and the men went quiet.

The driver walked to the edge of the circle and pushed to the front, Missy close behind him. In the center of a wooden-walled ring, two roosters, an enormous white bird with a vermillion comb and a small brown bird, leaped into the air. They spread their feathers and clawed at each other with stainless steel spurs. Their wings snapped and flapped. The handlers, a man in a black beret and a kid in a torn yellow T-shirt, hovered nearby, ready to pull them out or push them deeper into the fight. At the far end of the ring, a half dozen wire cages held other fighting birds.

The taxi driver saw a man he was looking for. He jogged across the dirt outside the ring, leaving Missy behind.

The handlers pulled their roosters from the fight. They checked them for wounds, then lowered them to the ground by their tail feathers. The man standing next to Missy put a sweaty hand on her and grinned with gold teeth. "You came for me?" he asked. She pulled from him. The roosters clenched and flapped and fell away.

The man moved close and put his hand on her again. "I think you did. You came to make me happy." His breath smelled of beer. "I think you're here just for me."

She leaned toward him. "Take your hand off or I'll give you something you won't like."

He stumbled into her. "I like anything you give me."

She reached into her duffel bag and brought up a nine-millimeter.

He fell back. "You're right. I don't need this."

The other men saw and circled around them, making a second ring, smaller than the one where the roosters fought.

The taxi driver reappeared along with the man he was talking to. He said, "Come on, come on, *chica*, let's go."

She looked once more into the cockfighting ring. One of the roosters, the enormous white, lay on its side. The little brown strutted away. The handler in the beret stepped into the ring and jabbed the big bird with a forefinger as if he might wake it from the dead.

* * *

The taxi bounced down the dirt road, the driver and his friend in the front seat, Missy in back. The men talked about her, the

Americana, in Spanish, and then the new man turned to face her. "Do you like the roosters? *Furioso*, no?"

"The story of my life," she said.

He nodded. "*Muy bien*. Like me. You will be fine with me, okay?"

"Okay."

"Why d'you want to go to Mexico like this, *chica*?"

"I'm looking for a Frenchman."

He laughed, and the driver said, "That's stupid."

"Story of my life," she said again.

They drove through town and into a tangle of backstreets. The sun would rise in three hours, but now the houses were dark, and they saw only the glistening eyes of a dog on the roadside. As the taxi approached the border, the houses gave way to a strip of businesses—a muffler shop, side-by-side pawnbrokers, a storefront church. Behind the buildings, a steel and barbed wire barrier separating Arizona from Mexico rose into the dark. "Your wall, *Señora*," the driver's friend said. On the U.S. side, the government had cleared houses and vegetation from a broad strip of land.

The friend directed the driver to a parking lot behind a tire repair shop called Bernito's. The parking lot dead-ended into a rocky hill, topped by the barrier. On the other side, plywood shacks and thin-roofed concrete houses stood in the still night air.

The man gave Missy an old yellow flashlight, removed a section of wooden fence, and stepped into the rocky waste. He and Missy climbed the hill. "I come and I go," he told her. "ICE is a bunch of *putas*." Halfway to the top, a few yards before the cleared strip began, he stepped into a thick patch of dead brush.

A piece of plywood, flush with the ground, opened into a hole. The hole looked too small for him to enter, but he crawled in headfirst. Missy followed, pushing her duffel in front of her.

The tunnel smelled of the dry earth. Rocks snagged her jeans and shirt and cut her knees.

"On hot nights, I sleep here," the man said.

They crawled for five minutes through the rocky hill. The unventilated air became thin and hard to breathe. At one point, the man asked again, "Can I ask you, why do you do this?"

"Love?" Missy said. "Fear?"

"I see no love in you," he said. "No fear either." He crawled onward.

Soon, the tunnel began to rise inside the hill. They came up through a panel of sheet metal into a house. The place was clean and spare, with cheap rugs, a wicker sofa, and a wooden table. Doors opened from the living area into two bedrooms. A young boy came out of one, a woman the other. "*Mijito*," the man said, "and *mi mujer*"—as if naming his son and wife brought them close to him and kept them safe while he crawled through tunnels and bet on American cockfights.

As Missy waited for another taxi, she cleaned the dust from her face and arms in the sink. The man, his wife, and his son sat at the table and watched as if a fascinating animal had wandered into their house. When the taxi honked outside, Missy thanked the man and moved toward the door.

He stepped into her way. "The three hundred dollars, that was for my friend. You give me three hundred too."

She shifted the contents of the duffel bag. He'd seen what she could pull out of it.

He stepped aside. "You can't blame me for asking."

• • •

Marcel Beauvien had a compound on the outskirts of Nogales Sonora—the Mexican side of a city cut in half by the border.

Missy knew the importance of moving hard, fast, and first.

Every competitor understood how an unexpected burst of power could knock rivals out of a contest. Sure, the ability to *respond* mattered, but best to surge ahead and never look back.

At four in the morning, the compound was dark. Missy crept around the outside, looking for signs of danger. She moved to the front of the main house and unzipped the duffle bag. She tucked a nine-millimeter into the band of her jeans. She hid the other guns in a gap under the brick steps to the front door.

In the dry dark, she climbed the steps and leaned against the door.

Silence.

She reached for the handle.

Then the door ripped open seemingly on its own.

As she raised the nine-millimeter, a chunk of metal—a pistol butt—cracked against her wrist. The nine-millimeter fell and clattered on the steps.

Beauvien gazed at her from the doorway. Then he grabbed her, pulled her inside, shut the door—softly—and pushed her through the hall to a living room. He drew curtains across the windows and turned on a lamp. "Sit down," he said.

There were a half dozen chairs and a white couch. Missy walked to the far wall and leaned against it.

Beauvien went to her and held his pistol barrel to the underside of her jaw. "You need to listen to me."

She stared through him to keep from staring at him.

He lowered the gun, took a step back, and nodded at one of the chairs. "Sit."

She relaxed her legs, slid down the wall, and sat on the floor.

He looked like he would kick her or shoot her. "You're hilarious."

Competitors learned to avoid showing distress—smiling icily through bone grind and torn muscles.

Beauvien shook his head. "Why did you come?"

"To kill you."

"You don't want to do that." He moved close enough to strangle or kiss her.

She lunged at him as if she would bite him, and he jerked away.

He stared at her with those eyes. "What a waste," he said.

"I'll do it first chance I get."

"You know what you are? You're a mystery. Good thing for you I like mysteries. But I need to deal with you, don't I? Long live the king but only if the king keeps order. So, what should I do?"

"Stick your gun in your mouth and pull the trigger?"

He grinned. "I like you."

A sound came from a room above them. Furniture moving. Footsteps.

Beauvien's grin fell. He held a finger to his lips.

"Why?" Missy said.

"Shh," he said. "You don't want to meet her."

"Her?"

"My sister," he said.

"You have a sister?" Missy shouted at the ceiling—"Hey!"

Beauvien aimed his pistol at her again. "You shouldn't've done that."

• • •

A woman came downstairs—skinny, black haired, in a white nightgown.

Missy eyed her the way she once eyed her toughest swimming rivals. "You look like a spider."

The woman stared at her. "Who is this?"

Beauvien said, "Missy Denners."

The woman appraised Missy, as if she might buy or sell her. "I know about you," she said. The shape of her mouth made her teeth flash. "You are the girl who is chasing my brother. Do you want to kill him—or make love to him?" She reached as if she would stroke Missy's hair. "Maybe you want to do both. When Marcel said he killed your husband but let you live, I thought he must be joking. He would never make such a mistake. Then I thought, you must be a pretty girl. Marcel is stupid around pretty girls. Men are stupid, don't you think?"

"Some men," Missy said. "Some women too."

"Yes, women who don't know when to stop. But I don't blame you. You and I are both persistent. We're alike in this way. I'm glad to meet you, Missy Denners. Welcome to our house." Then she snapped her skinny fingers.

A tired-looking maid emerged from a hallway.

"You will join us for coffee," Beauvien's sister said to Missy. "You will tell me why a pretty girl is visiting us in the middle of the night."

"I don't think so," Missy said.

But Marcel Beauvien aimed his gun at her, and then, he, his sister, and Missy went into a dining room and sat at a table.

The maid filled their cups from a chrome pot. Missy stared at the other woman's white nightgown.

"Who are you?" Missy asked.

The woman drank her coffee, her thin fingers wrapping like a spider's legs around her cup. "You miss the point," she said. "The correct question is, who is my brother? The answer is, he wants to be boss, but he's no one special. He has a convincing face, though. He's very handsome, yes? *Très agréable*. Hot, yes? And he can be terrifying when he must be."

Missy stared at her coffee cup.

"And I love him," the woman said. "As I imagine you loved your husband. Stupid men, but what are we to do? We tolerate them. We take care of them."

"*You* run the operation?" Missy said. "Marcel's a front?"

"A handsome front."

"He killed my husband."

"Your husband broke his promises. I can't let people do that. Now, I must kill you too. With regret—because I see something of myself in you. But I have no choice, do you see?"

Missy glanced around the room. Outside, the sun would rise soon, but she sat in a strange house with a beautiful, vicious man and a woman who took pleasure in killing. She had no weapon, no way to fight. So she swept her arm across the table, knocking her coffee into the air—toward Beauvien's sister. The coffee splashed across the other woman's face and down her chest.

She screamed.

Missy stood and ran. She went through the hall toward the front door. A gun fired behind her—once, twice, a third time. But she was out in front where she liked to be. She knew to look forward, always forward. Only losers looked over their shoulders.

She looked over her shoulder.

Marcel Beauvien—he really was very handsome, *très agréable*—squared his pistol to shoot her. He pulled the trigger, and the bullet sank into a wall with a spray of plaster dust.

She reached the front door, and then she was outside, the door splintering as another bullet hit it.

She went over the side of the porch as Beauvien came out. Her duffel bag lay in the gap where she'd left it. She pulled it open. As Beauvien came down the steps and spun toward her, she crawled into the open and shot the Remington and shot it again and again. The shots went everywhere. Mostly into the sky.

Then she ran. She scrambled up the hill beside the compound. Gunshots hammered the ground around her. Her ears rang. Her feet fell silently on the gravel. She sprinted along a concrete wall. She disappeared through a stand of ragged trees.

• • •

As the sun rose, Missy came down into a street a mile from the compound. A dog barked. Behind a house, a rooster crowed.

She turned onto a dirt lane sided by shacks. She cut across two similar lanes and returned to pavement for a block before dropping back onto dirt. The Nogales Sonora neighborhood smelled of burning wood and rotting vegetables. An orange cat raced across another lane. Missy turned onto a road that snaked up a steep hill. The air cleared and the shacks gave way to a rocky hillside barren of life.

All day, as the sun heated the dry town, Missy worked her way toward the border. She stayed on little streets and ran from alley to alley. When cars or motorcycles approached, she dipped into doorways or behind buildings.

She waited until the sun went down that evening before knocking on the door of the house with access to the tunnel. The woman who lived there cracked the door open and peeked out.

Missy shoved the door and stepped inside.

The woman's little son stood on a chair holding a shotgun. He aimed at Missy. He touched the trigger with a tiny finger.

"Whoa," Missy said, and raised her hands.

"You don't belong here," the woman said.

"I don't want to be here," Missy said. She gestured at a throw rug covering the tunnel entrance. "I need to get back across the border."

The woman shook her head. "They'll see you if you go now."

"Let me show you something," Missy said. With an eye on the boy, she lowered her duffel bag to the floor. She unzipped it, slowly. She reached past the guns to her remaining cash—four hundred dollars. She offered two hundred to the woman.

The woman looked disgusted by the money. "The guns."

Missy eyed her like she must be kidding but removed the guns from the bag and laid them on the floor.

The woman nodded at her son and he lowered the shotgun. Then she snatched the bills from Missy's hand. "Go," she said. "Be silent. Don't come back." She pulled away the throw rug and lifted the metal panel. The dry smell of the tunnel belched into the room.

Missy went headfirst into the dark. Rocks tugged at her clothes. The air thinned.

She went on and on.

Then she touched the plywood on the rocky hillside behind Bernito's tire repair shop. She emerged into the cooling Arizona evening.

She brushed dust from her shirt and jeans and boots. She ran her fingers through her hair. She walked down the hill and, slowing her breath the way she learned to do after extreme exertion, hiked a half mile to a commercial strip.

Standing outside Ángel Pizza, she called a taxi. When it came, a man with a gray ponytail looked at Missy from the driver's side window and shook his head sadly, as if he understood how to suffer. She got into the backseat, told him where to go, and said, "Don't say a word. Please."

An hour later, a block from the Siesta Motel, she paid him and got out. Standing on the sidewalk, she laughed—nearly out of her mind with fear and relief. For several minutes, she stood there. Then she slowed her breath again and, staying in the shadows, moved toward the motel.

A half block away, a deliveryman was filling a Coke machine in front of a laundromat. She waited until he got into his truck and drove away. Before the driveway into the motel, a Mexican woman pushed a stroller past an empty lot. A Tucson Electric Power truck—with a *We're there when you need us* motto emblazoned on its side and a man doing paperwork behind tinted windows—idled at the curb.

Missy hesitated—then walked, fast and hard.

She breathed in. She breathed out. She smiled through bone grind and torn muscles.

She crossed the motel parking lot.

When a couple, holding hands as they went to a car, wished her a good evening, she wished them a good evening back, as if it *was* a good evening.

She passed the front office and stepped into the courtyard.

Then, as she reached the swimming pool, a man called her name. She stiffened but kept walking. The man called to her again. He sat on a poolside recliner. He wore a red swimsuit and held an empty cocktail glass. A wolf tattoo reached from his back, over his shoulder, onto his biceps.

Missy breathed out. She sat down beside him on the pool deck.

"Where's your friend?" she asked.

He frowned. "He met a girl."

"And left you here alone?"

He nodded. "Alone and lonely."

So she asked if he would do her a favor.

"Anything." His eyes shined with an alcohol glaze.

"Go to my room for me," she said.

He grinned. "*With* you?"

She shook her head. "I want you to get my swimsuit. Bring it to me."

He looked at her out of the side of his eyes. "Why?"

"Just do it," she said. "Don't think too hard."

"You're going to change on the pool deck?" he asked.

"I've done crazier things."

He glanced around. The strings of Christmas lights cast a glow on the pavement and pool water. Though traffic passed on the street beyond the parking lot, he and Missy were alone. "Give me the key."

Missy hated to send him to her room, but why shouldn't she? If Marcel Beauvien was waiting for her, he would have no reason to hurt a drunk in a swimsuit who came in instead. And if no one was lying in wait and the man returned with her suit, what would she do then? She could plead fatigue and go to her room alone. Or she could swim in the pool. Steady her nerves. Give the drunk a thrill.

The man glanced at her from outside her room. Grinning like he couldn't believe his luck, he slid her key card into the door lock.

She moved onto the breezeway, away from the lights.

The man stepped inside Missy's room and shut the door.

Missy listened for voices, a struggle.

For nearly a minute, she heard nothing.

What was the tattooed man doing? Was he waiting for her. Had he convinced himself she would follow him into her room?

She waited.

She hated to wait.

She stepped into the light.

Then a muffled gunshot sounded in her room.

The noise seemed to throw her back into the shadows.

Her room door opened. For a long time, no one came out. Then Marcel Beauvien stepped onto the breezeway. He stood the way a man might stand while considering which direction his life would take him. The violent beauty of his eyes gleamed in the dark.

Missy froze on the breezeway.

Beauvien walked to the poolside. The pool water gleamed too. He inhaled deep, as if slowing his breath, and stared at the water.

Then, without turning to Missy—without signaling he even knew she was there—he said, "Run, baby. Run, run, run."

Without moving—without breathing—Missy knew she *would* run.

Away from Marcel Beauvien.

Out in front again, where she belonged.

Fast. Hard. First—always first.

Then, if Beauvien caught her—if she allowed him to get near—one of them would die in the grip of the other's deadly arms.

PATRON SAINT

Maura Yzmore

I WAS STILL A block away from the diner when I heard the crowd. The protests had been going on for months, first against the demolition of the old buildings across the street, now against the new development. Only the diehard protesters were still around, led by the local activist Jed Stevens, who was presently yelling about the evils of gentrification into a megaphone.

I focused on not getting my cane stuck in the cracks on the pavement. I loved the old buildings, but many had long been boarded up. People needed work. And the sidewalk needed repaving.

• • •

The construction crew filled most of the diner, as they had done every morning since they'd started the build. About a dozen contractors in hard hats, work boots, high-vis vests and pants, all clutching steaming mugs of coffee.

A small group sat in a booth by the front window, clad in business casual beneath safety gear. Probably the engineers in charge, from a big-city firm.

Sally arrived with my breakfast and set it on the table. "Here you go, Peter."

"Thank you, dear." I spread a napkin across my lap and nodded toward the construction guys. "How's this been? They giving you trouble?"

"Them and the Stevens boys," Sally said. "The other day, Stevens brought a few to pick a fight at lunchtime. Broken bowls, soup everywhere. I was about to call the cops."

"Jesus."

"Yeah, it's not good. And they're scaring the locals! Just yesterday, your neighbor Beth was here, about to come inside, when she saw those guys in the window booth, and she hightailed!"

"I'm so sorry, Sally."

She shrugged. "I keep reminding myself that they won't be here forever. And the new development will be good for business. I just gotta stick it out till then."

Sally left and I focused on my meal.

Then someone roared with laughter, and I looked up. It was one of the men sitting in the window booth. He was a big fellow, with thick brown hair that peered out beneath his helmet and the wide nose of someone who had taken a fist to the face more than once. With his mouth still stretched into a wide grin, for a split second he reminded me of someone, but I couldn't quite figure out who.

• • •

Beth and I sat in my backyard, enjoying the sunset and sipping sweet tea. Beth's son Mikey played with Tobias, my puppy in name only. I had bought him for Mikey, who stayed at my place every day after school and whenever Beth had to work extra shifts at the hospital. I loved having him over. Both him and his mom.

Beth and Mikey had been my neighbors for just a couple of months when my wife Mary passed away; Mikey was still a baby. Forty happy years of marriage, just Mary and me, until I woke up to her dead in her sleep. Beth saved my life. In the weeks after the funeral, she came over twice a day, brought me food, did the dishes, told me about Mikey and her job. She kept me tethered to this world.

Beth absentmindedly played with her necklace medallion. Saint Nicholas. It used to be Mary's, and it warmed my heart to see it worn again, glistening in the sun.

"Something bothering you, dear?" I asked. "You're quiet today."

"Sorry, Peter." She smiled weakly. "I saw something upsetting the other day. It's nothing."

Beth never talked about her past or Mikey's dad, and I never wanted to press. I hoped St. Nick, protector of children, would shield Beth and Mikey from whatever haunted them.

● ● ●

A huge crowd stood outside the diner as I arrived for my daily breakfast. The inside was packed, too.

When I finally made it to the counter, Sally looked frazzled. "Sorry Peter, your spot is taken. It's been crazy."

"What is going on? Who are all these people?"

"Folks are curious," Sally said. "They found a body at the construction site. One of the crew. Skewered on rebar." She made the sign of the cross. "Cops just dragged Stevens and a bunch of his guys back for questioning."

● ● ●

When Beth came to pick up Mikey that evening, she was pale, with dark circles around her eyes.

"You OK, dear?" I asked.

"What? Oh, yes. Of course." She sounded like I'd woken her up from a trance. "Thanks again for taking care of Mikey."

"My pleasure. You two have a good night."

Beth put her hand on Mikey's shoulder to gently lead him home. Just before she turned away from me, I noticed her St. Nicholas medallion was missing. She had never taken it off before, not since she'd first put it on six years ago.

● ● ●

"They still haven't let the Stevens boys out," Sally said as she poured my coffee. "The cops say the construction's back on next week. If Stevens killed that engineer to stop it, it was all for nothing."

"So it's murder?"

Sally looked over her shoulder, then leaned in and whispered, "This is all very hush-hush, but Rhonda from the sheriff's office says it might be over a woman. Says the dead guy might've been screwing someone. When they found him, he clutched a necklace pendant in his hand."

I felt my throat close at Sally's words.

I grabbed the mug and took a large swig of coffee.

"Peter, wait! It's scalding!"

As the liquid burned my throat, I remembered the laughing man in the booth, and I knew exactly who he reminded me of.

At least I could pretend that my coughing fit was over nothing other than too-hot coffee.

● ● ●

Beth and I sat in my backyard, sipping sweet tea. Mikey and Tobias were digging in the dirt.

Over the past few weeks, Beth's color had mostly returned, but the necklace hadn't.

"You never talk about Mikey's father," I said.

Her back stiffened. "Not much to say, really. I was young, and he was not a good man. I couldn't risk Mikey growing up with him."

"So you ran."

She nodded.

"Was he an engineer? Big-city construction firm?"

Beth eyes widened with terror. "Peter…"

I raised my hand. "You don't have to say anything. Just know that you and Mikey are my family, and I would do anything — *anything* — to protect you."

Her eyes softened and her shoulders relaxed.

I glanced at Mikey. His thick brown hair, his broad, familiar grin.

"I saw him at the diner, you know," I said. "Mikey looks just like him."

"He does," Beth whispered. "Is that…how you knew?"

"Not at first, no. But I put bits and pieces together. Mostly it was the necklace." I pointed toward where the pendant used to hang. "You'd never taken it off before."

Beth touched the unadorned based of her neck. "Peter, I'm so sorry. I know how much Mary's medallion meant to you. I never should've…"

"Don't worry about that," I said. "Saint Nicholas kept you and Mikey safe. That's exactly what Mary would have wanted."

Beth gave me a tired smile, tinged with relief and gratitude.

We sat in silence, looking ahead, sipping our sweet tea.

ABOUT THE AUTHORS

FRANCELIA BELTON writes character-driven crime fiction that cuts like a knife, but leaves you begging for more. Her greatest influences for writing short fiction come from watching the television anthologies of old like The Twilight Zone and Alfred Hitchcock Presents in her youth. Now, she's on a mission to write 1,001 stories before she dies. An audacious goal for a notoriously slow writer. You can read more of her stories at: https://Francel.Be/Writing-Stories.

JAY BUTKOWSKI is a writer of fiction, eater of tacos and amateur pizzaiolo living and working in New Jersey. He founded and serves as managing editor at Rock and a Hard Place Press, an independent publisher of dark fiction. His own writing has appeared or is forthcoming in Shotgun Honey, Vautrin, Dark Yonder, Yellow Mama, and other venues for noir and crime fiction. He's also a father of twins, doting husband, and middling pancake chef.

JAMES D.F. HANNAH is the Shamus Award-winning author of the Henry Malone series. His short fiction has appeared in publications including Rock and a Hard Place, Crossed Genres, The Anthology of Appalachian Writers, and the Lawrence Block-edited Playing Games. His story "No Man's Land" was selected for Best American Mystery and Suspense 2022. He lives in Louisville, KY. Annoy him on Twitter and Instagram: @jamesdfhannah.

KAREN HARRINGTON is a freelance writer and author from Texas. Her short work has appeared in Shotgun Honey, Mystery Tribune, and Ellery Queen's Mystery Magazine, where she won the 2021 Ellery Queen Mystery Magazine Readers Choice Award for "Boo Radley College Prep." Karen is the author of four novels, including Sure Signs of Crazy, a Kirkus Best Book of the Year, and Mayday, a Lone Star Reading List pick. Find her at www.karenharringtonbooks.com.

CURTIS IPPOLITO is the author of the crime novel Burying the Newspaper Man. He's an Anthony Award Finalist (2023) and Derringer Award Finalist (2023). His short stories have also appeared in Ellery Queen Mystery Magazine, Vautrin Magazine, Shotgun Honey, Mystery Tribune, and more, as well as being included in several anthologies. He is a member of Sisters in Crime and serves on the board of the San Diego SinC chapter.

MEAGAN LUCAS is the author of the award-winning novel, *Songbirds and Stray Dogs*, and the collection, *Here in the Dark*. She teaches Creative Writing at Robert Morris University and in the Great Smokies Writing Program at UNC Asheville. Meagan is the Editor-in-Chief of Reckon Review. She lives in Western North Carolina.

BOBBY MATHEWS is an award-winning novelist, short-story writer, and journalist who calls Birmingham, Alabama home. His short story, 'Negative Tilt' won the 2023 Derringer Award for 'Best Long Story,' while his novel Living the Gimmick and short story 'The Ghost of Buxahatchee Creek' each won top honors in the Alabama Media Professionals 2023 contest. His most recent novel, Magic City Blues, has earned rave reviews for its hard-hitting action, keen dialogue, and artful depiction of Birmingham. When he's not writing, Bobby is procrastinating.

CATE MOYLE writes mystery stories; she's won numerous recognitions, including the latest as a Silver Falchion Award finalist. She is also an award-winning poet, having been published in literary journals from The Southeast Review to Wicked Alice. Moyle's recent stories appear in Mystery Tribune, Bowery Gothic, Crimeucopia, and Bang!: an anthology of modern noir fiction. Find her on the web (and socials) at https://catemoylepens.weebly.com/

JONATHAN NEWMAN is a British writer. His stories have appeared in such places as Story Nook, Rock and a Hard Place Press and now Shotgun Honey. When Jonathan isn't typing, he's travelling. China, Japan, most of Southern Africa, and even North Korea, to name a few highlights. If it's on the map, there's good chance he's already been or it's on his list just waiting to be ticked off. Unfortunately, Jonathan isn't able to travel all the time, so he lives near London, England.

Nestled in the foothills of West Virginia, **RON EARL PHILLIPS** lives with his wife, their daughter, a German Shepherd named Freya and one too many cats. He is the co-founder and publisher of Shotgun Honey, specializing in short crime fiction, from flash to novella and short novel-length stories. He is also the primary editor and anthologist of the Shotgun Honey Presents series. When not managing Shotgun Honey, Ron pursues passions as an artist, designer, and writer.

LORI ROBBINS is the author of the On Pointe and Master Class mystery series and is a contributor to The Secret Ingredient: A Mystery Writers Cookbook. She won the Indie Award for Best Mystery and the Silver Falchion for Best Cozy Mystery. Short stories include "Leading Ladies" which was cited in the 2022 Best American Mystery and Suspense anthology. Lori is co-president of the New York/Tristate Sisters in Crime and an expert in the homicidal tendencies everyday life inspires.

J. ROHR is a Chicago native with a taste for history and wandering the city at odd hours. To deal with the more corrosive aspects of everyday life he makes music in the band Beerfinger. Currently, he writes articles for Film Obsessive and Horror Obsessive. His Twitter babble can be found @JackBlankHSH.

JESSICA SLEE studied English Literature and Creative Writing at the University of North Carolina at Chapel Hill. She is a Claymore Award finalist, and in 2022 she was longlisted for the CWA Debut Dagger and the First Pages Prize. For more, visit sleesquared.com.

ROB D. SMITH is a common man attempting to write uncommon fiction in Louisville, KY. His work has appeared in Shotgun Honey, Pyre Magazine, Bristol Noir, Thriller Magazine, Tough, and several other crime, horror, and speculative anthologies and online magazines. He also edits at Rock and a Hard Place Press. Find more about him at https://robdsmith.carrd.co/

MARY THORSON lives and writes in Milwaukee, Wisconsin. She received her BA in Creative Writing from the University of Wisconsin-Milwaukee and her MFA from Pacific University in Oregon. Her stories have appeared in the Los Angeles Review, Milwaukee Noir, Worcester Review, Rock and a Hard Place, Tough, among others. Her work has been nominated for Best American Short Stories, Best American Mystery, a Derringer, and a Pushcart Prize. She hangs out with her two daughters, husband, and dog when she isn't teaching high school English, reading, or writing ghost stories.

JULIE TOLLEFSON is a lifelong Kansan whose short fiction has appeared in Alfred Hitchcock Mystery Magazine and in anthologies, including Life is Short and Then You Die: First Encounters with Murder from Mystery Writers of America and Flash and Bang: The Short Mystery Fiction Society Anthology. Find her at http://julietollefson.com.

ILYN WELCH (she/her) resides in the vast and varied Inland Empire with extended family, beloved dogs, red-eared slider turtles and goldfish. She writes crime stories, horror, and creative nonfiction. Her work has been published with PANK, Shotgun Honey, Pomona

Valley Review, and in Step Into the Light, a Bag of Bones Press Anthology. Her debut crime fiction novella Signs of Pain was published in 2023 by Shotgun Honey. Connect with @IlynWelch on Twitter or Instagram.

HOLLY WEST is the author of the Mistress of Fortune historical mystery series and the Anthony Award-nominated editor of Murder-A-Go-Go's: Crime Fiction Inspired by the Music of the Go-Go's and Killin' Time in San Diego. Her short fiction has appeared online and in numerous anthologies, including The Big Book of Jack the Ripper, Florida Happens, and The Eviction of Hope. Her novella, The Money Block, is out now from Down & Out Books. Learn more at hollywest.com.

MICHAEL WILEY writes books in four mystery and thriller series, including, most recently, The Long Way Out (Franky Dast #2). His short stories appear often in magazines and anthologies, including Best Mystery Stories of the Year (2022). He won the Shamus Award for A Bad Night's Sleep and has been a Shamus finalist for three other novels. He's a native Chicagoan, who has lived for the past twenty-five years in Jacksonville, Florida.

MAURA YZMORE is a Midwest-based writer and career math nerd. She pens short fiction across genres (horror, sci-fi, mystery, lit fic, and humor), some of which has appeared in Mystery Magazine, Flash Fiction Online, The Arcanist, and elsewhere. Find out more at https://maurayzmore.com or on Twitter @MauraYzmore.